D0007917

THE
ART *of*
SAYING
GOODBYE

Center Point
Large Print

**This Large Print Book carries the
Seal of Approval of N.A.V.H.**

THE
ART *of*
SAYING
GOODBYE

ELLYN BACHE

CENTER POINT PUBLISHING
THORNDIKE, MAINE

This Center Point Large Print edition is published in the year 2011 by arrangement with William Morrow, an imprint of HarperCollins Publishers.

The text of this Large Print edition is unabridged. In other aspects, this book may vary from the original edition. Printed in the United States of America on permanent paper. Set in 16-point Times New Roman type.

ISBN: 978-1-61173-174-3

Library of Congress Cataloging-in-Publication Data

Bache, Ellyn.
The art of saying goodbye / Ellyn Bache. — Center Point large print ed.
p. cm.
ISBN 978-1-61173-174-3 (library binding : alk. paper)
1. Female friendship—Fiction. 2. Middle-aged women—Fiction.
  3. Large type books. I. Title.
PS3563.A845A78 2011
813´.54—dc22

2011022388

ACKNOWLEDGMENTS

Many thanks and much love to:

My North Carolina writing group, for nurturing this project—and so many others—from the beginning.

My Pennsylvania critique group, for seeing it through to the end . . . and most of all, for believing in it.

My extraordinary agent, Jenny Bent, and editor, Carrie Feron, for making me refine and deepen it.

CHAPTER I

October 14

On this warm October night, if you turned into Brightwood Trace beside the handsome brick entryway, and followed the graceful curve of Brightwood Circle past the three culs-de-sac that branch off like fingers, you'd notice even through the gathering fog that a white bow with long streamers, one that might look good atop a large wedding present, has been secured to a tree in front of every house. Every house. This is not because of hostages in some foreign country or a deeply felt political cause. The residents put them up to support one of their own. Paisley Lamm lives at the top of Lindenwood Court, the highest point in the development, and has to pass this way on every trip in or out.

No one is sure who tied the first ribbon to a tree this afternoon. Most people think it was Andrea Chess, Paisley's longtime friend, who knows her better than anyone in Brightwood Trace except Paisley's husband, Mason. Andrea is the one with the mushroom-colored hair falling in a bowl around her face, and those odd gray-green eyes that seem somehow colorless, like slightly dirty water. You wouldn't imagine Andrea as Paisley's best friend, but she is. For twelve years they've shared secrets, seen each other through every crisis, given each other space. In Andrea's view, this has led to a special, dignified friendship few women ever enjoy. Andrea loves Paisley like a sister.

Most of the neighbors are much more ambivalent. Paisley is pleasant to everyone, so affable and good natured the women find it hard to stay jealous even after their husbands stare longingly at her at a party and it ruins their night. They burn hot for a day or two, incensed that a woman of forty-six should look so good. It's unnatural. Then on Monday or Tuesday they run into Paisley at the supermarket or in the gym, where she offers a tomboyish wave and spills benevolence onto them from her snappy blue eyes. "Hey," she trills, and "Hey," they call back, and at that moment their ill will vanishes like smoke. There's something irresistible about Paisley. There's something that makes her seem the gracious hostess even in the grocery store. The next time Paisley issues an invitation for coffee or wine, the neighbor will say, yes, of course, and forget until it's too late the way her husband looked at Paisley that time and probably will again.

Of course, Iona Feld doesn't feel this way. At sixty, Iona is practically old enough to be Paisley's mother—maybe not quite—and hasn't been much interested in men since her husband died. The only man in her life now is her grown stepson, who is trouble enough. Iona isn't jealous of Paisley, and she knows too much to be an ardent admirer, but she enjoys her all the same. At Paisley and Mason's many social gatherings, she watches with wry amusement the way Paisley works a room. The more aware Paisley is of men eyeing her, the more conscientious she is about distributing her charms with judicious fairness, a little for John, a little for Eddie, some for the women, too. It's almost an art form. Iona is sure Paisley's parents impressed on her that it was important to *be nice to everyone*. She sees Paisley teaching this same lesson to her two daughters. The younger girl, Melody, isn't much interested yet, but Brynne, at fourteen, already exhibits more social savvy than some women ever acquire.

This morning, Iona fought alarm, irritation, and an actual lump in her throat while driving to A. C. Moore to buy the biggest white bow she could find. Afterward, she didn't stop at the Quick-Mart to get the coffee she can barely live without or pick up the dry cleaning that has been sitting there for a week. She was furious at being sucked into this ordinary, unexotic tragedy. She's had her own tragedy. She doesn't need this. At home she tied the ribbon around the enormous willow oak in her front yard, a tree she has always despised, while its rough gray bark practically glowered disapproval at having to wear a shiny white bow. In a few weeks the tree will retaliate by shedding thousands of tiny pointed leaves onto Iona's lawn, impossible to rake up. Much as she likes yard work and believes it keeps her limber, she'll have to call the lawn service. It isn't the expense she begrudges; it is the admission of defeat.

By nightfall when the fog begins to gather, Iona is so worked up that she'd like nothing better than to take one of her long treks through the undeveloped field behind Lindenwood Court, her usual way of burning off energy. But it's dark, and the ground back there is too uneven to negotiate without a flashlight. She doesn't want to walk on the street. Just her luck, she'd run into some gossipy neighbor who'd whisper about Paisley for twenty minutes. She goes into her house instead, picks up the newspaper, and fumes.

Up on Lindenwood Court, across the cul-de-sac from Paisley's house, Ginger Logan stands rigid at her bedroom window, watching her twelve-year-old daughter, Rachel, slip quietly out into the front yard. It's all she can do not to follow Rachel outside. They had their family discussion about Paisley's situation at dinner. Theoretically, there's nothing more to say. Ginger wishes Paisley well, of course; they've been across-the-cul-de-sac neighbors for more than nine years. But mostly, she's concerned about her children. Well, not so much about Max who at fifteen wants only to drive. She worries more about her daughter. Twelve is such an impressionable age. Lately Rachel has become thoughtful and quiet, no longer a jabbering child. Ginger wants to act before it's too late. *Do something. Make sure her daughter is not scarred by this, whatever happens.*

It's so misty out in the yard that Ginger can just barely make out the way Rachel touches the ribbon tied around their oak tree and then turns to stare at the nearly invisible Lamm house across the street. The Lamms and the Logans are neighbors but not exactly friends. Paisley's daughter, Brynne, is two years older than Rachel, a barrier thicker than this fog. For as long as anyone can remember, all Rachel has wanted to do is *be* Brynne. Tonight she's probably thinking that if this terrible thing is happening to Brynne—well, to her mother—then it could happen to anyone.

Ginger watches as Rachel hugs herself against air fluffy as wisps of cotton, soft but creepy. She watches as Rachel turns her attention to the indecipherable sky. Until she donned her mask of silence, Rachel often gushed dramatically that, on an ordinary, cloudless night, the bowl of sky above Lindenwood Court revealed more stars than anywhere else in the neighborhood. Some of the lights moved and even blinked, because

Lindenwood Court was in the middle of the landing pattern for the airport down in the city. It was hard to tell the difference between planes earthbound for landing and fixed points of light that stayed forever in the sky. "Imagine!" Rachel would say. There was something mysterious about this, and thrilling.

But tonight, Ginger doubts her daughter believes in a benevolence that allows stars and planes to share the heavens so comfortably. She doubts she believes in anything, beyond this claustrophobic fog.

She waits until she hears Rachel come into the house and go up to her room. Then she heads down the hall to comfort her. But there is such silence behind Rachel's door, it's as if Rachel is hardly breathing. As if she's thinking with all her might, Don't come in. *Don't come in.* Almost a prayer.

Ginger moves away.

It's only a little after nine, but all of Brightwood Trace is home now, too distraught for meetings or errands or visits with friends. They are all inside, sheltering themselves, cocooning into postures of comfort that don't actually help. Andrea Chess sits on the lip of the garden tub in her master bathroom, hiding from her husband and daughter, clenching and unclenching her fists. Iona Feld reads and rereads the front page of her paper, not taking it in. Ginger, who hasn't gone to church for years, phones a friend who belongs to a prayer circle and asks her to add Paisley's name to the list.

In the third house on Dogwood Terrace, Julianne Havelock paces back and forth in her kitchen for such a long time that her seventeen-year-old son, Toby—the only one of her three sons who still lives at home—turns off the TV and comes in to ask if she's all right.

"I'm fine. Just upset," she says, though she hasn't been fine for days. More than anyone, Julianne knows what's going on. She knew how things would turn out even while Paisley and Mason were waiting for the definitive word. She knew from the beginning. And this . . . this *foreknowledge* . . . is eerie. She might as well be a palm reader or a gypsy with a crystal ball. Moving into the front hallway, she squints out the window toward her maple tree with its bow. She doesn't see it. She is like everyone else. It is not invisible just because of the fog.

As they put up the bows today, Julianne thinks, everyone in Brightwood Trace must have acted by rote. None of them could possibly have thought about what they were doing. The situation is, in the most literal sense, *un*thinkable. They are in shock. At the beginning of this unknowable journey, they sense—especially Julianne, Andrea, Ginger, and Iona—that this is happening not just to Paisley, but to them all.

CHAPTER 2

Ten Years Earlier

They were drunk. Some of them really, truly drunk for the first time in years. Sitting around the hot tub in Paisley's backyard on Dogwood Terrace, they marveled at the way everything looked soft edged and wobbly in the twilight, like something seen through beveled glass. They marveled at the way their skin tingled as if it were being massaged from within. Why didn't they drink more often?

It was the dead-hot end of summer, everyone back from vacation, the weather relentlessly sunny. The children in the neighborhood were restless. The mothers, too. The march of long, oppressive days before preschool began again spread out before the young women of Brightwood Trace like a trek along the Great Wall of China. Much as they all loved their children, devoted as they were to their husbands, right then their good fortune felt like a constricting band of silk, binding them into such a narrow routine that they could hardly breathe. For the past week Ginger had dreamed every night about flying the coop, hitting the road, riding off, solo, into the sunset. What did *that* say about a person, when she could think only in clichés? Andrea had imagined herself walking down a runway in a glamorous, bright-yellow suit, a color she never wore. Iona, who knew perfectly well she was older and ought to be wiser, kept thinking, *Another month of this damned heat and I'm going to move to Alaska.* As for Julianne—well, she had pretty much stopped eating.

And then—yes! Paisley had rescued them. Up and down Brightwood Circle and into the culs-de-sac she'd marched, delivering invitations despite the heat and the laments of her four-year-old, Brynne. "Remember *The Little Engine That Could*," she reminded the girl. " 'I think I can, I think I can, I *know* I can!' " Paisley chanted with such enthusiasm that soon little Brynne was chanting, too. The invitations Paisley dropped off were a perfect summer yellow, decorated with bubbly champagne glasses and printed in bold pink type, *Happy Hour for Hot Moms in the Hood . . . We deserve it!*

Oh, they certainly did!

Then there they were, a gaggle of hot moms in the hood, tipsy as fools, trying to keep their balance on the edge of Paisley and Mason's hot tub as they dangled their legs into the swirling water.

For Ginger, the only imperfect note in the chorus of the evening was that the hot tub had been purchased not long before from Ginger's husband, Eddie, who referred to it as a spa. *Tub* sounded common. *Spa* sounded classy. This was the mantra of every salesman in the business. But Eddie was not a salesman. He was a computer expert who could troubleshoot even the most difficult software. He was a man who wrote computer programs for fun—fun!—including teaching aids for his sister, who taught elementary school, and a counting game for their five-year-old son, Max, that every child in the neighborhood wanted to play.

Now Eddie had given all that up. He'd quit a job he loved to take over the family's hot tub business because his father, Leonard, needed bypass surgery. The irreverence Ginger loved most about Eddie had been cut out by the same scalpel that opened his father's chest. Ginger felt alternately hurt, angry, and deprived—although not right now. Right now she was too drunk to care. All around her, the yard began to rotate slowly, like the first moments on a carousel, which she had always loved. She fumbled on the edge of the hot tub and picked up her cup.

Paisley's invitations had said five to seven, but it was after eight and the four women who'd stayed were sitting exactly where they'd been an hour ago, not inclined to budge. Iona kept telling herself to get up and go. She was fifteen years older than these women and had been invited only out of politeness. She should have stayed

16

home. She had no social life. The buzz in her head was pleasant. She stayed because of her inertia.

The only one who moved was Paisley, who had never dipped more than her legs into the hot tub but was wearing a bikini that showed how genuinely slender she was, how delicately long limbed and . . . well, beautiful. The others stared at her openly every time she hoisted her feet out of the tub onto the deck, flung her ridiculous white feather boa over her shoulders—"My cocktail waitress getup," she called it—and retrieved the pitcher of what she referred to as Painkillers. Circling her guests to replenish their drinks, she swayed dreamily to the oldies on the CD player, and sometimes sang along.

"Anybody recognize this one?" she asked. " 'Earth Angel' by the Penguins."

Iona nodded. "I remember dancing to it in somebody's basement with a guy from my English class." But the image that swirled into her head was not of the boy she'd known thirty years ago but of her husband, Richard, dancing her around their living room. A few long, unguarded seconds passed before she remembered that Richard was dead.

Paisley pulled the pitcher toward her as if twirling a dance partner and crooned, slightly off-key, "Earth angel, earth angel . . ."

Iona tried to smile.

"Here's something I bet you didn't know," Paisley said. "At first they thought the flip side, 'Hey Señorita,' was going to be the big hit. Can you imagine?" She waved the feather boa to the music. "The Crew Cuts also did a version of this, but I never liked it. I was surprised it did so well on the charts."

"How do you know all that?" Iona asked. "Some of that obscure rock 'n' roll trivia dates back to the '50s before you were born."

"My mother was a big fan. Still is. I grew up listening to the original records, the old 45s. Ask her about them next time she visits."

Paisley danced over to Julianne, plucked her cup from her hand, and refilled it nearly to the rim before handing it back with a flourish.

"Very nice, the way you serve a drink," Julianne said, slurring a little. "I'd pay you handsomely if I could get this kind of service at home."

"We can negotiate, but I warn you, I don't come cheap. I waitressed most of my way through college." She two-stepped toward Andrea, draped the feather boa around her neck, and bent toward her with the pitcher.

"I think I'm too drunk to have any more," Andrea said.

Paisley poured anyway. "It's just what the doctor ordered. Exactly like a piña colada except made with orange juice. Practically a health food. A healthy dose of vitamin C."

"Here's to vitamin C!" Julianne tossed the long hair she'd been growing for a year, a dozen sun-streaked shades that always looked messy. Bill, her husband, hated it. For this reason she intended to let it grow until the end of time.

Wobbling a little, she jumped into the waist-deep water and stood on tiptoe to call attention to her flat, tanned midriff, punctuated by a tiny sterling ring. "Check out the navel decor, ladies," she said, pointing. "You can do it, too. Have a piercing or two and make a jewelry statement!"

Ginger peered at Julianne's stomach, which was impressive for a woman who'd popped out three sons. Of course, none of her boys were babies anymore. She'd had plenty of time to get back in shape. The ring looked like it belonged on a teenager. So did Julianne's skimpy bikini. Ginger herself wore a stylish one-piece suit, as did Andrea and most other young mothers who no longer wanted to show their midsections. Not Paisley, of course.

"Weird," Ginger told Julianne. "Not my kind of jewelry statement."

"Mine, either." Iona patted her belly. "Too flabby in the middle. Too old." Ginger noted that Iona was not in swimwear at all, but in the body-concealing uniform of walking shorts and short-sleeved shirt she'd been wearing ever since she moved into her house last spring, revealing only a pair of feet crying out for a pedicure, and a set of knobby knees. Everyone knew Iona's husband had died in an accident a year or two ago, but she seemed determined to look like she was still in mourning.

"Where's your little girl?" Iona asked Paisley.

"Mason has her. He took her for pizza at a sit-down restaurant where the service is notoriously slow. It's a big treat for a four-year-old. I told him to keep her out as long as he could."

Seeing she'd lost the group's attention, Julianne stopped pointing to her belly and seized the bra top of her bikini. With a mischievous grin, she yanked it up to expose a perfectly formed small, tanned breast. "I'm piercing my nipple next!" she shouted.

Andrea and Ginger and Paisley and Iona exchanged glances.

Iona decided Julianne's husband must be having an affair, for her to turn into such an exhibitionist.

Andrea wondered what would happen if she exposed her own breasts to the sun. Just her luck, she'd probably burn to a crisp.

Ginger wondered what Eddie would think if he could see this. Would he prefer to spend his nights with breasts like Julianne's instead of Ginger's, which were larger but less perky? She immediately censored the thought. She hated getting jealous like this. *Of course,* Eddie looked at other women—all men did—but as far as she knew, he was faithful. He loved her. He loved their children. He was the kind of man who'd leave a job he loved, a prestigious job you'd be proud to tell people about, in order to fulfill a family duty in a damned *hot tub* store. She took another sip of her drink.

"Did it hurt?" Andrea asked Julianne. "The belly, not the breast, which I'm assuming was a joke." Andrea put her cup down, held her back against the edge of the tub, and let her spindly legs float out in front of her.

"Not a bit," Julianne said.

"I don't believe that. Piercing a body part with a steel instrument—that's got to hurt."

"It didn't, I swear to God."

"Well, hell. I wouldn't want to do it anyway." Why would anyone choose mutilation if they didn't have to? Andrea's daughter, Courtney, had a mark on her abdomen, too. She hadn't chosen it. A year ago, when she was only three, she'd been diagnosed with a Wilms' tumor, a kind of kidney cancer. She'd had surgery and then chemo. There was still no certainty how it would turn out. The scar would last forever.

Andrea had loved this night, up until now. For the first time in a year she hadn't thought of Courtney once, until Julianne started talking about piercings.

"Oh, shit," she said, remembering. "I have to get going. I told John I'd be home by nine. He's doing me the great favor of watching Courtney."

"Well, here. Call him." Paisley offered her phone.

Andrea felt her features lock into a pose of determination. "No."

"Why not?"

"Let *him* worry, for once." She seemed to have made this decision without thinking. Too drunk to think. "It won't kill him to take care of his daughter for a while. Then I'll take care of *him* later. If you know what I mean."

Hearing her talk like that, the others realized that Andrea was every bit as drunk as Julianne. Well, good! Andrea deserved an evening of escape, after what she'd been through. Even though the chemo was finished, Courtney was still bald. Did anyone know how *pathetic* a bald four-year-old looked? The last time Ginger's son, Max, had to take an antibiotic, he'd nodded solemnly before swallowing the spoonful of thick pink liquid and said, "This'll make me better. And then my hair will fall out like Courtney's, right?" It was all Ginger could do not to burst into tears as she took her son into her arms. "Oh, not at all, Max," she'd murmured. "Your hair won't fall out at all."

A silence fell. Julianne tried to pull herself together. What was she doing, taking off her top? Dark thoughts sloshed around in her head. Next thing she knew she'd be showing them the still-tender tattoo on her butt. *What was she doing?*

Ginger closed her eyes and let herself ride the slow carousel of alcohol around Paisley's twilit yard. She used to like Julianne so much. A doctor's wife should be classy, not trampy, and Julianne *had* been classy. Until lately. She wasn't beautiful like Paisley, but she was a natural blonde. Men found that irresistible, even Eddie. Of course, it was mostly Paisley Eddie looked at. Ginger wasn't going to dwell on that. She was forever looking at Paisley herself. Being jealous made no sense.

The gate opened just then, and in walked Mason, a lanky, bespectacled man who looked exactly like the newspaper editor he was, with a skinny little girl half-asleep against his shoulder. "Good evening, ladies. Good evening." With his free hand, he pretended to tip his hat. "I hope you're having fun."

"Oh, we are, honey." Paisley kissed him on the cheek but didn't move to take her daughter. "Put her to bed, all right? Then come back and see us."

"Well, I surely will." The way Mason smiled as he opened the door to take his daughter inside, Iona thought he was making a joke she didn't quite get. She wasn't part of this group; she was too old.

Then, as sometimes happened, the fact of being drunk lifted Iona right out of herself, into a perfectly clear vision of what she'd become. Her age wasn't a hindrance here. It gave her some perspective. All these young women, Andrea and Paisley and Julianne and Ginger—every one of them was drowning in estrogen soup. Thirtysome years old and their lives were about nothing but kids and sex. Sure, they probably had hobbies they loved and volunteer work they thought was important, but mostly they were just trying to keep themselves one step ahead of their hormones.

Iona, on the other hand, was beyond all that. Her head was clear. She was lucky.

Then the liquor turned on her, as it always did. She wasn't lucky. She had been like these women once, coupled and comfortable. And now she was alone.

In the gathering dusk, Paisley lit a citronella candle against the no-see-ums that had begun to plunge from the sultry air onto their shoulders, hungrily nibbling. The door to the house opened and Mason came out, carrying a little box. He made a great show of lifting off the top. "Something special for you, ladies," he said. "I wouldn't offer this to everyone."

"Cigars!" Andrea cried.

Sure enough, there they were—long, fat, unladylike cigars circled by paper rings.

"Oh, me first!" demanded Julianne, who extracted one and put it in her mouth. Paisley produced a lighter. Mason bowed, clowning, and went into the house. Julianne lit the cigar, sampled it, and handed it around. "Now, don't inhale," she warned.

"Oh, I won't." Andrea took a puff and blew smoke rings into the air. Lovely. She hadn't had a cigar in years. Iona made a face and refused. When it was Ginger's turn, she drew the dry, bitter smoke into her mouth and tried valiantly not to cough.

"I thought it'd taste more like a cigarette," Julianne said, "but it doesn't. It's more like smoking reefer." She fixed her gaze on Andrea. "You smoked a lot of pot in college. Doesn't it taste like reefer?"

Andrea saw Iona's expression of surprise at hearing about her checkered past. She understood. After a year with little Courtney in and out of hospitals, Andrea had gotten so scrawny and flat chested that she looked like she ought to be wearing starched white dresses like Florence Nightingale's, and doing acts of purity rather than drugs or sex.

Leaning against the edge of the tub, she gazed up into the night—a moonless, starless dome of charcoal gray—and told them the truth. "I haven't smoked pot or done any other kind of drug for so long I wouldn't know if it tasted like cigars," she said. "Once I had Courtney, I was always afraid I'd get so stoned I'd pass out and something terrible would happen and it would be my fault. And the responsibility would be with me for the rest of my life." She was quiet for a moment. "Then the cancer happened anyway."

Julianne had to hold on to the lip of the hot tub so she wouldn't fall. A mean thought flitted through her mind, which she was too drunk to censor. She hadn't worked as a nurse since the kids started coming along, but she still thought like one. Maybe the drugs had something to do with Courtney's illness. They very well might. Being a druggie for a couple of years might translate into a genetic defect you passed along to your child. A defect that would attack your child's kidney. If she did a little research, she bet she'd find out that was true.

"Well, Courtney's going to be fine," Paisley said. "She practically *is* fine."

Feeling guilty for what she was thinking, Julianne said, "Bill says Wilms' tumors are the most curable. He's really pleased with Courtney's prognosis." She was trying to be supportive, but her voice wavered with the liquor so badly that she sounded anything but.

A stab of envy knifed through Ginger at the idea of Julianne's husband being a doctor. A surgeon. Bill Havelock, the man you wanted in the operating room if you got a bone disease or broke your shoulder or blew out your knee. A man who could make pronouncements about kidney cancer, which wasn't even his specialty, and people would believe him.

Every woman in this tub was living a life of privilege, Ginger supposed, able to stay home with her children instead of going to work. All the husbands made enough money to support them. But only Julianne was married to a prominent surgeon.

Whereas Eddie sold hot tubs. Hot tubs, which he always referred to as spas, like every other cheap salesman on the planet.

"Hey, this is a party!" Paisley reminded them. "No negative thoughts!"

Julianne laughed. "No negative thoughts! No sir! Not me!" What a lie. She waved her drink around so forcefully that she lost her balance on the edge of the hot tub and fell right in, went all the way down until she was sitting on the bottom with her long hair streaming up above her. For the briefest moment she thought, *I could stay down here forever*. Then the most powerful urge for air came over her, and she propelled herself to the surface, spluttering and giggling. She didn't feel like giggling—but there she was. She put her hand to her navel. "Oh, no! I think my ring fell out!"

"I'll get it!" Andrea shouted.

"I will!" Ginger propelled herself forward, jumped in with a splash.

"No, don't!" Paisley waved her arms at them

from the side of the tub. "It's too dark and we're too drunk. I don't want somebody to end up drowned. It'll turn up in the strainer."

Julianne raised her arm in a jubilant power fist. "Too drunk!" she shouted gleefully.

Paisley motioned Julianne to sit down. "You," Paisley told her gently, "are drunk as a skunk."

"As a skunk." Julianne felt the gleeful expression drain from her face. "We've all been living in Brightwood Trace like a bunch of friends, and you tell me I'm a skunk."

"Not a skunk, Julianne. Just *drunk* as—"

"You might think I'm a skunk but I'm not." A dull throbbing began behind her eyes. "Julianne Havelock has an important role in this neighborhood. She's a vital link." Sloppily, Julianne pointed around the group. "If you want advice about giving parties, you ask Paisley. Or if you want to know about pediatrics, you go to Andrea," she said. "But years from now when your kid comes home with a tattoo or your daughter wants an abortion, you'll come to me."

No one said a word. Silence shrouded them like noxious fumes. Finally Andrea hoisted herself out of the tub. "It's getting late."

"What? Leaving so soon?" Julianne accused.

"Well, I told John—"

"John is probably asleep by now, Andrea. Sound asleep. Off to la-la land. Tired of waiting for you to come home and *take care* of him."

Paisley set a hand on Julianne's shoulder. "Girlfriend," she muttered softly, "you sound like you're in la-la land yourself."

"You think so?" Julianne heard her voice degenerate into a slurry whine. "You're right. I'm thirty-four years old and I have three children under eleven. I have a bachelor's degree in nursing, but I can't work because Bill makes too much money and we don't need more income. I'm thirty-four years old, and I'm finished."

"You're not finished, Julianne. You're just starting."

"Of course you are," said Iona. "Before you know it, they'll all be grown and gone and you'll still be young enough to do whatever you want. You ought to enjoy them while you can."

"Well, I can't stay in the same house with him that long," Julianne said. "I can't."

"You mean you and Bill are—"

"I can't stay with him," Julianne said.

Andrea wondered where Mason had disappeared to. If he'd just come out and ask how they liked his cigars, all of this would stop. Julianne couldn't mean what she was saying.

"You know what? I think this party is over," Iona said.

Ginger held tight to the side of the tub. The yard had stopped feeling like a merry-go-round and begun to spin in earnest.

"Here, let me help you," Paisley said. With a

strong grip, she pulled Ginger out of the water.

Everyone but Julianne stood on the grass and toweled off. Julianne sat where they'd left her, head bent, wet yellow hair hanging over her face. She was weeping into her hand. Andrea headed over to comfort her, but Paisley put a hand on her arm. "She'll be all right. She's just drunk. We all are." Paisley's voice was like a lullaby.

Unsteadily, Ginger wrapped herself in her towel while the others told Paisley what a nice party it had been. Her thoughts wandered to Eddie. She remembered him saying goodbye when she'd left the house this evening, leaving him with the children. He always sounded much huskier and sexier than she expected. It still made her tingly even after seven years of marriage. Even when she was sober. Even though he was running a hot tub store. For a second she wished he were right here in Paisley's yard, touching her all over her wet bathing suit. Sometimes she had these thoughts even though the pill made her sick and birth control was her greatest worry. It was crazy.

"It's late. Let's walk down the street together," Andrea suggested. "Safety in numbers." There was no danger in Brightwood Trace, but everyone agreed. Paisley would tend to Julianne, who lived right next door.

They all walked as steadily as they could. Iona felt almost sober. Andrea wondered if she could fake passing out so John would leave her alone. Ginger was plagued by dizziness, which had brought on the first wave of nausea. As soon as she got home she was going to throw up. Eddie would hold her head and say, "Honey, I know you had too much to drink, but you can sleep it off and you'll be okay tomorrow."

"Maybe *late afternoon* tomorrow," she'd say.

He would rub her back. If her stomach felt better, maybe they'd make love.

Even so, she was as sad as the others that the party had ended so abruptly. It felt unfinished. As if they'd come close to a bond that wasn't ever going to happen now. Maybe they hadn't really expected it. Except for Iona, they were women who had room only for husbands and children in the too-full chambers of their hearts. Probably this was exactly as it should be. But they regretted the sisterhood they might have had, and they would always yearn for the wildness.

CHAPTER 3

October 6

The week before the ribbons go up, Julianne Havelock walks into Examining Room Two where Paisley is waiting to have her pre-op workup for bunion surgery. She isn't expecting anything unusual. Julianne has worked for the same podiatrist for six years, ever since she got her nurse-practitioner degree. By now she's done so many of these histories and physicals that she's a wiz at spotting a bad cold or other condition that might make surgery risky. These are elective operations, after all, and if there's the least question about the patient's health, the surgery can be postponed.

She opens the door and finds, as always, that Paisley looks beautiful enough to make Julianne's heart skip a beat, as it did even when they were younger and her admiration was tinged with envy. Paisley's tennis tan still glows golden even though it's October. Her hair is ruffled but stylish, a little damp. Julianne pictures her jumping out of the shower, dressing quickly, finger-drying her hair in the car. Her short dark locks shine.

"So you're having bunion surgery," Julianne murmurs as she checks Paisley's chart. "What made you decide?"

Paisley holds out her right foot, where a good-size bunion has begun to push the big toe to the right. It's not pretty, but Julianne has seen worse. "Does it hurt?"

"No, but my tennis game is off, and I think this is the culprit. It's gotten so that I have to buy shoes a whole size wider. It's great for the right foot, but it makes the left foot slosh around so I run like a gimp."

Julianne smiles at the idea of elegant Paisley as a gimp. "Even with your foot sloshing around, I can't imagine you clumsy."

"You'd be surprised. Sometimes I have the sense to buy two pairs of shoes in two different widths, but do I remember to wear the right size on the right foot? No. I'm always rushing out of the house thinking of ten other things. I figured if I have the bunion removed now, Mason can take off on Columbus Day, so I get an extra recovery day not to cart the kids around. Then I can take a break from tennis over the winter and by spring I'll be a whole new person."

"A whole new person?" Julianne arches an eyebrow. "I thought the old person was doing all right."

"Oh, she is. She is." Paisley laughs. "And how is *this* old person doing?" she asks, shifting the focus to Julianne. "I can hardly believe Toby's a senior this year. And *you*. Do I sense wedding bells in your future?"

"Bite your tongue, Paisley. Everything's on hold until Toby starts college. Right now we don't broach the subject even in the smallest whispers." It's interesting how patients will try to change the subject, even patients who aren't also neighbors. Nerves, Julianne thinks. Anyway, she's not ready to make wedding plans, much less discuss them. "Now. Tell me. How are you feeling?"

"Okay except for a touchy stomach. I had an ulcer years ago and sometimes it comes back full force in the fall. I don't know why. Usually it bothers me for a couple of weeks and then goes away. I wonder if it's scientific to have ulcers only with the change of seasons."

"Who knows?" Julianne says. "I'll check out the literature. Have you seen your doctor for this?"

"Not yet."

"I bet you already know the standard advice. Bland foods. No hot spices. Be careful what you drink." It's been years since Paisley lived next door to Julianne on Dogwood Terrace, before the Lamms moved to the larger house up on Lindenwood, but in those days the weekly overflow of bottles in the recycling bin showed that Paisley liked her liquor. Even now, at parties, she always has a glass in her hand. "Do you know that some studies show cooked cabbage can heal an ulcer?" she asks.

"Oh, Lord. I think I'd rather suffer!"

"Or it could be a bacterial infection and you need an antibiotic. Most ulcers are caused by bacteria."

"I've read about that."

"Here. Lie down. Let's check out the sore belly."

Over the years, Julianne's hands have learned to palpate and probe so skillfully that she tends to close her eyes and let the organs beneath yield up their secrets like words in Braille. But she's surprised when the pins and needles begin in the tips of her fingers as they sometimes do—that tiny current that always signals illness. She isn't alarmed yet, only alert.

Then her hand makes contact with Paisley's brick of a liver. At that instant a hellish wave of darkness washes over her, a bilious tsunami of liquid night. A liquid firestorm of wet, toxic heat, unleashed from some hidden, secluded place within. It rides her bloodstream, drowning her but fiery, too, invading every vessel, cutting off her breath.

"What's wrong?" Paisley asks, frowning.

Julianne can't answer, can't move. Her flesh feels singed wherever the darkness has passed. Her ears fill with a sizzling she knows is no earthly sound. Hanging on to consciousness by a supreme effort of will, she gasps, struggling to draw air. She's going to collapse. Just as it threatens to crush her heart, annihilate her brain—just then, instead, it passes out of her, a literal *thing,* the embodiment of darkness. Gone.

"Julianne?"

Julianne gulps air and lifts her hand, trying not to snatch it back, away from Paisley's flesh. "It's nothing. Just concentrating. I always do that. Didn't mean to scare you." She inhales again.

"Time for Dr. Dunn to come in now. Back in a minute."

In the corridor outside the examining room, Julianne plasters herself against the wall and waits for her head to clear. She knows what this is. It happened once before.

She'd thought it was a fluke. It couldn't possibly repeat itself. That's what she'd thought.

It had been one of those tender, warmish mornings with everything in bloom, when the last place anyone wanted to be was a doctor's office—including Julianne, who was doing a pre-op for hammertoe surgery. The patient's name was unforgettable even without the drama. Eudora Nestor. How was Eudora feeling? Oh, fine, fine, just the usual allergies that bothered her every year. Julianne made a notation on the chart, checked the patient's sinuses, found a swollen gland in her neck. The pins and needles began then in Julianne's fingers, a tingling that happened sometimes, that signal of illness she'd grown accustomed to over the years. What was it? Maybe simply a reaction to her surprise at finding anything amiss. Peter Dunn's patients tended to be vibrantly healthy. Only the diabetics had underlying health problems—poor circulation, ingrown nails that escalated into infections, occasional rotting, gangrenous toes. But they were the exception. Most of the patients simply wanted to have something fixed. They wanted to start jogging again, improve their golf game, play tennis. Like Paisley, they aspired to be a whole new person in the spring.

In that room with Eudora, the tidal wave of darkness replaced the tingling with the suddenness of an electric shock, flaying her with twin punishments of water and fire, like a visitation from hell. She couldn't breathe, couldn't move. She must be dying. Poisoned? A heart attack? A stroke?

Then it passed, exactly as it had today.

Excusing herself, Julianne had fled into the same hallway where she stands now, as much confused as panicked. What had happened? It had been a physical thing and yet . . . not. Her heart drummed a frantic cadence, but otherwise the physical effects of the assault seemed to be gone, leaving behind only a dull headache. She was, remarkably . . . all right. Then she understood that, in some profound way, Eudora Nestor was not. She grabbed Peter's lab coat as he swished by between patients. "Come into number three," she demanded. He had to follow because she wouldn't let go of his sleeve. After palpating Eudora's swollen gland, he raised his eyebrows, puzzled. A swollen gland could mean anything or nothing. Julianne trailed him out of the room. "I know you think I'm overreacting, but I'm sure it's something serious. I have a feeling." Julianne never had "feelings," so Peter ordered follow-up tests. Eudora turned out to have an aggressive, undiagnosed form of leukemia. Why the first, routine blood tests hadn't picked up something, no one knew. Eudora Nestor was fifty-one years old. Eight weeks later, she was dead.

Now again she waylays Peter and takes him into the room. While he repeats the examination, Julianne studies her patient more closely. What has she missed? Perhaps Paisley's too-golden tan is not from early-autumn sunning. Perhaps it's the beginning of jaundice. Paisley has always had remarkable skin, toned and flawless, with an almost apricot tint even in winter. Jaundice would be easy to miss. Perhaps the whites of her eyes harbor an incipient yellow tinge, disguised by the wide-awake blue of the irises. Julianne is too shaken to know. To Julianne, Paisley simply looks beautiful. Paisley looks fine. Only the hard liver says no. But even then, even as Peter consults with Paisley's primary physician and orders further tests, even as they wait for the results that won't come back for days . . . even then Julianne lives in the shadow of the darkness that assailed her . . . and she knows. She doesn't for a moment think: hepatitis, parasite, something simple. She knows.

"I heard about Paisley," Julianne's ex-husband, Bill, says when he brings Toby home after taking him to dinner that night. This is Monday, not his usual Wednesday with their youngest son, who at seventeen is satisfied with their one night out a week and doesn't need more. Julianne is sure Bill heard from her boss, Peter, how upset she is about what happened, and he's come to check up on her. "From what I hear, it was pretty awful," he says.

"It was. Try being the first one to touch the obviously diseased liver of your ex-next-door-neighbor. Try watching someone who thinks she's opting for elective surgery end up with orders for a slew of serious tests."

"I know." But of course he doesn't know, he has no idea—and she's certainly not going to tell him.

He looms in the doorway even after Toby bolts off to his room, a man just shy of six feet but looking taller because of his long-limbed build. When Julianne first met him at the hospital where she worked after nursing school, part of his appeal was his status (up-and-coming surgeon) and part was his aristocratic bearing that reminded her of an Episcopal priest—aquiline nose and blue-gray eyes, narrow face with impossibly high cheekbones, a smooth, mellifluous voice and languid, graceful walk that has degenerated over the years into a shorter, pinched-looking stride. It saddens her to see how quickly he's aged. At forty-eight, Bill is only four years older than Julianne, but tonight he looks like a man of sixty, jowly and gray. Odd, how once she stopped desiring him physically, her attraction to him was over so completely that she can't imagine ever feeling differently.

"Are you okay?" he asks in his practiced doctor voice, which she would resent if he didn't look so world weary.

"Fine. Just a headache." She rubs the area between her brows with thumb and index finger. The dull throbbing has stayed with her all day just as it did after the incident with Eudora Nestor, when it didn't go away until morning. As on that other occasion, aspirin hasn't helped.

"I wish I could do something," Bill says.

"Really. I'm fine." Generous Bill. He makes her feel like a force-fed goose, forever stuffing gratitude down her unwilling throat. During the divorce proceedings, Bill deeded their house to her without asking her to buy him out. He agreed to liberal child support. He let her have custody of the boys but offered to watch them anytime she asked—and actually *did* watch them, even after he remarried and had a daughter. When Julianne went back to school to become a nurse-practitioner, she sometimes needed whole weekends to study. Bill was always available. His openhandedness was boundless. He was a paragon, wasn't he?

Ask him in, Julianne tells herself. When you've

known someone half your life and shared the task of raising sons, that's what you do. But she doesn't. For another thirty seconds, she lets the renowned but humble surgeon and model father lean wearily against the doorjamb. "What about Doug?" he finally asks. "Did you tell Doug?"

She's too startled to say it's none of his business. "I told him. Of course. Yes."

Bill shifts in the doorway and seems to be struggling to hold his ground. "You've been seeing Doug a couple of years now."

She crosses her arms over her chest. "Three. Why?"

"I was just wondering if you had— Do you have any plans in the works?"

Bill sounds so uncomfortable that instead of getting angry, for an instant Julianne is pulled out of herself and laughs. "How did we get on to the subject of Doug?"

"It's been almost ten years since you and I separated," he says. "The boys are pretty much grown."

The laughter retreats from her throat. "I'm aware of that."

"You know how much I admire you for sticking with them all these years. Going to school. Working. When I heard you and Doug were serious—"

"You heard we were serious? Where? From Toby?"

Bill shrugs. "I just want you to know that if you decided to make an announcement, I wouldn't object."

As if she needs his permission! As if he himself hadn't moved on years ago, married Joyce, had another child, lived his life!

"Well, thank you." She senses that he doesn't in the least detect the note of sarcasm in her voice.

Now he's studying the newly sanded hardwood entryway so intently that Julianne thinks he's about to criticize the finish. "You've worked for Peter a long time," he says to the floor. "You do pretty much the same thing every day." Determinedly, he lifts his eyes to meet Julianne's. "You're good at it. Peter says you're a treasure. But aren't you bored?"

"Bored? No. Of course not."

What's he saying? That her job is so dull that when something dramatic and unexpected happens, as it did with Paisley, she behaves unprofessionally? Not so!

"Besides, you were the one who got me the job," she tells him.

"Yes, but that was six years ago. The idea was that you'd keep it while you were deciding what to do with your nurse-practitioner credentials, and then you'd move on."

True enough. Peter Dunn was Bill's colleague, a respected foot surgeon. He'd understand if she left once she'd made a career decision. The offer had seemed so generous, on both Bill's part and Peter's, that she'd accepted.

"It's just that I never thought you'd stay there this long," Bill says.

"Neither did I. But I didn't count on Will"— their oldest—"needing tutoring in calculus, or Joe going through that grumbly, throwing-things-around phase after he didn't make the golf team at school. All that took up a lot of time and energy. I wasn't thinking about looking for other jobs." She cocks her head coyly, hoping to hide her irritation at needing to explain herself at all. "I guess I got hooked on foot ailments. What can I tell you?"

Bill doesn't respond right away. More than any other man she knows, Bill has mastered the art of speaking softly and in a level tone, no matter what. He has become a man who can pull his mask off after surgery and tell the anxious family, "Well, we didn't get it all, but I think with chemo and radiation he might do well." Not *be fine*. Not *recover*. Just do well. The family wouldn't hear bad news. They would hear the soft voice, the mellifluous tone, the air of quiet authority. Nine times out of ten, they wouldn't ask questions. They would never sue.

And Bill was a genuinely good surgeon. So why did Julianne so resent the demeanor that keeps him out of trouble?

He draws a long, resigned breath. "I know what a job the boys were. But that was years ago. They're all right now. Toby's no trouble, is he?"

"No." The ache behind her eyes is beginning to feel like a hangover. "I think I'm going to turn in, Bill," she says. "You look tired yourself."

"Yes. Busy week." He turns to go, then swivels back. "Will you think about it, Jules? About how you really feel about the job?"

"Sure." He's the only one who's ever called her Jules. She hates it. She feels like he's issuing a warning, or maybe a command.

"Thanks for taking Toby to dinner," she calls when he finally heads down the walk. "See you next week."

He nods, always the gentleman, but she's trembling when she closes the door. She wants to be free of him. Has she ever been? She thinks, *If he could still control everything I do, he would.*

After he's gone, she pours herself a glass of wine but can't drink it. Another job—*why?* She divorced Bill partly to get to the point where she could do this one. He would have liked her to remain the privileged suburbanite she'd been then, with too much money and no accomplishments except her ability to produce sons. It had helped for a while to take out her restlessness in wild hair, piercings, and a tattoo of a butterfly on her butt . . . and then it had gotten to a point where that sense of being caged had put her, literally, on the brink of violence and even madness.

She had divorced him so she would not go mad.

She wonders if Bill has any clue that it was Paisley—*Paisley*—who had helped her back then. Who had showed her she was not psychotic, just under stress; not evil, just upset. It was Paisley who had brought her back to herself. And in the most shocking way.

The memory of that makes her smile . . . until she remembers the tsunami of night, the disease that has been gathering inside Paisley like a storm.

Setting the empty wineglass in the sink, she turns out the light in the kitchen and goes upstairs. In her bedroom, she catches sight of herself in the mirror—a woman who wears her hair short now, whose piercings are gone except in her ears, whose embarrassing tattoo was long ago lasered off at considerable expense and pain . . . a woman who spent years doing nothing but going to school, raising children, and working. Now, finally, here she is, living the productive life she always wanted, useful in an intelligent way. Even Doug fits tidily into her plan, a man she met just as she was beginning to see through her tunnel of busyness to a time when her sons wouldn't need her, when it would be important not to cling to them, or give the appearance of clinging. She has a social life, and she has a career. What right has Bill to suggest she needs more? She knows nurse-practitioners can do more than she's doing now. Of course she does. She stays at this job Bill thinks is too dull for her because it is safe. Or *was* safe until her fingers began to feel what fingers can't feel.

And after all, what *do* her fingers feel? What's happening now might be an extension of the hypersensitivity she didn't even realize was unusual, growing up, until it became clear that others didn't share it. Unlike her friends in high school, she was utterly unable to borrow other girls' sweaters or jewelry, and later, as a poverty-stricken nursing student, she'd been unable to buy used furniture for her apartment, even though used furniture was all she could afford. The vibrations emanating from other people's possessions were too overwhelming, that sense of the bodies they'd touched or houses they'd been in, their whole history of joys and sorrows. Once, in an antique shop, after she'd shied away from a particular chest of drawers that gave off the very aura of doom, she'd learned from the owner that the chest had come from a bedroom where someone was murdered. The only used furniture in her house, even now, is the graceful Queen Anne dining room set her mother gave her, which has belonged to various relatives for three generations and gives off only a peaceful, familial air of contentment.

Who would have known that such an odd sensitivity would mature into this horror in her fingers? Or did it? There might be some other explanation entirely. Either way, this is an awful gift.

Julianne does not believe in psychics or fortune-telling. What has happened twice now makes no sense. It frightens her. She won't be able to sleep, but she's too muddled to think anymore. All she knows is, if she could give back the gift of prophecy in her fingers, she would. No one wants to touch a person's flesh and feel their death.

CHAPTER 4

October 15

The day after the ribbons go up, Andrea Chess stands at her kitchen sink peeling potatoes while her daughter, Courtney, sits on a stool at their breakfast bar, arranging a variety of bottles, pumice stones, emery boards, and other nail implements on the counter.

"Go somewhere else, Courtney," Andrea says. "Did it ever occur to you that a kitchen is not an appropriate place for a manicure?"

"A pedicure," Courtney corrects.

"A pedicure! Absolutely not! Take this project to your room."

"I'll clean the counter later. I'll scrub it down with Clorox." Courtney chooses a cuticle cutter from her collection. She braces her left foot on the newly scrubbed counter.

"Courtney."

"What?" With muted savagery, the girl begins to pull pieces of skin from around her big toe. Andrea forgets what she was going to say. In any case, it no longer matters. She sees what's going on. Courtney, a cancer survivor herself, a child about to go for the dreaded annual checkup that will determine if she's still free of disease, needs the guise of this pedicure to steel herself for Paisley's news. In Courtney's mind, she *is* Paisley. She shares Paisley's fate.

After waiting hours for Paisley's call, Andrea is almost as unsettled as her daughter. Although the ribbons went up yesterday after Paisley's firm diagnosis of cancer, there's still no word on where it originated, how aggressive it is, or what kind of treatment she'll need. Paisley is supposed to find out all that today. She has promised to phone Andrea as soon as she hears.

Shoving a handful of potato peels into the disposal, Andrea practices breathing exercises as she listens to them grind away. By the time the noise stops, Courtney has put down the cuticle cutter and is viciously scrubbing the bottom of her foot with the pumice stone. She sets the pumice stone back on the counter, seizes an emery board, and files her toenails. It's like a film on fast-forward. Catching Andrea's eye, she tosses the emery board away and lifts a bottle of polish for her mother's approval. The color is a maroon so dark it could pass for black.

"No. Use a lighter shade. Didn't we talk about this? Ultradark polish doesn't allow your nails to breathe properly. You can get a fungus."

"I'll take my chances." A flame of anger sparks under Courtney's light tone.

Well, fine, every fourteen-year-old in town favors this color, what's the harm? Andrea watches Courtney stroke polish onto the nail of her little toe, her tongue sticking out a bit, her face scrunched, a pose of concentration. Anxiety radiates from her like heat. Compared with previous precheckup outbursts, black polish is not so serious. Better than temper tantrums or cutting school. A countertop can be disinfected. A fungus can be treated. Paisley's is a new cancer, not a recurrence, but to Courtney it's all the same, a knifepoint of danger cutting through everything. If Paisley is incurable, so is all the world.

Andrea can no more talk to Courtney about this than she could bring herself to give a speech to an audience of thousands. She's simply going to assume that, like Courtney, eventually Paisley is going to be all right.

Eleven years ago when Courtney was diagnosed with the Wilms' tumor, everyone but Paisley thought the child was done for. While other people studied the ground and muttered platitudes about Courtney's prognosis, Paisley looked Andrea straight in the eye and said, "She's going to be fine," with such fire of recovery in her voice that her certainty passed to Andrea like a torch.

It was a great gift, because Andrea's husband, John, had gone stony. In his most rational, lawyerly tones, he went over the treatment options with Andrea a dozen times—surgery first and chemo later; it was the standard protocol. He did hours of research. But feelings? He wouldn't admit to any. The most he'd do was pat Andrea awkwardly on the shoulder, as if she were a stranger he was obligated to touch.

The night before Courtney's surgery, John's mother flew in from Indianapolis and disappeared with him into the hospital waiting room to talk. When Andrea returned to get them so they could tell Courtney goodnight, she heard the sound of weeping drifting into the hall. Her mother-in-law? She hadn't shown much emotion up to now. But no. It was John. John was weeping! "They're going to cut open my *baby*," he gasped between sobs. Andrea stopped short. *She* was John's wife. Didn't *she* deserve his tears? His outpouring of fear? Didn't she deserve the chance to comfort him, to let him comfort *her?* Oughtn't the two of them muddle through this together? Dazed and numb, she retreated down the corridor. Andrea lost him then, or he lost her, and whatever it was between them that went missing that night, they've never gotten it back.

It was Paisley, not John, who got Andrea through the nightmare that followed. Who warded off the gloom-and-doom neighbors. Who spread hopefulness like angel dust. During those first frantic days, when Paisley heard John make some comment about Courtney's dire condition, she turned and snapped at him, "For heaven's sake, John, don't start burying her just yet!" Never before and never since has Andrea heard Paisley be short with anyone. It stopped John in midsentence.

Surgery, chemo, checkups—dreadful, but Courtney survived it. Losing John was terrible. The smooth, mannerly surface of the relationship they've maintained ever since is terrible, still— the emptiness of a marriage running on autopilot. Andrea doesn't often dwell on this, but on the rare occasions when it opens like a draining wound, she decides that, on balance, keeping her daughter, and gaining Paisley, was worth it.

Andrea discovered later that Paisley had an instinct for knowing when people were in trouble. Andrea was only one of her projects, maybe the first. When Paisley saw Courtney sick and John paralyzed and Andrea cowering, there was nothing for her but to step in. It was not even a conscious decision. To cheer Andrea on her lowest days, Paisley would tell stories about herself she swore no one else knew, so unlikely, so funny that Andrea would find herself once more the self that could put on a happy face for her ailing daughter and anyone else who happened to be looking.

Their lasting friendship was a fallout no one expected. By the time Courtney had begun to recover, Andrea had discovered beneath Paisley's sparkling surface a thoughtfulness, an *innerness* she wouldn't have guessed at. And Paisley—though she wouldn't have admitted this—had found Andrea *easy*. Easy to talk to. Easy to trust. "Lagniappe" Paisley liked to call their bond, a New Orleans term for something extra that you didn't pay for, thrown in to sweeten the deal. It's certainly been sweet for Andrea. She peels another potato. There are enough here to feed all of Brightwood Trace.

Until today, Paisley has been good about giving Andrea regular updates about the tests she's undergoing. Their conversations haven't been long, but they've been purposeful. "More liver-function studies. Big issues with the liver, but they're not sure what."

Or, "Another biopsy. I'll call you later."

Or simply, almost lightly, "Cancer. But no details until tomorrow."

Tongue-tied into silence, Andrea was as shocked as if she herself had brought their story full circle, from Courtney's illness to Paisley's. When she bought a white ribbon and tied it around her maple tree out front, she knew the neighbors would do the same. It wasn't much, but all of them knew Paisley would see them as she traveled through the neighborhood to her house. Andrea hoped their purity and festiveness would somehow temper the sharpness of the news.

Courtney is so quiet, so absorbed in painting her toenails, that the ticking of the kitchen clock sounds like something out of a suspense scene from a murder film. Maybe no news is good news.

Maybe not.

So when the phone rings just as she's rehashing this in her mind, Andrea nearly drops the paring knife. Courtney looks over, polish brush dripping sticky liquid onto the counter, face frozen in expectation. Andrea picks up.

"Paisley?" But it's Mason. "Paisley's wiped out, so she asked me to call you," he says.

Andrea is too stunned to breathe. She knows what this means. It means he's reverting to a code that says, *This is private. This is too painful. This is something we will never discuss.*

It dates from a time when Paisley had the last in a series of miscarriages and couldn't bear to talk about it. She hadn't confided in Andrea—or even, as Andrea learned later, in Mason. She'd retreated into a silence that lasted four months. Her withdrawal and its aftermath had proved a disaster. A shiver of fear scoots up Andrea's spine at the memory. Doesn't Paisley remember?

Or is Paisley protecting Andrea from hearing news she doesn't think Andrea can bear, having been through cancer with her own child? She hopes not.

"She's had too many tests and too much waiting," Mason says. "You know how it is."

This is hard, but Andrea takes her cue. In the blithest tone she can muster, she chirps, "Oh, Mason, tell her I'm sorry. Tell her I'm looking through my cookbooks right now, trying to find my super-duper energy potion to make for her."

"She'll appreciate that."

"Let me know when she's up for visitors," she adds lamely. But then . . . no! A steel bar of defiance knifes through her. She is not going to be cowed into silence the way she'd been after Paisley's last miscarriage. Abandoning the cheery tone, she says, "At least tell me what the specific diagnosis is. The neighbors are already speculating. Would you rather have *that?*"

"Pancreatic cancer," Mason says flatly, "with metastasis to the liver."

"Oh, Mason." Andrea notes in her peripheral vision that Courtney, hearing that, quickly turns her attention to the counter, pouring polish remover on the spilled polish.

"It's always grim when it progresses to the liver," Mason goes on, so professorially Andrea can almost feel him putting on his objective newspaperman's face, "but there's plenty of research being done and some clinical trials. I'm taking Paisley to see a specialist tomorrow. We'll be gone overnight. Two nights at the most."

"Then let the girls stay with me. Courtney would love it." This is a lie. Although they're the same age, Courtney and Brynne tolerate each other but aren't friends. And Melody is only eight.

"Rita is coming to watch the girls," Mason says. This is Paisley's mother. "She should be here any minute."

"Then what can I do?"

"A little while ago I drove Paisley around the neighborhood to see the ribbons again. She said she can't even express how moved she is. She asked me if you'd thank everyone for her."

"Well, of course I will. *Of course.*"

That's the extent of it. Thank the neighbors. Make small talk. Don't rub it in.

Andrea hangs up. On the other side of the kitchen counter, Courtney uses a cloth to absorb the puddle of polish remover she poured to remove less than three drops of polish. She doesn't ask what Mason said. Her lips are a tight, thin line.

"They're going to a specialist," Andrea tells her. "I guess we won't know anything definitive until they get back."

Courtney nods almost imperceptibly. Andrea supposes she and her daughter will have a moratorium on open talk, as mothers and daughters often do. She won't talk to Paisley and she won't talk to Courtney. It will be an exercise in solitude. Blinking back tears, she tosses the peeled potatoes into a huge pot. She swallows and swallows, trying to reassure herself she can still do this, that the lump in her throat won't choke her.

Then her mind spools back nine years to that other phone call from Mason, after Paisley came out of the anesthetic from her D&C. At the time, the whole neighborhood knew Paisley had had two failed pregnancies in the five years since Brynne had been born, but only Andrea knew about this third one. Paisley had almost made it to the end of her first trimester. She'd planned to tell everyone the good news as soon as she reached twelve weeks.

She came home from the hospital as pale as if she'd lost a gallon of blood.

Then Mason phoned with his cryptic message—*Paisley's wiped out, so she asked me to call you*—and the topic of the miscarriage became taboo. For four months, Andrea and Paisley danced around it, avoided it, pretended it didn't exist. Then, in a tearful rush, Paisley broke her silence. She told Andrea about the horrible doctor who had handled the miscarriage and its aftermath, about her despair, about the act of desperation she'd been driven to, an act that shocked her—that shocked Andrea, too. Would it have happened if she'd confided in Andrea earlier? Andrea didn't think so.

It was a long, slow healing for Paisley, painful to watch, even after Melody made her untroubled entrance into the world—the child Paisley had waited so long for—and grew into a sweet but willful little tomboy with Mason's cleft chin and Paisley's springy dark hair.

Does Paisley really think silence, now, will be any better?

Finished cleaning up her mess, Courtney caps her bottle of polish and holds out both feet for inspection.

"The most fertile fungus breeding grounds I've seen in ages," Andrea says. "Now get up and clean the counter with Clorox like you promised." She puts the potatoes on to boil. "Wipe it six or seven times so we don't all get gangrene."

"Gangrene isn't contagious!"

"With those feet, I wouldn't be too sure."

"I'll do it in a minute." Courtney gathers the manicure things into a green-and-white cosmetic case that was part of a bonus gift from Clinique. "I'll be right back." She walks out of the kitchen on her heels, trying to hold her toes apart to keep the polished nails from touching each other and smearing.

Andrea knows she won't see her daughter again for hours. She ought to call her back. As often happens when she means to stand firm, especially before Courtney's annual screenings, she's visited by an image of her daughter at three, being lifted onto the gurney for surgery, her face frozen with terror and trust.

She conjures a picture of Paisley in those days, saying over and over again, always with that note of certainty in her voice: *She's going to be fine.*

Getting the disinfectant from under the sink, Andrea sprays the countertop so thoroughly that no germ will have the slightest chance.

She knows the word that forms in her mind very rarely applies to her daughter, but it comes to her all the same: carefree. Let Courtney be carefree while she can.

CHAPTER 5

October 17

When Iona goes to her front door and sees Marie
Coleman standing there, her first inclination is to
slink back into the house and pretend she's not
home. Marie, in a simple but expensive-looking
brown sweater and trendy jeans that hug her
shapely bottom, doesn't look like the local do-
gooder church lady, but she is. Marie doesn't just
go to church, she lives and breathes it.

If this is a God thing, Iona thinks, *I'm out of
here.*

But how can she hide? Her car is in the
driveway. Her blinds are open. If Marie looks
hard enough, she'll see Iona's half-full coffee
cup on her desk in the office. When you work at
home, in a room right off the front hall, you're
easy to find. Iona notes the clipboard in Marie's
hand even before she fully opens the door.

"Marie!" she says brightly. "What's up?"

As Marie begins to offer the clipboard, Iona
backs away, using her hand to motion Marie
inside.

"I can't come in. I have a lot of ground to
cover." Polite, but all business. "I guess you
know Mason and Paisley are out of town seeing
a specialist. They get back tonight."

"Of course I know. Everybody knows. The news was probably in this morning's paper. Mason probably wrote the article himself."

Marie endures this with placid forbearance.

"I made this sign-up sheet for people who want to make dinners for them." This time she thrusts the clipboard into Iona's hand before Iona can react. A handsome Excel spreadsheet lists available dates and provides space for the donor's name, phone number, and e-mail address. Fastened at the bottom of the clipboard is also a stack of instruction sheets for the volunteers, giving pointers on how to deliver the meals without disturbing the family during this difficult time.

"I thought Paisley's mother came to watch the kids. Doesn't she know how to cook?"

"Of course she does. But Mason goes back to work on Monday, and Rita will have the whole household to run. She'll be busy driving the kids around and taking Paisley for her treatments."

"Sometimes it's good to be busy." Iona knows this for a fact. "What kind of treatments are we talking about?"

"Some kind of experimental drugs, I think. I'm not exactly sure." She lowers her voice. "It sounds like it's pretty far advanced." Then, perking up, Marie cocks her head. "One meal? What about that delicious potato salad you brought to the neighborhood picnic?"

Iona is on the verge of being drawn into this.

Marie has a rare talent for calling up guilt. Uncharitably, Iona wonders if Marie also elicits this emotion in her husband, Dean, who actually *is* a dean of student affairs at the community college. His title draws forth sly smiles from the neighbors because Dean has long been rumored to have actual affairs with both students and staff members. Iona isn't sure she believes this. Marie stays busy raising their eleven-year-old twins, a boy and girl with disturbingly similar faces, which Iona assumes will change once they hit puberty. Marie arranges carpools, serves as parent liaison at their Christian school, hosts a prayer circle from her church, and runs a bible study group that meets weekly at different people's homes, like a floating crap game.

"It's nice of you to think of this," Iona finally replies, "but I doubt the Lamms are going to need dinner or any other meal. They have more friends than anyone I know. Even without a sign-up sheet, people are going to bring enough cakes and casseroles to fill a garage full of freezers."

"Well, if you're too tied up . . ."

"I'm not tied up."

With maddening gentleness, Marie retrieves the clipboard from Iona's hand. "Thanks anyway."

Closing the door behind her, Iona is irritated because she's vowed not to be sharp with Marie and always is, annoyed because she feels she's somehow been gotten the better of, and angry because she's been forced to take a stand on casseroles. *Casseroles,* for God's sake. Twelve years ago, after her husband, Richard, was killed in a freak accident, her house had been overrun with them. Keeping track of whose dish was whose made Iona forever grateful for people with the sense to use disposable bakeware. At first there was the usual parade of visitors who came to pay their respects and eat some of the stuff. After a while, there were just Iona and her stepson, Jeff, Richard's nineteen-year-old from his first marriage, who was there for the summer. Somehow the food kept coming, endless containers of lasagna, three-bean salad, tuna-noodle casserole, chicken divan, chili, cookies, cakes.

One day Jeff wandered into the kitchen in scruffy cutoff jeans and a T-shirt, scratching a three-day beard with one hand while running the other through his greasy straggle of shoulder-length hair. Opening the refrigerator, he peered in for a long time as if mystified by the contents. Iona was about to tell him to close the door, they didn't need to refrigerate the whole kitchen, but before she could speak, he picked up a casserole from one of the shelves, turned around, and flung it onto the floor, where it broke into a dozen pieces. "What are we going to do with all this fucking *food?*"

Iona was too stunned to do anything but watch the shards of the fluted casserole dish, someone's good stoneware, scatter across the vinyl, sending crockery and glops of macaroni and cheese into every corner. The commotion brought Richard's dog, Chance, from the backyard to the porch, where he nosed at the screen in hopes of a snack. Iona ignored him. She stared at Jeff. Jeff stared back, waiting for a reaction.

"Let's throw all the damned stuff out," she said.

They mopped up the macaroni and cleaned out the refrigerator. For ten years, from the time Jeff was nine and Iona had married his father, until that day in the kitchen, the two of them had been wary of each other. Jeff resented Iona because she was not the real mother who had left him. Iona resented Jeff because he was living proof of Richard's fertility, evidence that her failure to get pregnant year after year was her own fault, not her husband's. Disposing of the funeral food together proved therapeutic. They reduced the refrigerator to bare white walls that reflected the bare-bones truths of their newly altered lives. "If my mother had given the first damn about me, she would have come to the funeral," Jeff had said, stuffing a red velvet cake into a trash bag with some force. As for Iona, she was now a widow, nearing fifty, who was never going to bear a child. These were the raw facts.

The dog, Chance, sat on the porch, watching hopefully as the bountiful feast disappeared. Occasionally he pawed expectantly at the screen. Scraping a blob of green Jell-O into the sink, Iona waited until it went down the drain and then said to Jeff, "I can't keep that dog."

"I know." He tossed out a package of lunch meat. "I'll take Chance back to school. I'll live someplace where they let you have pets."

Jeff was nothing if not unreliable, so Iona was doubtful. But as it turned out, he would make good on his promise. He would keep Chance until the dog finally died of natural causes, six years later. It was the beginning of a time of trust.

Now Iona watches from the window as Marie Coleman, procurer of casseroles, disappears down the street. She gets her coffee cup from her office, zaps it in the microwave, and returns to her desk to make out the week's paychecks. She'll deliver them to Jeff at the job site right after lunch. The irony of their partnership always makes her wonder what Richard would think if he knew his wife had ended up in the real estate rehab business with his son. He'd probably be delighted.

Maybe he'd be less delighted if he knew their odd pairing was precipitated by his death.

Iona is usually a logical woman, so she still believes that, despite the thorough cleaning she and Jeff gave her kitchen after the mayhem of Richard's passing, the scent of funeral food lingered for months. Friends said it was her imagination. She knew it wasn't. It got to the point where she couldn't even go into the kitchen to brew coffee.

Like any well-educated widow, Iona planned to follow the standard advice not to do anything for a year, but the odor drove her out. She found herself buying meals at places that, philosophically, appalled her but realistically were cheap enough for her budget: McDonald's, Kentucky Fried Chicken, Taco Bell. She began looking at houses idly at first. She knew that if she stayed where she was, she could live comfortably on Richard's insurance and social security and her own small income as a part-time real estate agent. This argument aside, she was soon looking at real estate every day, seeking new lodgings with a vengeance.

She would never have ended up in Brightwood Trace, where the houses were all too big for her, except that the one on Hazelwood Way sounded like a steal. The owners had moved out a year before. The property had languished on the market. The price had been reduced for the third time.

Well, no wonder, she'd thought at first. Although lovely from the outside, the house was thirty years old and needed work. The floor plan was nothing special. The bathrooms hadn't been updated. The Formica counter in the kitchen was about to collapse.

"I'll do it for you," Jeff had offered when she described it.

She regarded him skeptically. By then Jeff had dropped out of school. He was working for a builder. Every Sunday he came over for dinner, for reasons neither of them could fathom, except that for a few hours it connected them both to Richard. He had the good sense never to bring the dog.

"You'll do what?" she asked.

"Remodel the kitchen if you decide to buy the house. Fix up the bathrooms."

"You wouldn't have the first clue."

"Try me," he said.

She thought, *What the hell*. If she didn't get away from the smell of casseroles, she'd be a dead woman, not just broke.

Jeff had always been a mediocre student, but he turned out to be a fine carpenter and handyman, and wise beyond his years in the matter of hiring subcontractors. The new kitchen and baths were a pleasant surprise. The plumbing worked flawlessly. The cabinets and countertops looked far more expensive than they were. Encouraged, Iona bought a second house. Her background in real estate had honed her eye for value. Over the next few years, she and Jeff

66

formed a business, Real Estate Reborn. She found the houses. Jeff rehabbed them. They sold some and rented the rest. Jeff was paid to keep them up. For a while, Iona was as rich as the surgeons who lived in the neighborhood, but during the downturn she made the mistake of buying high and having to hold longer than she liked. She wasn't as rich now, just more cautious.

In this year's slow market, the only house she felt confident enough to invest in was a decaying junk heap that would have been worth almost nothing except that it was located in an otherwise-decent neighborhood. After finishing up in the office and eating a sandwich, Iona drives out to take a look at it. A few months before, it was a fall-down pile of rubble. Now it's a nice suburban house with a spacious, grassy lot some young family will find perfect for a vegetable garden and a swing.

Jeff has been supervising the carpet installers this morning, not painting or sawing or climbing around on rafters, so he ought to look more put together than usual but, as a matter of principle, doesn't. If his father's death twelve years ago cut off the long tail of his rebellion, he's pridefully retained its stub. Except at his wedding, he has unfailingly looked like poor white trash, giving himself away only when he talks. His long hair is gathered in its usual limp ponytail, his frayed jeans ride far too low on his hips, and today's T-shirt features a large, menacing-looking motorcycle above a faded logo too washed out to read.

"Paychecks?" he asks, fingering his signature silver earring as he strides toward her across the construction-littered yard with its eco-friendly Real Estate Reborn sign sprouting from the dried mud. Jeff knows she has the checks but leaves the matter in question for the workers emerging from the house, milling about in the distance until the moment they can grab their pay and then take off early, as on Friday they always do.

"Paychecks," Iona confirms, and adds as she always does, "Next time I'm going to let you do them yourself. You need to learn, sooner or later."

"Later would be nice."

"One of these weeks I'll drop dead before they're ready, and then you'll be in a fix. You'll have subcontractors sitting in your living room when you get home, harassing your wife and unborn child."

"I'm not worried." He takes the checks from her and flips through them to verify the names and amounts, which he invariably commits to memory. "You're going to live to ninety, Iona."

"I'm going to retire long before then and spend my golden years sipping margaritas."

One of these days she's going to take a firm stand about this. She's going to make Jeff learn all the office functions—the accounting software, her filing system, the taxes. It's ludicrous for someone whose name is on the account to be incapable of doing the payroll. Like most skilled carpenters, Jeff is good in math. If everyone were paid in simple cash, he'd take over in a second—ten dollars an hour times eight is eighty dollars, no problem. But when it comes to figuring taxes and other deductions, he isn't interested. He doesn't like office work. He hates computers. Iona clings to the hope that when Lori gives birth to their daughter next month, he'll change his mind.

After she leaves Jeff, she goes to the bank, picks up her dry cleaning, and stops at Whole Foods for lettuce and walnuts. She's nearly forgotten the ribbons until she turns onto Brightwood Circle and practically has the wind knocked out of her by the sight of the streamers dancing in the breeze around the trunk of the small maple at the Kelly house at 109.

She will have to see this every time she turns into this street. She will have to prepare herself better. Sit up straight. Look straight ahead. Breathe.

Last night, when she couldn't sleep, she spent hours at her computer, scanning medical websites from which she learned very little. Doesn't cancer come on slowly? Not always. Doesn't it give signs? Only sometimes. She hasn't seen much of Paisley since school started last month, but on those few occasions, Paisley looked fine. Energetic. Cheerful. A pretty woman who eats right and exercises. Paisley can't have cancer; she's too damned healthy. If her liver is "hard as a rock," as Julianne is reported to have said, something else must be at work. Biopsies can be wrong. You read about it all the time.

It occurred to her, in the spooky hour between two and three A.M., with only the ghostly light from the computer screen illuminating the room, that Paisley has always been too beautiful, and too flirty, for her own good. She's done some things she shouldn't have. Many people probably wish her harm. Iona googled "poisons." She was vaguely aware that she was going in the direction of murder not for Paisley's sake but for her own, hoping she could make sense of it in a way she had never been able to make sense of what happened to Richard. But "poisons" gave her no help. Almost anything can be a poison. Solvents. Antacids. Furniture polish. *Tylenol,* for God's sake. As to symptoms, anything goes. She googled "damage to pancreas and liver." She didn't learn much.

Still, she persisted. Who's around Paisley enough to make her eat or inhale or absorb sufficient quantities of something to kill her? Her kids. Her mom? No. It has to be Mason. He's always reminded Iona of Clark Kent, the mild-mannered newspaperman who turns into Superman every time he passes a phone booth. Once, at the swimming pool, he took off his glasses and was instantly transformed from writer nebbish to Handsome Dan, revealing a fine profile and strong jaw along with his unusual, deeply cleft chin. Gym-honed biceps, too, which Iona never noticed while the glasses were in place, and a six-pack she didn't expect. A man like that could be dangerous. Even his editorials sometimes had a surprising kick. Who's to say he's not more diabolical than anyone thinks?

She went to bed satisfied and slept for a few hours on the strength of her theory, only to awaken slick with what felt like sweat but was actually a fine sheen of shame. Mason, a murderer? No. Making Paisley's illness into a homicide will not put reason to what happened to Richard, or ease, even one iota, the bitterness that sits eternally on her tongue.

If she's not careful, she thinks as she passes the ribbon-bedecked trees on her own block, these bows and streamers will cease to be just about Paisley and become a reminder of Richard and all the gruesome details she has promised herself to put behind her. Pulling into her garage, she takes the interior door into the house, not wanting to risk another glimpse of white ribbon. Leave it alone, she tells herself. Let it be. But she's already back in the summer of twelve years ago, too far gone to push it away, and already sickened by the memory.

It was a Saturday morning, the end of an interminable three-day rain from a tropical storm that had blown inland and up the coast. She and Richard hadn't exactly fought, just been antsy and irritable. Jeff, too, was in one of his weather-induced snits, although for Jeff that wasn't unusual. When the sun finally peeked out around noon, Jeff disappeared in his car, Iona fled to the grocery store, and Richard took Chance to the park for a walk. None of them said goodbye to each other. They were too glad to escape one another's company, after so much enforced togetherness. Imagine that now.

The park where Richard took the dog had a mile-long walking path, bordered in part by a U-shaped water-retention area with a culvert at the far end to carry storm water beneath the road and down to the creek. Usually it emptied quickly and stayed dry, but that afternoon, so soon after the flooding rains, it was nearly three feet deep with water rushing toward the culvert and its two-foot-wide drainpipe with a current fast as a river.

As might be expected, Chance went to investigate. A good-natured dog, part golden retriever but smaller, he loved water almost as much as he loved Richard. He sniffed around and

72

then, straining at his leash, waded into the pool, liking nothing better than a summer swim. Almost at once the current grabbed him, propelling him toward the culvert. Rushing down the embankment, Richard held tight to the leash and tried to yank the dog back up the hill. The current was too strong. Chance disappeared, sucked into the pipe. Richard stumbled, belly flopping into the pool. In a rush of confusion, he was dragged headfirst into the pipe himself, his right arm still above his head as he clung to—and then let go of—the leash. His shoulders crowded against the edges of the pipe as he was dragged slowly forward, unable to back out or move through more quickly, his legs kicking helplessly behind him.

A woman named Laura Beckwith, jogging along the nearby walking path, saw what was happening and rushed to help. Splashing into the water, she grabbed hold of Richard's feet. One of his shoes came off, but his body didn't budge. His legs went limp. Panicked, she screamed, thrashed her way up the bank, found the cell phone she had dropped, and called 911.

By the time Richard's body was recovered, he had been under water about half an hour. Chance had been swept through the pipe and out the other side, suffering only minor injuries. The detailed story in the next day's paper described the accident as "bizarre" and the Good Samaritan's efforts as "valiant." At the funeral,

Iona thanked Laura Beckwith in a voice that sounded, even to Iona's own ears, icily formal. Why didn't the woman make the 911 call first, then rush into the water? Why didn't Richard let go of the leash before it was too late? Why hadn't they said goodbye that day?

A few months later, Laura appeared at Iona's door with a chicken casserole in hand. Iona didn't recognize her at first. She introduced herself again, and when Iona still stood in the entryway and stared, she added, "The person who . . . who saw your husband in the water."

"Oh, yes." Numbly, Iona took the offered casserole dish. She invited Laura Beckwith in. After carrying the unwanted food into the already-odorous kitchen, she returned to the living room and handed the other woman a glass of wine. Laura set it on a coaster and left it there. She asked how Iona was doing. Fine. How about Laura? Also fine. All lies.

After a while, Laura leaned forward with some urgency. "I should have called 911 first," she said. "I've been thinking about that ever since it happened."

"Yes." Iona supposed she was expected to say "No, no, you did what you could." When she didn't blush or gush, Laura Beckwith sighed.

"It's nice, for once, not to have to pretend to be a hero."

"Heroine," Iona said.

"Heroine, yes."

They spoke for a few more minutes about unrelated issues, Iona aware that this was the oddest possible meeting but feeling that a window had opened briefly onto a morass of hypocrisy and pain.

When Laura Beckwith rose to go, Iona said, "I don't eat casseroles. If you have a family and can use it, you might as well take it."

"I don't eat casseroles, either," Laura said. "I didn't know what else to do. It's in one of those dishes you can throw away."

"Thank you," Iona said, and meant it, about providing a dish that could be thrown away. She did not mention the futility of trying to provide comfort food full of cream soup and noodles, when comfort was not an option.

Now, back inside her house, she goes into the office and closes the blinds against the detested willow oak tree festooned with ribbons. She won't allow them to remind her, every time, of anything but Paisley. She won't.

She closes her browser and turns off the computer, still ashamed of her midnight ride through all those medical websites and her cockamamy poisoning theory. What difference does it make? Cancer. Poison. High water. They all kill you, eventually. Maybe she'll take a nap. Maybe not. All she knows for sure is this: she's not going to make Paisley any damned casseroles.

CHAPTER 6

October 17

At three thirty on that same Friday afternoon, Ginger and Eddie Logan are in their car on their way to the Riverview Plaza Hotel in the city, where Ginger will attend the annual Pool and Spa Convention that begins tonight and lasts through Sunday morning. Ginger wants to check out the exhibit hall, meet with her suppliers, maybe take in one or two seminars. Eddie, who hasn't worked in the spa business for years, has brought his laptop so he can catch up on a few things in their hotel room. Ginger knows he's mainly here for the sex.

"Remind me what part of our personal fortune we gave away to get Sally to keep the kids for two nights," he asks as they turn off the parkway into the maze of downtown streets. Sally is Ginger's younger sister.

"Devon is going to stay with us on their anniversary weekend," she says, naming their four-year-old nephew.

"Perfect. You offered to keep the son of the devil."

"Devon will be fine. He always goes into zombie mode if you let him watch a movie. We'll rent something innocuous, like *March of the*

Penguins. Animals. Adventures. G-rated. He won't budge for an hour."

"Right. Lots of shots of the big eely-looking seal opening its mouth and showing its teeth, but nothing of him actually taking a bite out of the mother penguin or making her blood spurt. He'll be bored."

"Eddie, he's four."

"All he'll see is Mama Penguin trying to climb out of the water onto the ice and being pulled back. He won't be fooled. What ever happened to Big Ugly Bad Guys Have to Eat, too?"

The light turns green, but the traffic sits. Ginger knows why Eddie is trying to sound outrageous about a topic too ludicrous to provoke a real argument. It's part of the bravado he assumes every time they go to a pool-and-spa event—a reminder of a battle that was never fought, actually, because each side was ready to surrender to the other before it began.

Years ago, when Eddie quit his computer job to run the store, Ginger had been furious. Why hadn't he consulted her? Because his dad was sick. Because there was no choice. Ginger didn't forgive him. Being married to a hot tub salesman embarrassed her. Worse, he was no good at it. When out of desperation he began asking Ginger for advice, she discovered that she usually knew what to say. Selling spas (she soon learned to call them spas and not hot tubs) was not so bad. The clientele was upscale, moneyed, polite. Why, half of them were friends, neighbors, social acquaintances, people she'd known for years. Working part-time at the store was more interesting than staying home. Years before either of them thought the time was right, Ginger was ready to take over the business, solo. Eddie wanted to fine-tune his computer program, the Teacher Toolshed, and send it to market. Both of them felt guilty. Selfish. Frustrated.

Then along came Paisley, the catalyst. For all Ginger knew, the way she'd talked both of them into doing exactly what they wanted to do, it might have saved their marriage.

In the months after Eddie's father died, Paisley overheard Eddie telling at a party how Ginger had saved the store from floundering by suggesting they stop selling swimming pools. Pools were expensive and risky. Better to concentrate on hot tubs, which were profitable. Better to expand their line of pool chemicals, which provided the bulk of their repeat, bread-and-butter business.

"Now's your chance, girl," Paisley whispered to Ginger. "Your father-in-law is gone, so you don't need to keep up appearances. I bet Eddie would go back to computers if you'd tell him you'll run the store."

"There's nothing I'd like better. But I'm going to wait until Rachel's in school."

"Wait two more years, and your hair will turn gray and you'll be living on antidepressants."

"That quickly?" Ginger had tried to joke.

"Oh, yes. Coarse, unruly hair—the texture changes when it turns gray—and pills that put you in la-la land. *Then* you'll wish you'd taken over the store. You surely will."

In the oddest way, this had seemed to Ginger absolutely convincing and true. Not three months later, she was managing the store and Eddie was working in an office on the top floor of their building, putting the finishing touches on a web-based program for teachers that he now sells to school systems up and down the East Coast.

And here they are, driving to a luxury hotel in the city, away from their children for the first time in what seems like decades, anticipating a carefree weekend, while Paisley is on her way home from a cancer treatment center where they've told her God knows what.

"I just hope they have options for her," Ginger says, knowing Eddie knows what she's talking about. "Andrea says even before they left, Paisley was pretty wiped out."

"You or I would be wiped out, too. Doctors aren't gentle anymore. Nobody comes in and tells you not to worry. Now it's all about being straight with patients. Now it's, 'Well, it's just as we thought. The big C. The poisoned apple. The angel of death.'"

"Eddie, don't." But she asked for it. He can't stand being serious at times like these. The worse the situation, the more outrageous his jokes. She struggles between wanting to take his hand and tell him it's all right—which, of course, it isn't— and shouting at him to shut up. She gentles her tone. "Let's just hope we hear some good news."

"And what would that be? She's fried, isn't she? Pancreatic cancer? Also in the liver? Come *on*."

"Okay! Enough! Stop it, Eddie. I'm serious. *Stop*."

Traffic moves, and he steps on the gas so hard that the car lurches forward, forcing him to brake.

"Marie Coleman thinks she's going to be in one of those clinical trials," Ginger says. "There are all kinds of new treatments these days."

"Well, let's hope so." He inches along toward the hotel, only a hundred yards away.

"Of all people, why did this happen to her?"

"Why am I a computer guy?" Eddie asks. "Why was I standing on the street when the window fell out of the building? Why did the bus run over me? Because it was my turn in the barrel, that's why." His voice is strangled.

With a whoosh, the cars surge forward.

Under the hotel's marquee, they are delivered into the hands of parking attendants and bellmen in formal, maroon-colored uniforms, offering services for which they will pay extraordinary rates. Next to the registration desk, a huge silver coffeepot dominates a highly polished mahogany table, set with real china cups and saucers, apparently to provide a pick-me-up for the long line of guests waiting to check in. But the pot is empty. "First class," Eddie whispers. "It's prettier, and it costs more, but it doesn't mean they don't treat you like shit."

"Shhh."

Just then a sour-faced bellman seizes the small overnight cases they intended to carry themselves and sets the bags on a movable cart, practically daring them to refuse the service. Eddie clutches his computer case to his chest and impales Ginger with a wide-eyed stare and a Groucho Marx lift of his eyebrows.

In their room at last, the bellman sets down the bags and holds out his hand for a tip, without the least show of embarrassment. Looking down at the bills Eddie gives him, he nods but doesn't say thank you. "First class means never having to be grateful," Eddie murmurs when he goes.

"You didn't have to be so generous."

"And have him come back and slit our throats in the night?"

On either side of their bed, on the heavy cherrywood night tables, a small square of chocolate, wrapped in gold foil, sits on a tiny porcelain saucer. "Ah," says Eddie. "Feed them chocolate and expect them to pant and blow."

But Ginger can tell he's already losing interest in his attack on first-class service. Even as he speaks he's easing Ginger down onto the silky bedspread of their plush, king-size, first-class bed and running his hand up her thigh. Desire twists in her belly the way it did when she was twenty. Two hours later, they're still lying on the bed, naked now, Ginger partially wrapped in a silky sheet with an obscenely high thread count, Eddie propped up on one elbow beside her, tracing circles with an index finger around her flattened-out right nipple.

"Is this foreplay?" she asks. "Or postcoital play? Or just idleness in the face of exhaustion?"

"The latter, I think." After having oral sex on the fully made bed the moment the bellhop left, they had pulled back the covers to enjoy what Eddie terms "regular" sex, then napped briefly, then did it all over again. Now the bedspread is on the floor and the sheets are rumpled, and Ginger is too relaxed to contemplate getting up. Eddie seems to share her lethargy. "Maybe we should skip the opening dinner and order room service," he suggests.

Ginger grunts, or hums. It's all she can get out of her mouth, though not exactly an answer. She can't remember the last time she and Eddie had this much unbroken time together, alone, without sexually aware children within earshot. Max can't barge in to demand a driving lesson, or

82

brandish his learner's permit in their faces if they refuse. Rachel, safely across town at Sally's, can't spend her day staring mournfully at the Lamm house, thinking grim thoughts about Paisley's condition and her beloved Brynne.

Experimentally, Eddie pinches Ginger's nipple to make it stand up. From where she lies, she gets a fine, close-up view of his profile—russet hair as thick and wavy as it was eighteen years ago when she met him, pug nose just as youthful looking, chin still firm. She chose wisely. So many men fall apart.

After all their activity, Eddie's sheet has inched its way down far enough to leave him fully exposed from the hips up. Ginger finds this interesting. Although she knows his private parts in detail, she doesn't think she's looked this closely at the rest of Eddie's unclothed body for years. He's always had nice skin, tan even in winter, more olive toned than you'd expect on a man with that much red in his hair. The skin seems to fit him more loosely now. Although not tall, Eddie has always been rather muscular. A mesomorph, they used to call it. Well, not so *meso* anymore. Without a shirt, the hard cut of his torso used to be impressive, even with the curly chest hair, whose color Ginger found somehow comical, on a chest. In a T-shirt or button-down dress shirt but no jacket, the younger Eddie was clearly someone whose muscles wanted to burst out from the confining cloth. Not now. All his edges have softened, his chest and midsection especially. He's lost the hardness of his youth. When did it happen? Why hasn't she noticed this before? Does it bother her? Well, no. She rather likes it. Eddie's shape is becoming—what? More welcoming, somehow. Friendlier.

Friendlier! What a thought.

"This is more action than we've had in months," Eddie says, his voice thick, sexy, not at all friendly, in that gender-neutral sense. As exhausted as she is, Ginger feels once again the first twinge of desire.

"More action than we've had in months? Is that a declaration of devotion?" She grins at him. "You know what your trouble is, Eddie? You're not romantic."

"I'm a techie, not a poet."

"See? You sound like you don't even care." In what feels like slow motion, Ginger moves his hand away from her breast and sits up. There was a time when her breasts would have stuck straight out when she did this, instead of slumping tiredly toward her stomach, but she's too relaxed in a dreamy, postsex way to worry about this.

She tells him, "Say, 'Oh, my sweet darling, you are the love of my life. Without you I would be desolate.' Say that."

"Did anyone ever tell you you're a pain in the ass?"

"Is that your final answer?"

"It is," he says.

"Well, fine." Ginger slides back down onto the mattress, the effort of sitting being too taxing. She arranges the sheet to bare her breast again, so Eddie can resume his attentions to it.

It isn't until later, after the dinner they knew all along they had to attend, after socializing with dealers and sales reps whose names they won't remember once they leave the ballroom, that they grow serious again. "When my father was sick, he looked so awful," Eddie says. "So old."

"Well, he *was* old."

"Remember his fingernails?"

Ginger does. They were thick and yellow, unwholesome looking.

"Paisley has nice fingernails," she says. "She doesn't even polish them unless she's going to something big, like a wedding. Doesn't have to."

"And nice teeth," Eddie adds.

"Teeth?" Eddie has been noticing Paisley's *teeth?*

"Straight. White. Her parents probably spent a fortune on orthodontists. I've always thought she had them bleached by a dentist."

"I never noticed," Ginger says stiffly. The sweet aftermath of sex curdles in her belly. Why should she be surprised that Eddie admires

Paisley's teeth? He's been studying Paisley every day since she and Mason moved to Lindenwood Court nine years ago when Brynne was still their only child. Even before that, when the Lamms lived down the hill on Dogwood Terrace, Eddie liked being near Paisley every chance he got. By now he's memorized the length of her legs, the curve of her hips, the swell of her breasts, the sweep of her dark eyelashes that sometimes cast a shadow on her cheek. Ginger has memorized these features herself. If the value of a woman is her looks, Paisley is worth more than Ginger. It's that simple.

Ginger fears she might be secretly relieved that, if Paisley is out of the picture, she won't have to be jealous anymore. Can she really be this petty?

But there's this, too: that in one small, perfect paragraph, spoken at the perfect time, Paisley set the two of them to rights about their careers. She has Paisley to thank for that. She won't forget it.

"What are you thinking about?" Eddie asks.

"Nothing. Well . . . Paisley being sick. Same thing you're thinking about."

He doesn't deny it. Should Ginger care? Eddie isn't going to run off with Paisley or vice versa. If that had been the plan, they would have done it years ago. For all of Paisley's appeal—the charm and charisma that captivated Ginger as much as it did Eddie—for all of that, Paisley has always seemed devoted to Mason and their daughters, just as Eddie has been devoted to Ginger and Rachel and Max. Paisley likes other men only so much; she doesn't want them except in the most superficial way. Look at me. I'll be nice to you. I'll listen to what you say. Don't touch, though. Ah—don't touch. The fact that Eddie is aware of Paisley's teeth—they aren't talking about breasts or private parts here—shouldn't mean a thing.

But it does. Over the years, there have been times when Ginger knew Eddie was not only watching Paisley but found her exciting—the way he followed her with his eyes, wanting her, perhaps fantasizing about her. Or did Ginger read more into it than there was? It hadn't mattered. It was exciting to know he'd be going home with Ginger, wanting Ginger, making love to Ginger, staying with Ginger—and if it was Paisley he thought about when his eyes were closed, all the better. Ginger *was* Paisley then. A silky fire snaked through her belly when she came. How can she explain that now, even to herself? There was something powerful about it. Paisley was Ginger's fantasy, too.

But not tonight. Not this weekend. Not with Paisley sick. If Eddie is thinking about Paisley now, that's not a matter of simple lust; it's something else entirely. For Ginger, the glittery evening turns to ash. All she wants to do is sleep.

The next morning, they don't make love when they wake up, though Eddie is more than willing. "Too late," Ginger tells him, pointing to the clock. "I promised I'd stop in at that water-purity seminar." She doesn't, though. She speaks to a few of the salespeople she knows and spends the rest of her time on the exhibition floor. Wandering the aisles under the too-bright fluorescent lights, she studies the specs for the new spas in the displays and takes notes on the latest innovations. Without intending to, she also makes entries into the mental journal she keeps but never writes down. All right, she tells herself, here is what you feel when your neighbor is sick, who has lived across from you for years yet has always been an acquaintance, not really a friend, because your husband is more interested in her than you'd like him to be.

You feel like a traitor.

You feel two-faced because you like her quite a bit, even though you wouldn't mind being rid of her. She's always been nice to you. She's always been fun. You don't want her to get cancer. You just want her to gain fifty pounds or acquire a disfiguring scar on her face.

You feel helpless. This is the thing Ginger hates most. Whenever there's a problem, she likes to act. Action has always been her salvation. Think how scornful she once was about hot tub stores. Think of how hard it was for her to admit her family was falling apart after Eddie's father died. Think of how hard it was to say, okay, Eddie, you need to go back to computer work; you need to let me run the store. Think of how well it turned out.

But with Paisley, Ginger inscribes in the journal in her head, there's nothing you can do for her, not really. You work, so you can't even offer to keep her kids after school, not that she would want that. Your kids aren't the same age and don't hang out together. The most you can do is take over a plant that won't get watered or a bouquet of flowers that will make everybody think of funerals. The best thing is probably just to send a card.

Mainly, you feel guilty. What kind of person is glad her neighbor is the one in trouble and not her? What kind of person lives only two houses away from someone in mortal danger, and in spite of that spends a weekend down in the city, having *fun?*

"Can I help you? Do you have any questions?" a man with an exhibitor name tag asks. Ginger feels like someone being shaken from sleep. She supposes she's been staring all this time at a spa festooned with a large, red sign proclaiming, "Consumers Digest Best Buy Award! Extremely energy efficient! Four-hundred-gallon water capacity! Seating for six adults!"

"No. No, thank you. I was just looking." She

moves on, chastened into alertness, her mind bristly and sharp. She checks her watch. Almost lunchtime. There's nothing she can do for Paisley. For the moment, she lets it go. There's someone she *can* do something for. She heads up to the room.

Eddie looks up from his computer with a sly grin when she comes in. Rising from the desk where he's sitting, he's completely naked below the waist. This is exactly what Ginger expects. Even so, she's impressed by the size of his erection. "Gross," she says as she opens her arms to him. "Truly, truly gross."

Even after all their activity yesterday, his mouth is hungry for hers and hers for his. Their hands stroke each other for a long time before they actually make love, and when they're finished they hold each other much longer than they usually do. In some way, this is because Paisley is in peril and she and Eddie are not. It's a celebration. Afterward, Ginger wants to feel awful. The truth is, the memory will always make her smile.

CHAPTER 7

Paisley—Flying

Tell us something about you we don't already know.

It was a game we played, on and off for years. Sometimes a bunch of us, bored but watchful, gathered at the playground or the pool. Mostly just with Andrea when Courtney was sick.

Distractions.

Here's one I never told.

When I was twenty-one, I learned to fly.

My first day in a small plane, the wind blew hard and the pilot shot me anxious glances, expecting nausea, hysteria, I'm not sure what, given the loud motors and the wild ride. I loved it. Loved it! Next time, I'd fly that plane myself. I did, too. A graduation gift from my parents.

I was deciding what to do about marrying Mason.

The sky seemed a good place to think.

I soloed at twelve hours when other students took twenty or thirty. Up there with just the firmament and the sound of the motors, I had a whole new perspective. I could see everything. Up in that plane, I felt free.

So how I missed the deer . . . well, I have no excuse. It was October, a beautiful day, and I was turning from the downwind leg of the landing pattern to the base leg, thinking, well, we don't have to get married in June. It could wait another year. I was so lost in this that I hardly registered the small forms on the runway. Maybe in the back of my mind I thought they were dogs or even people. Then the woman in the control tower told me, "One two seven November, you better circle one more time. We don't want venison for dinner down here—at least not tonight."

I saw them clearly then—three deer, running across the tarmac with great, graceful strides. "Venison for dinner! Well, certainly not!" I said. Climbing, circling, I was saving them from all harm, keeping them uninjured and free, so euphoric I might have been given a glimpse into some elusive secret I never would have known if I'd stayed on the ground. I might have been listening to music so powerful it practically made me burst out of myself. Sort of like an orgasm, only more spiritual. This wasn't something I could explain to Mason.

The deer leaped across the blacktop and disappeared into the surrounding trees. Then the controller came back on the radio and gave me clearance to land.

It was the most marvelous day.

It didn't occur to me until later that the deer might not have fared so well if the controller hadn't warned me about them. I might not have fared so well, either.

The weather stayed warm and calm right through November. I got my logbook signed as often as I could, landing on a dozen little airstrips and then flying back home. Mason was always waiting when I landed. He'd applaud silently and give me a thumbs-up sign, gestures that make a man hard to resist.

One afternoon I headed for Front Royal, the Blue Ridge mountains bathed in the same magical, amber sunlight that had shone for days. My map showed a factory on one side of the airport and a forest on the other. Focusing on the forest, acres of bare trees with a lovely maroon cast to them in the sunshine, I decided there must be a thousand deer down there and cautioned myself to keep an eye out for potential casualties. I knew I must be getting close to the airfield, but with all my attention on venison, I didn't see it. I picked up the UNICOM frequency of my radio and asked where it was.

"Are you lost, one two seven November?" a man's voice demanded.

"Negative, Front Royal. I know I must be close."

"If you're lost, maybe you should turn back." When you got lost, you were supposed to remember the three C's—confer, confess, and climb. I didn't want to climb. Didn't need to. I was sure I was *right there*.

Then I saw it—the flat top of the factory, the forest, the airstrip, right where they were supposed to be. Not a deer in sight. "I'm not lost," I said. "I see the airport now."

"Do you also see the factory?" The voice was edgy, unsure.

"Roger, Front Royal. I see the factory, too."

"Lady, are you sure you know what you're doing? Because you can still go back where you came from, where you know the airport."

Usually people called you by your numbers and used the standard radio talk, but this man sounded like he thought I was some dumb kid standing right there in front of him.

"Sure I know what I'm doing."

I could hear him take a breath. "Runway nine is in use and there's no known traffic." If there was no traffic, why did he sound so nervous?

I turned into my final approach, dropping low over the threshold. Maybe I was too anxious to get in after all that, or more shaken than I thought, but I flared just a little too late. I hit the blacktop hard and bounced, jolted. Even without thinking, I opened the throttle, closed the carburetor heat, did a touch-and-go, climbed back up.

Okay, it was humiliating, but I would go around again. If the airport wasn't busy, it never hurt to do a touch-and-go, my instructor always said—never hurt anything but your pride. When you had to fly out of a bounce, you took a few deep breaths, thought a few cool thoughts, got your act together. My instructor had a lot of touch-and-go stories.

"One two seven November, did you do any damage?" the man on the radio asked.

It hadn't occurred to me that I'd done any damage. I was sure I hadn't. I'd hit the ground harder than that before. But when my voice came, it was smaller than I expected, a tiny chirp. "I don't think so."

"One two seven November, maybe you better make a low pass over the field so we can take a look," he said.

Make a low pass over the field? Ridiculous! But I—who was never afraid of *anything*—was all of a sudden shrinking inside. "All right," I whispered. "Affirmative."

My head pounded as I flew low over the runway. I expected to see one or two people below me, looking up at the belly of my plane—but when I passed there were not two, not three, but maybe a dozen. All of them stood below me with their arms crossed, as if I'd interrupted a party. I broke into a sweat. They might have been watching *my* belly, not the plane's, giving me disapproving, judgmental looks, making sure there'd be hell to pay if they spotted some imperfection. I pushed the throttle forward and climbed.

"One two seven November, no visible damage," the voice said. And then, condescending, "Lady, you can still go back where you came from if you want."

Anger started up in me then like it did sometimes, a small blue flame in the pit of my belly. Mason said it served me well. I was never so sure. Either way, I couldn't help it. "One two seven November is turning final for runway nine to land," I barked at the controller.

For a second, he sounded more official. "Everything's clear." And then not so official: "You sure you want to try this again, lady?"

"Yes, sir, I certainly do."

My anger didn't diminish, just cooled into raw efficiency. I thought, *This has got to be the best landing of my life.*

Throttle back, a seventy-knot glide, first flaps lowered, plane retrimmed. I pushed the voice on the radio aside, focused on what I was doing. I was not incapable, and I was not lost.

Descending through 350 feet, coming in on final, I felt fine. Came over the threshold, leveled out the glide. Controlled the rate of sink as if I'd been doing it all my life. Wings level . . . glide halted . . . just a few feet off the runway. Then the flareout: nose up just a little, power reduced. Main wheels down, nose wheel. Done. Rolling out.

I'd greased it in there. I really had.

The people who'd examined the plane's belly were waiting on the tarmac, anxious to see who I was. When I finally emerged, their posture changed—it always did—as they got a good look at me. The women pulled into themselves, and the men registered approval. The judgmental looks disappeared.

They kept staring at me. I was used to that. I let them get a good eyeful and then said, "Somebody sign my logbook. I'm working to get my license."

At home, Mason applauded when he saw me and gave me a thumbs-up sign. "You'll have your license before you know it." But I knew even then I'd gotten all I needed from flying that little plane. I told him yes, a June wedding would be fine, I'd always wanted one. I told him about the people who thought I was too dumb to land without mishap and he said, exactly as I knew he would, "Those bastards. Well, you showed them, didn't you?" I'd loved him for a long time by then. It was a day of triumph.

When you're down, remember your triumphs. That's what I need to tell the girls. Sometimes you get in trouble and crash. Other times: just a bumpy landing.

CHAPTER 8

October 23

For the first week after Paisley returns from the specialist, most of the neighbors avoid her, except for Andrea, who wants to be with her as much as she can. After their shared experience with Courtney years ago, Andrea thinks Paisley will understand everyone's reticence, but she seems totally baffled every time the doorbell rings and yet another well-wisher drops off a cake or casserole to Paisley's mother, Rita, and then flees without coming in to say hello. "Oh!— look!" the neighbor will say breathlessly, tapping the face of her watch. "I wanted to see Paisley but I'm late picking up Jenny at soccer. She'll have a fit if I don't go *this second*." Brandishing her car keys, she'll add, "Give Paisley my love. Tell her I'm thinking about her." Or if she's religious, "Tell her I'm praying for her." Then she's out the door and down the driveway, racing as if chased by wolves.

Practically every day, Paisley puts on a comic face to hide her disappointment and says to Andrea, "Tell people they're welcome to visit, not just drop off food." Andrea promises she will. She never adds, "Be real, Paisley. They're too scared. They're afraid what they might find out." After five days, during which Paisley becomes decidedly more jaundiced, Andrea says quietly, "They don't want to bother you, Paisley. They think you're tired. They think you want time with your family."

To which Paisley replies, "Oh, I have plenty of that."

Andrea is not so sure. This is exactly what is in doubt.

At the end of the week Paisley pats Andrea's hand, squeezes it for emphasis. "Tell them I'm going to the doctor and getting plenty of rest."

Andrea nods. But what does this mean? No one knows what kind of treatment Paisley is getting, even Andrea. In spite of everything, they seem to be honoring the vow of silence Andrea wanted to ignore.

Does it really matter? *Any* kind of cancer treatment takes its toll. Think of what it did to Courtney. Paisley's hair isn't falling out like Courtney's did, but her skin is a darker yellow every day, and she's more worn out than Andrea's ever seen her. She spends her days in the big leather recliner in the family room, attached by earbuds to her iPod, with the volume turned up so high that sometimes when Andrea arrives she can hear a tiny beat of the music even from across the room. One day when Andrea walks in, Paisley's eyes are closed, her mouth slightly agape and her breath so noisy that she might be snoring. In all the years they've known each other, until this moment Andrea has never seen Paisley asleep.

Paisley's eyes jerk open. She smiles to pretend she's been awake all along. Removing the earbuds, Paisley sets the iPod in its docking station and turns the volume down to practically nothing.

"I was listening to a song by Frankie Lymon and the Teenagers," she says. "Remember them? Late '50s, one of the first big groups?"

Andrea nods, though she has no idea. Paisley is such a fan that it never occurs to her that some people don't listen to oldies.

"The Teenagers' song 'I Want You to Be My Girl,' was a big hit, but I always liked their recording of 'The White Cliffs of Dover' better. A World War II song. Can you believe it?" She speaks with such intensity—*healthy* intensity, Andrea thinks—that Andrea feigns wide-eyed interest. "Anyway, instead of singing it slow and mournful the way it was done during the war, they upped the tempo. And it's great. *Great,* even though it was never a big hit. The up-tempo makes it even sadder. Listen." Paisley turns up the volume. Her eyes sparkle. She bursts into song, something she can never help doing, which has got to be a good sign. *"There'll be bluebirds over / the white cliffs of Dover / tomorrow / Just you wait and see . . ."*

Paisley's voice is perfectly pitched, despite a small tremor. The song *is* sad. You don't expect bluebirds tomorrow, over the white cliffs of Dover or anywhere else, but the music makes you long for them all the same.

If Paisley can still sing, how sick can she be?

Before Andrea leaves, Paisley reaches down to the shelf under the end table beside her and pulls out what at first looks like a handful of fluff and then, as Paisley shakes it, becomes the old white feather boa Paisley used to wear at parties, claiming it was part of her college cocktail waitress outfit.

"You still have *that?!*"

"Brynne found it in the attic and brought it down to cheer me up. It *does* cheer me up." Paisley drapes it over her shoulders, where it looks as ridiculous as always. "Tell people I'm almost ready to boogie."

"Well, I will. I certainly will." Andrea struggles not to let her voice break.

She is *so* glad to get out of the house. So filled with conflicting emotions—elation, dejection, relief that the visit went as well as it did, despair that it didn't go better. The way Paisley was singing, she was certainly still *herself,* in spite of the jaundice and fatigue. And that feather boa! Even so, Andrea isn't going to be able to attract visitors unless she drags them there. Not yet. Eventually they'll come on their own. She remembers. They won't show up until they digest the fact of Paisley's condition. This might take another week.

In the gathering twilight, Lindenwood Court seems unnaturally quiet, even with Paisley's daughter Melody kicking a soccer ball around the yard while Trinket, her little dog, chases it. There used to be two or three cars in front of Paisley's house almost any time of day, not just Rita's Tahoe. When the Logans' old Ford careens into the cul-de-sac with Ginger's son, Max, at the wheel and his father beside him, Andrea is grateful for the commotion. The boy makes a wide turn into their driveway, hits the brakes with a screech, and stops just in time to avoid crashing into the garage door. The tumult is so welcome, so cheerful, that it chases the ghosts away.

At dinner, Courtney grumps and glowers as she usually does while waiting for the results of her medical screenings, but so unrelentingly tonight that John loses patience. "If you're finished eating, go do your homework until it's time to clear the dishes." Courtney stomps out. John shrugs apologetically. "She's hard to endure for a whole meal."

"She's a teenager," Andrea defends lamely, aware that John's tough-love approach in the face of the medical ordeal is probably the only thing that keeps the family out of therapy. Not that they couldn't use therapy.

She waits for the miasma of Courtney's sulking to lift. John remains restless. He hasn't changed his clothes after work. He taps his plate with the tines of his fork.

"What?" she finally asks.

"You know that company in California where I've been doing those seminars?"

"Yes, of course." John is a lawyer who reviews contracts for museums and historic homes and other semipublic organizations that sponsor events with an element of danger—children's overnighters, glass-blowing demonstrations, hayrides. He has a reputation for being good at reducing an organization's liability. Sometimes other firms hire him to teach their lawyers his methods.

"Do they want you to go out there again?" Andrea knows he likes the traveling. It keeps him from getting bored. He's stayed with the same company his whole career because of its health insurance. When you have a child with cancer, that's what you do.

John puts down his fork. "They want to offer me a job."

Andrea opens her mouth. Nothing comes out.

John smiles. "It turns out, according to them, that I'm an expert in a 'tricky, specialized, growing field.'"

"Tricky, specialized, growing?" Now Andrea is smiling, too. It seems like a joke.

"So they say. The new position would mean going to meetings all over the country, doing training seminars, supervising a staff. It would mean more prestige. More money, too."

"Enough to live in Southern California?" Andrea hears her question, quite logical, but she can't quite imagine any reality in it. She can't quite take this in.

"I think it would take a while to negotiate the money."

"I'm sort of . . . stunned."

"Me, too."

"Did you see this coming?"

John shrugs, enigmatic. "Yes and no."

It's a dream, of course. A scene viewed through shifting waves of heat, an oasis turning into a mirage. Is John really considering this? Andrea has lived here all her life. She went to high school not ten miles away, attended college down in the city, drank too much, experimented with every drug anyone offered her, and suffered no consequences whatever. After graduation, she had a couple of interesting jobs, met John at a party, married him in the white dress she'd been dreaming about since she was ten, and two years later gave birth to their daughter after an easy four-hour labor. Until Courtney was three, Andrea's days had draped around her like a filmy layer of chiffon, pleasant and amorphous and soft to the touch. When Courtney grew limp and sickly and peed blood, Andrea's life grew as focused as light through a magnifying glass. But it was still a life lived *here*. On the East Coast. In Brightwood Trace. With Paisley.

And yet . . . Sometimes she thinks the hot light that came with Courtney's illness is still shining on her, following her around this house, this neighborhood, still trying to burn into her . . . what?

If they left, would that hot point of magnified light stay right here, behind them, where it belongs?

As if at a signal, both she and John rise from the table to clear the dishes. Neither suggests they call Courtney to help. They don't talk. Moving away from here for the first time at age forty-six seems—too enormous. John is pushing fifty. They can't do it. They can't leave everyone they know. More important, Andrea can't abandon Paisley. Especially now.

All the same, everything has changed. Twenty minutes ago Andrea didn't know this was there, ripe fruit waiting to be plucked. No matter what happens, for now, for this instant, the air vibrates with possibility.

Andrea rinses the dishes; John loads the dishwasher. "I guess you went to Paisley's," he says after a time—an offering, not just because it changes the subject that now seems too tender to touch for a while, but also because John knows

Andrea visits every day and rarely mentions it. "How's she doing?"

"Pretty jaundiced. Pretty tired. Otherwise, she seems okay."

John rolls up the sleeve of his shirt. "Treatments make you tired."

"Yes, but what seems to bother her most is people not coming to see her." This is the gist of it, isn't it? It keeps nickering at the edge of her mind. "She was so understanding about all that when Courtney was sick. About people not coming to visit and not looking you in the eye. Now she doesn't seem to remember."

"She wasn't the one it was happening to, back then. It's easy to forget, if you're not the one."

Andrea regards him sidelong. How does he know this? She recalls only his absence during Courtney's illness . . . his analytical coolness, the distance that opened between them and persists to this day. Eleven years after the crisis, they still live in separate limbos, suspended between hope that Courtney's health will last and fear that it won't. They haven't leaned on each other in all that time.

"I remember the averted eyes well," John says, as if trying to convince her. He pauses with a slippery plate in his hand, then puts it into the dishwasher, wipes his hand on his trousers, and touches the back of Andrea's neck. "I remember very well." His fingers are still slightly damp from the dishes, but they sit so tenderly against her skin that tears spring to her eyes, which she has to blink away. All at once, after all these years, she believes him.

They're awkward again when he drops his hand. He makes a great show of finding room for a glass on the already-full upper bin. After a while he says, "If we can come to terms, what do you think? Could you do it? I mean, after Paisley is better? After we sell the house?"

Andrea turns off the water and faces him. He looks so—well, hopeful.

Superstitiously, she's half-afraid to say what's on her mind, so close to Courtney's annual screening. She says it anyway. "It might not hurt for Courtney to go to a school where nobody knows about her medical history and thinks they need to feel sorry for her."

"Where she can learn to attract flies with honey instead of vinegar?"

She nods but keeps her eyes on the sink.

"It might be good for all of us," he ventures.

She doesn't answer that. She doesn't know.

Julianne can't bring herself to stop by the Lamm house every day, but she tries to go two or three times a week. She stops in right after work when she can stay for a few minutes and then say, truthfully, that she needs to get home to make dinner for Toby, or that Doug is taking her out to eat. At work, when she asked Peter if he knew what had been decided about Paisley's treatment, Peter held out his hands in a gesture of helplessness, which meant that no one in his network of doctor friends had told him, or that they'd told him and he didn't want to discuss it, or that he felt the case was hopeless. She hasn't asked again. Chemo, she supposes, though she's not sure what it will accomplish.

The family has done a good job of making Paisley comfortable, setting her up in the big recliner in the den, surrounded by sound equipment and CDs, with the television right across from her, the remote at hand, and the bathroom just across the hall. The jaundice Julianne didn't see in the office two weeks ago is very much in evidence now. And there's enough weakness that it keeps Paisley in her chair. What heartens Julianne is the feather boa Paisley is sporting today. The sense of humor.

Beyond the confines of the den, life goes on in the house as if nothing unusual has happened. Paisley's mother, Rita, moves through the rooms with such calm efficiency, such an air of serenity, that this is almost possible to believe. The girls are encouraged to wander in and out as usual with their friends. Mason arrives home from work at his normal hour, meals are served on schedule, records are kept of gifts and cards, the fluffed pillow or glass of ice water brought in exactly when Paisley might need it. Soccer practices, piano lessons, a birthday party—no one misses a beat. Homework schedules are posted on the refrigerator. If, as Julianne suspects, Rita's show of tranquility is the result of a gargantuan act of will, she's not letting anyone know.

Julianne also suspects much of this effort has gone toward sheltering Melody and Brynne, and she's not sure this is such a good idea. Ten to one they haven't been told much beyond *Mom's sick. That's why her skin is so yellow. Grandma is here until she feels better.* Julianne feels like a fraud, participating in this show of "business as usual." It's all she can do to make it through ten minutes of chitchat before she hurries out.

Today a hand touches her arm just as she reaches the door. "Mrs. Havelock?" It's Brynne, standing stock-still beside her and nearly as tall, a straight line of arms and legs and a sheet of light-brown hair like a silk cloth against her back. "Can I ask you something?"

"Sure, honey. What?" Brynne glides around Julianne to open the front door and usher her out onto the porch, apparently for privacy. Although long limbed and still a bit gawky, not quite finished growing, Brynne has an air of serenity that makes her seem older than fourteen, in a sad sort of way. She isn't going to be as pretty as her mother, Julianne thinks, but she has a quality of substance Paisley lacks—an observation that makes her feel slightly disloyal.

"It's about Mom," the girl says. "She doesn't like to let on, but I think her back hurts even though she takes a bunch of Tylenol. Do you think it's because she sits in that recliner so much? I thought since you work in a doctor's office you might know."

"Her back, not her stomach?"

"Her stomach hurt even before, but now I think it's her back—from the way she touches it when she thinks no one's looking. From the way she fidgets. Do you think it's the recliner? Or is it part of the cancer?"

She says *cancer* with the same inflection she might use for *flu* or *cold*. The guilelessness of the question takes Julianne's breath. Brynne's aura of calm fills the space around them with a kind of peaceful willingness to listen to whatever Julianne has to say, no matter how long it takes her to say it. Purposefulness radiates from Brynne exactly as it does when she's retrieving the family's mail from the overstuffed box at the curb or reasoning with her volatile little sister. It's unnerving.

"I think it's fine for your mother to be in the recliner," Julianne says, deliberately not answering the question. "But she ought to mention it to her doctor. Tylenol might not be the ideal painkiller for a backache. He can probably prescribe something better."

110

"He can prescribe something better," Brynne says—part statement, part soothing chant. Julianne can't tell if she's really as tranquil as she seems or just impenetrable. Never having raised daughters, Julianne isn't intuitive about them. Before she can censor herself, she thinks that Brynne will be a fine hostess someday, but no one will ever call her a party girl, as they sometimes term Paisley.

Mason pulls onto the other side of the driveway just as Julianne begins to back out. They're far enough apart that they don't have to talk, just wave. Back when Paisley and Mason lived near Julianne on Dogwood Terrace, before Melody was born, Mason had always seemed delighted but a little bewildered by the fact of fathering a daughter like Brynne. He'd been raised in a family of raucous boys and seemed unsure what to do with such a composed and serious child. He swung Brynne around, carried her on his shoulders, tried to make her laugh. Tomboyish Melody is easier for him, you can see that— though Julianne suspects that when Melody reaches puberty she'll mystify him every bit as much as Brynne does now. It would be one thing if Mason were left with boys, she thinks, but teenaged daughters? Julianne had a hard enough time raising three sons alone, even ones who always had access to their father. Thinking this, she forgives her ex-husband, Bill, for at least three or four of his crimes.

• • •

An hour later she's in a car with Doug Fenster, the man she may or may not love, heading for a restaurant where there may or may not be anything she wants to eat.

Does she love him? After three years, you'd think she'd know. Does he love *her?* When his paw of a hand reaches over to stroke her cheek, she wonders if this is a gesture of affection or an attempt to detect wrinkles. She knows that's unfair, a thought born of her own insecurity and not his. Getting out of the shower earlier, stroking on mascara, Julianne had peered in the bathroom mirror and thought, *Well, I certainly know a middle-aged face when I see one.* Much as she loves having natural blond hair, she's already paying the price of having the fair, early-to-age skin that goes with the pale locks. She looks older than most of her friends, her face beginning to line, her neck growing slack. No matter how much lotion she applies, she's drying up in places both public and private, just as the books always said she would. Perimenopausal at the age of forty-four, who would have imagined? She knows as a sort of hard, unsentimental truth that in a few years she won't even be pretty.

Maybe she doesn't love Doug. Maybe she wants him because it won't be long until she can't attract a man at all.

"What do you think? Should we go to Caruso's?" he asks.

"Sure." When he first took her there, she thought from its unassuming exterior it was a cheap pizza place, which would have suited her fine. She was a bit disappointed to find that it served the best Italian cuisine in town.

Doug grins, reading her mind. "Or is the food there lost on you?"

"I can't help it if I like spaghetti." She'd eat spaghetti with marinara sauce every night if she could. But since Doug is a gourmet, a big man, not fat, who approaches a fine dinner with such gusto that Julianne feels awed when she watches him eat, she tries to adopt a more all-inclusive diet. It's not easy for her. Doug likes sushi, but the thought of raw fish turns her stomach. Escargots? Snails are disgusting enough in the garden. Thai cuisine? She feels no guilt about shunning spices that could cauterize an entire digestive system. Most of the time she orders something simple and takes her pleasure from observing the way he studies a menu, savors his wine, samples a bite of fish. But she wishes, tonight, that instead of Caruso's he'd suggested a place that serves plain American dishes.

Settling back against the plush upholstery of his car, Doug continues a story he started earlier about a financial transaction his office handled today. He's a stockbroker. Excited, his voice rich with inflection, he launches into his tale with a passion for finance that's almost a match for his zest for food. Ordinarily, Julianne enjoys this. For the past three years, he's brought a whole new dimension of information to her life, about money markets, expensive brandies, exotic waters that yield the healthiest fish. Tonight, she can barely keep track of what he's saying.

"You're distracted," he says.

"Tired."

"Worried," he corrects.

"I was at Paisley's this afternoon. Her daughter came up to me when I was leaving, upset because her mother's back hurts."

"So?"

"It's from the cancer. Pancreatic cancer can affect the nerves in your back."

"*You* get backaches."

"Only when I twist something from exercise. This is different. One of the big issues in pancreatic cancer is pain. It gets worse."

Doug brakes for a light, then leans over to take her hand, engulf it in his palm. He squeezes, then lets go. "I'm sorry, honey." Julianne senses—the way she could always sense when Bill was subtly ordering her to do something—that Doug's warm fingers mean not just to comfort her, but to smother her words with so much affection that she'll shut up. He's queasy. Illness is abhorrent to him. Once, when she tried to tell him about a plantar fascia surgery that should have been simple but went terribly wrong, blood had drained from his face as if someone had opened a vein. He doesn't want to hear about Paisley. Too much information.

She'd lied that night she told Bill that of course she'd told Doug how upset she was about Paisley's condition. They hadn't discussed it at all. Doug has the rough outline of the situation now only because Julianne spends time at Paisley's after work and feels she owes him an explanation on the nights she can't go to dinner until later. She'll never tell him about her electric fingers that pick up illness with a touch. It's not so much that she *can't* talk about it as that she's *spared* from it. Doug allows her to leave the worst of her fears at the office.

It's just that, tonight, she'd be grateful for a chance to discuss Paisley's backache with someone who'd listen without looking like he was about to throw up.

"Okay, be pensive if you want to," Doug says, cajoling. "Sometimes I'm pensive myself."

"Never." He's so loquacious, she can't help but smile. In the half light of the car, he turns to her with eyes that seem almost patent-leather black, cow eyes but more intelligent, caressing her with a lambent gaze full of feeling. It makes her believe he's concerned about her in some deep, heartfelt way that has nothing to do with the cause of her distress, only with his desire to ease it. She recognizes this as the most extraordinary kind of gift.

Does she love him? She doesn't know. All she knows is that she's no longer interested in having dinner. She wants to go to her house and have an hour alone with him before Toby comes home. Doug puts on his blinker, then does a U-turn as if he's reading her mind. He gives her a smile that turns into a leer and makes her laugh. She's not so interested in the actual sex anymore, given the dryness that makes it painful. What she longs for now are those warm moments of flesh on flesh that sometimes, on the worst days, are the only way to obliterate the dark. She's glad Doug doesn't want to know about blackness that invades her less as a premonition than as a certainty, traveling the blood with the very touch and feel of death. She's *glad*. If he knew about the darkness, maybe his touch wouldn't chase it away.

"Better step on it," she whispers. Even if something is missing—that urgent, clenched fist of desire she used to feel when she was young— she's grateful for what is left. If an interest in finance and food is healthy, think of the benefits of making love.

CHAPTER 9

Paisley—Swimming

Here's another one I never told. I met Mason when I was twelve.

Funny, how some people fall in love. Sort of like being hit over the head with a baseball bat, in the nicest possible way.

I never tell anyone how young I was. I just say I met him at the swimming pool, which is true enough. I'd never liked swimming, but there I sat, an early bloomer in a lawn chair, dazed and hormone drenched, soaking up the sun. My mother had practically kicked me out of the house. I'd been checking my reflection in the mirror a dozen times a day, tossing my hair, stomping through the rooms.

"Go swimming," she told me. "Do exercise. Take a cold shower."

The only sport I liked was tennis. Still, you got to wear fewer clothes at the swimming pool. I went every day.

I was so sure of myself, *so* sure. It was a new feeling. Heady stuff, having people look at you. Boys. All I wanted was to hang out with the high school girls. I thought I was ready for them. Not so. Even the freshmen were two years older than I was. The only ones who paid me any attention were Stacey Johnson—think Rizzo from *Grease*, but without the soft side—and her two tough sidekicks. All three of them teased me, asking every day if I had a boyfriend yet. They knew I didn't. I was fascinated by the boys, but wary, too, of the harshness in their eyes, hunger mixed with admiration. Later, I'd understand that better. I'd develop a technique.

"Well, you find your boyfriend yet?" Stacey would ask. Her lips curled into something closer to a sneer than a smile. For a while I pretended not to notice. Then one day in a rush of indignation I said in a haughty tone, "As a matter of fact I *did*. See that blond boy over there?" I pointed to a nice-looking high school boy standing by the diving board.

Stacey glowered. "Not funny, Paisley. Mason's *my* boyfriend. You fool with him and I'll tear your eyes out."

I thought she really would. Her expression turned stony, her hands curled into fists. Mason sprang high off the board, dived in, and swam to our section of the pool.

"Hey, what's going on?"

"Nothing," Stacey said. "Keep away from her," she hissed to him, nodding in my direction. "Tell her you're spoken for. Tell her you belong to *me*."

"Don't you wish." Mason laughed. Stacey laughed. Her cohorts laughed. They'd been putting me on—though Stacey's expression said she wished her story were true. Briefly, Mason regarded me with more interest than he probably would have otherwise, to see what he was supposed to avoid. A sweet cramp fluttered through my belly. I couldn't have stated in words exactly what it meant, but I knew.

"And here I thought he was *my* boyfriend!" said another voice, throaty and mellow, coming from a sweet-faced girl who'd walked up behind us. Molly. I'd seen her before.

Mason winked at me. "Molly loves me because I'm such a hunk."

He flung his arm around her, his thick tanned hand connecting with the tanned skin of her slender arm. The air whooshed out of me, the baseball bat connected with my head, my vision went blurry. I would have knocked his arm away and taken her place, if I hadn't gotten my wits about me just in time. In a flash of intuition, I understood that Stacey was no threat for Mason's affections, but Molly was.

I found out he helped coach the swim team. No one joins the swim team at twelve and hopes to compete with kids who've been at it since they were eight. I signed up anyway. Workouts were at seven in the morning. I didn't know until I got there that Molly was a swim coach, too.

I made a fool of myself. Practice, practice, practice, but for the life of me I couldn't perfect my breast stroke. Invariably, in every length I swam, without being aware of it, I'd do a scissors kick instead of the frog kick. I was disqualified at every meet. Mason would come over and say, "It's all right, it'll come, it just takes time." Sometimes Molly would get into the water, sleek and calm, her low voice reassuring. "Let me show you again, Paisley. I'll do it and you copy." Over and over. Frog kick. Frog kick. And sure enough, at the last meet, when I made it the full length of the pool in correct form, Mason was waiting at the other end, applauding silently, giving me a thumbs-up sign. Molly, too.

I might have been their slightly clumsy younger sister.

Over the winter I saw them at basketball games at the high school. Mason's blond hair had grown out brown, no longer streaked by the sun. Molly's hair stayed light. Bleached, I thought, but I wanted that hair, that resonant voice, that sweetness. In a way, I loved her. I wanted her for a friend. It was complicated. I wanted Mason more.

They broke up now and then. I wasn't allowed to go out with him for two more years. "And not *exclusively,* Paisley," my mother would say. "You're too young. For that matter, so is he." Sometimes we met in secret, which added to the allure. Then I'd find some other boy and he'd find some other girl, often—guess who?—

Stacey. Which didn't bother me. Then he'd get back together with Molly, which did.

The year I was a senior in high school, I ran into Stacey in JCPenney. "You think just because you look the way you do, you can get anybody you want, don't you?"

She didn't know Mason was going out with Molly at the time. I didn't tell her. I was surprised she'd held a grudge so long. Probably she really had planned to tear my eyes out, back at the swimming pool. A worm of misery ran through me, knowing as I did that Mason might be somewhere with Molly at that very moment. Maybe he loved her. If that were true, it followed that sometimes the things you wanted most and thought you couldn't live without were precisely the things you couldn't get, no matter how you looked or what you did. A harsh epiphany. Even so, I sneered at Stacey the way she'd sneered at me back at the pool. That was the best I could do.

His junior year in college, Mason broke up with Molly for good. Or vice versa; I never knew. She transferred schools and moved to another state. I loved him. And finally I *had* him, which frightened me. For a while, I thought I wanted to be free of him, or at least untethered. That didn't last long.

The week our engagement announcement was in the paper, I saw Stacey Johnson for the last time. "Well, I guess I should congratulate you," she said.

"I guess you should."

"Maybe you have everything you want right now," she said. "Maybe you do. But someday it's going to catch up with you."

Maybe she didn't just mean Mason, though she couldn't have known that, then.

Maybe she meant now.

CHAPTER 10

October 27

As often happens in the verdant hill country that stretches from the South into the mid-Atlantic and the lower Northeast, the on-again-off-again humidity and heat are finally swept out to sea by a blast of dry, cold air that rushes down from Canada, crisping the leaves and letting them show their colors under the sudden clarity of the autumn sky. It is the best time of year, people say. It is the great, glorious flash of color before the dimming of the light.

Iona is with her stepson, Jeff, on one of these days, the two of them sitting in her office arguing about what he considers her underhanded effort to introduce him to the accounting program that tracks their business.

"You got me here on false pretenses," he

protests. "I thought we were going to discuss that house on Bailey Street."

"We will. This first." She points him toward the computer screen, where she has just generated expense reports for nails and lumber. "You need to know what you're spending. It's critical. This isn't hard."

"Lori's coming here after the obstetrician," Jeff informs her. "She'll be here any minute."

"Listen," Iona says, "I'm not kidding when I tell you I'm going to retire someday. If you don't learn to do this, Real Estate Reborn will be bankrupt in a year. I'll feel sorry about it, since by then you'll probably have a couple of kids and a mortgage. But I'll be damned if I'll feel obligated to work until the end of time."

"Nobody's asking you to." Jeff shifts in his seat, looks hopefully out the window toward the driveway.

"And I'll tell you another thing," says Iona. "You're going to have to look the part sometimes. Wear a dress shirt. Real trousers. It shouldn't matter, but it does. Go into the bank looking like that"—she waves a hand at his stonewashed jeans, his unbuttoned flannel shirt flapping over a Hard Rock Cafe T-shirt, his ponytail hanging below the back of a New York Yankees baseball cap—"and they'll talk to you about a loan only if you're having a good year and are holding the paperwork to show it. If there's any real reason to be borrowing, forget it." She slashes her throat with her index finger.

"Who's being murdered?" Somehow Lori has come into the house without their noticing, stopping them cold as the enormous lump of her belly precedes her into the room, encased in a form-fitting black shirt that perfectly outlines her eight-month pregnancy.

"Good God," Iona says. "You're beginning to look like a beach ball."

Lori laughs, which Iona thinks is the proper response. Many women would take offense.

"What does the doctor say?" Jeff goes to her, puts a hand protectively on her stomach. He regards her with a new—Iona hates to call it tenderness—a new *softness* that's grown between them now that Lori is pregnant.

"She says we're on schedule. She says all is well."

Jeff offers her a chair. Sitting down, Lori sighs and fans herself with a hand. "I've turned into my own personal furnace," she says, prompting Iona to get up and open the window behind her. Instantly the room is chilly. Lori keeps fanning.

"Another month and you'll be freezing," Jeff says.

"Another month and the baby will be here," she says, "or else I'll have to buy bigger maternity clothes." The afternoon sun, partially obscured by the willow oak outside, falls in a gently dappled pattern onto the chair where Lori sits, light and shadow shifting with the rustling leaves and the movement of the ribbons still secured to the tree. In the ever-changing light, she's the perfect image of a soon-to-be Madonna.

"You've just rescued me from becoming an accountant," Jeff tells her, pointing to Iona's computer.

"You?"

"That's what I told her."

Iona might as well be in the next room.

Lori hoists herself out of the chair, waddles over to the desk. "QuickBooks?" She studies the screen, wiggles the mouse, brings up a financial statement. "This is what I did at Becker's Trucking." She sounds wistful, already having doubts about quitting her job with the idea of becoming a full-time mother. She clicks through a few more screens, nods to herself. "I could do this," she says.

"What do you mean?" Jeff frowns, but his voice is bright with expectation.

"After the baby is born," Lori tells him. "I could input all the financials. Run the reports. It would only take a couple of hours a week."

True enough, Iona thinks. Lori turns in her direction, as if it has just occurred to her that she's been present all the time.

"What do you think, Iona? After the baby

comes, you can take her anytime you want and I can mind the office for a couple of hours. It will give us both a break." She sounds as hopeful as Jeff does.

Iona shrugs noncommittally and doesn't reply, though it has already occurred to her that this might work. Lori and Jeff are a good team. When they're together, he seems so centered that it's impossible to imagine him as the truant he was at ten, or the petty thief he became at twelve, dissuaded from serious crime only by the trauma of being hauled into court for stealing a carton of cigarettes, or the miserable wreck he was as a teenager. When he gets too intense, Lori calms him down. When Lori gets depressed, Jeff makes her laugh. Who would have thought Lori also takes to business the way Jeff took to drywall and plumbing? If this works out, Iona can drop dead at will, Jeff can run the job sites, and Lori will handle the finances and keep them from becoming destitute. Thank God.

Not that Iona believes in God.

Lori could also go to the bank with Jeff if it ever becomes necessary. She's the sort of conventional, sensible-looking young woman who looks like the perfect candidate for getting a loan and making the payments on time.

"Sure," Jeff says to Iona. "Not only can Lori can get out of the house to do your books, but it will give you a chance to indulge your grandmotherly feelings." He burps an imaginary baby against his shoulder.

Iona smiles politely. She doesn't expect to have any grandmotherly feelings. She intends to be kind to the baby, and as attentive as necessary, given that Lori's parents live in Wyoming and Jeff's mother isn't interested. But as to "feelings"—no. It will always rankle with her— it rankles even now—that the child to whom she's being linked as the sole, indulgent grandparent is no blood kin to her. Just as she had no child of her own, she will have no grandchild. If her emotions are foolish and petty, she can't help it.

"Let's not rush into this," Iona says. "Let's see how Lori feels in a few weeks."

But all at once the imminence of the new arrival makes her feel, as she hasn't since Richard's death, *barren*.

Barren. For Iona the word conjures up the vast winter landscapes of Russian novels and the bleak emptiness of her own body. Until Richard, men had generally considered Iona fierce rather than feminine, so she didn't marry until she was thirty-eight. She never used birth control, but she never conceived, either. Maybe she was just too old. This was before there was a hormone for everything that ailed you. Richard never cared much about having another child. Given his troubles with Jeff, he harbored few illusions about parenthood. When month after month Iona's periods arrived on schedule, despite all the tests and treatments, he was sympathetic but not heartbroken. The Silence of the Womb, he dubbed it. They tried to pretend it was a joke, but it wasn't, not to Iona.

Her oldest sister, the one who'd moved to Alaska, had two husky sons. Her other sister, also many miles away, had a daughter. She was never close with either of them, but their fertility made her feel *lesser*. She will never get over not having a child of her own. Even today, fond as she is of Jeff, there are times when she is keenly aware that he is not her son, and that his child will not really be her granddaughter.

Lumbering toward the window, Lori stands in front of the screen and inhales deep draughts of air. Maybe it's her petite, small-boned build and not the tight shirt that makes her belly look so disproportionate. If it weren't for the sonogram showing one female child, Iona would be sure she was having twins. Lori lifts her hair off her neck, lets the breeze blow against it, fidgets a little. Then she grows still and points toward the street beyond the willow oak, beyond the white ribbons whose streamers are dancing in the wind. "Look."

Lori is not the first one to witness the spectacle outside. Ginger is. Fifteen minutes before Lori points out the window, Ginger is rolling her empty trash can up her driveway after picking up Rachel from school with a stomachache. She turns because she hears the garage door at the Lamm house go up with its usual muted growl. Mason and Paisley emerge onto the driveway, not in the car but in person. It's the first time Ginger has seen them in nearly two weeks. Paisley's skin is a deep yellow. She sits in a wheelchair. Mason is pushing.

Ginger stands transfixed.

The Lamm driveway angles down sharply toward the street, and for a second the chair threatens to get away from him and careen into the cul-de-sac, spilling Paisley onto the asphalt. With an expression of alarm, Mason pulls back on the handles.

"Whoo!" Paisley says as the wheelchair halts.

"You were almost a goner!"

Both of them laugh.

If the situation were really as dire as it looks, would Mason be making comments about being a goner? Would they be laughing so merrily? Slowly, Mason rolls the wheelchair down the driveway into the street.

"Paisley! It's great to see you!" Ginger calls as they approach. "How *are* you?"

"Great. Great!" As if everything is normal. As if she's not aware of the wheelchair or her yellow skin. As if she hasn't noticed that Ginger hasn't been over to see her.

"I hope your treatments are going well. It looks like they must be." After all, chemo, radiation, all those experimental therapies—they sap your energy. It's temporary. The wheelchair was probably rented for a month.

"We're doing the leaf tour," Mason says, nodding toward the bright trees.

"So I see."

"I'd stop if I could, but this thing has a mind of its own."

Ginger can tell how hard he's working to keep the chair from pulling him down the hill.

"Come see us," Paisley says as Mason whisks her along. "I know you're usually at work. But come whenever you can."

"I'm only home right now because Rachel is sick." As if Paisley hasn't already given her an excuse. As if more protest won't just weaken her case.

"Anytime is good. Anytime." Paisley lifts her long arms and stretches them toward the sky, as if to embrace its bright blue cloudlessness and the tangy air. "Look at this," she says. "Just look at this!"

"Yes," Ginger agrees. It is the perfect autumn afternoon. They are lucky—all of them—to be here to see it.

As Mason and Paisley head around the corner, disappearing down the hill, Ginger makes a mental note to tell Eddie that, except for the jaundice, Paisley seems to be doing well. Her voice is strong. She's laughing. It must be the combination of her red shirt and the black sweater draped over her shoulders that accentuates the yellow in her skin. She can't possibly be that yellow.

At the intersection of Applewood Drive, halfway down the hill, Andrea sees them from her laundry room. For a moment she's so shocked that she's frozen at the window, clutching a warm sheet just out of the dryer. She understands what's happening. If the neighbors won't come to Paisley, she'll go to them. Andrea knows how Paisley thinks. She'll overcome their shyness by letting them see her in her present state. See, it's not so bad. She'll make everyone feel at ease with her, as she always does.

But will she? In a wheelchair?

Andrea's throat aches with bitter, gathering tears. Nearly every afternoon for more than a week, she's kept Paisley company in her family room, thinking Paisley was spending all her time in that leather recliner because the chair is comfortable, not because she's too weak to walk. Until this moment, at the same time that all the neighbors are witnessing what the situation is, Andrea, too, is finding out for the first time. This is how estranged they've become.

But why?

Does Paisley think that Andrea, having gone through cancer once with Courtney, is too fragile to do it again?

Or does she just not feel close enough to Andrea to lean on her?

Lifting the fragrant, clean sheet to her face, Andrea brushes away the tears she's determined not to shed. She's not going to stay here, locked in her house, and do nothing. She studies the streak of mascara on the fabric, then bunches the sheet in her hand and throws it back into the hamper before heading outside.

"Paisley! Mason!" she shouts.

"Too pretty to stay indoors," Paisley says when Andrea gets within earshot. Almost, but not quite, apologetic.

"You could have called me. I would have taken you out." Mason usually doesn't get home until five thirty or six. As publisher of a morning paper, he occasionally stays late, but only if there's a big, breaking story.

"You have no idea how heavy this chair is," Mason says. "Takes great brute strength to manage it."

Andrea scowls. If Paisley had trusted her enough to handle today's outing, instead of calling Mason home from work, Andrea would have suggested they cruise the neighborhood in a car rather than on foot, stopping to say hello to anyone who was outside. This would have gone over better than the wheelchair. It would have brought visitors to Paisley's house sooner than this cheery invalid parade.

It strikes Andrea as an act of desperation, genuine desperation, for Paisley to make Mason come home in the middle of the day.

Distracted, Paisley waves to someone. It's old Mr. Adler, shambling over from across the street. "Glad to see you out and about. How you doing?"

"Great. Great!" Paisley replies. A child on a bike rides into view, the Nelson girl, pumping hard to get up the hill. She stops. "Mrs. Lamm. You're *yellow*."

Paisley laughs. "I know. It looks awful, but it doesn't hurt."

Mr. Adler, looking horrified, laughs, too.

"It doesn't hurt?" the girl asks.

"Not even a little."

A silence of skepticism, and then the child rides off.

Mason hovers. For the moment, Andrea hates him. Well, no. Hate is too strong a word. She resents him. Resents that he's around so much. Resents how easy it is for him to leave work early, now that he's the boss. Years ago, when he was managing editor, he had to put the paper to bed every night, sometimes coming home at two or three in the morning. On those nights, if John had a late meeting as he often did, Andrea would

133

take Courtney to Paisley's for a pajama party, no matter that Brynne and Courtney weren't the best of friends. The women would let the children fall asleep in front of the TV, then tiptoe into the living room and drink wine and talk. All that loose-tongued talk—Andrea still misses it. If Paisley could tell Andrea about her illness, if Andrea could tell Paisley about the job John is negotiating . . . if they could discuss these things, the issues would become less momentous. Even the cancer. Talk about anything long enough, and you cut it down to size.

"Well, take care, Paisley," Mr. Adler says. "I mean it. Take good care." The undertone of affection in his voice is something people seem to reserve strictly for Paisley. Affection and worry. Mr. Adler heads for his house.

Paisley smiles up at Mason as he stands behind her. Something private happens between them, from which Andrea is excluded. Have they always been this way, locked into their own closed and private world? Or did this happen only after Paisley got sick? After all these years thinking she and Paisley were best friends, Andrea feels she's never known her at all. She's never known either of them, except in the most distant way.

They are the kind of people who, when you say, "Hey, how're you doing?" will reply, "Great. Great!"—even now, with Paisley that odd yellow

134

color, too weak to walk, and Mason wheeling her around the block in a wheelchair.

"Great. Great."

Which seems completely wrong to Andrea.

Or completely brave.

Iona goes straight out into her front yard when she sees what's going on, Jeff and Lori trailing her. It's awkward, the three of them like puppies curious to sniff around. But what else can they do?

"Paisley, it's good to see you up and about," Iona says. A lie. Being in a wheelchair isn't exactly *up,* and Paisley's color is horrible.

"The weather's so gorgeous, I couldn't stay inside." Changing the subject, Paisley gestures with a graceful hand toward Lori's stomach. "I guess it won't be long."

"A couple of weeks."

"Late fall's a good time to have a baby. You'll be inside during the winter when he needs to be in anyway, and by the time it's spring, he'll be ready to be out and about."

"She," Lori says.

"Even better."

Paisley holds her arms up and out to the flawless sky. "Look at this!" she says. "Just look at this!"

"It's wonderful," Iona agrees.

"Come see us," Paisley says. As if at a signal, Mason flashes a parting smile that looks about as merry as a dog baring its teeth and begins to push the wheelchair again. His color is worse than Paisley's, white instead of yellow, as if he's just completed a workout that was a little too much for him. A wheelchair is not a stroller but a heavy, cumbersome thing, meant to be confined to flat interior surfaces. It's no match for a bumpy road. How Mason got it down to Hazelwood Way, and how he's ever going to get it back up to Lindenwood Court again, Iona isn't sure. You have to give him credit. If he's having trouble maneuvering the thing, he's trying his best not to let it show.

Iona turns once they're out of sight and walks back into the house. Jeff and Lori are right behind her. She wishes her hands would stop shaking. The truth is, Paisley is so spunky that once you get used to the jaundice and the wheelchair, you convince yourself she doesn't look half-bad. It's Mason's ravaged face that tells her how sick she is. His look of exertion. Of forbearance. Of love. How could she have imagined the man was trying to poison Paisley?

"Iona, you okay?" Lori's voice comes at her from a distance.

"Fine." She sits down at her desk, wishing they would leave. She feels Lori's hand on her shoulder, solid and warm.

"You're not going to start boo-hooing, are you?" Jeff asks.

Iona looks at him sharply. "Did you ever see me boo-hooing about anything?"

"There's always a first time."

"Huh," Iona growls.

"Leave her alone, Jeff," Lori says. There's a hint of a smile in her voice. She thinks he's so funny.

Iona used to think Richard was funny, in almost this same way.

Even though she was supposed to meet with one of her suppliers this afternoon, Ginger is glad she didn't ask Eddie to go get Rachel when the school called. Rachel had made it through lunch, which meant she'd suffered through half the day, hating to ask anyone to call her parents. By the time Ginger got there, Rachel was practically doubled over with cramps. "There's a nasty stomach virus going around," the school nurse told her.

"I spent all morning running to the bathroom, but nothing was happening," Rachel confessed on the way home.

"The nurse said it only lasts twenty-four hours," Ginger assured her.

"I sure hope so."

When they got home, Rachel said she'd lie down on her bed, but moments later she raced to the bathroom and called for Ginger in such an urgent tone of voice that Ginger had to make herself breathe before she could bolt up the stairs. Rachel had taken off her underpants. She lifted them to show Ginger the brownish smear of blood.

So soon? Ginger thought. Ginger was thirteen, maybe fourteen when this happened. Not such a child.

"I don't think it's a virus," Rachel said.

"No."

They smiled at each other.

Ginger thought—and she thought Rachel was thinking it, too—*this is the most momentous day.*

Reaching into the medicine cabinet for painkillers, rummaging through the linen closet for the box of pads stocked for just this purpose, Ginger found herself on the verge of tears, filled with more emotion than made sense. "Do you want to lie down for a while?" she asked after she got Rachel situated. Rachel shook her head no, so they sat on Rachel's bed and had a little talk, rare and most welcome. Not a birds-and-bees talk, beyond the mechanics of pads and tampons. Not about much of anything. The nice weather. How lucky Rachel is to have Mrs. Winstead as her English teacher. How Max will probably wreck the car before he ever learns to drive.

"I'll do better," Rachel said. "I'll have the knack. He doesn't."

Ginger has to agree.

Rachel grew drowsy then. For the first time in years Ginger watched her daughter's eyes close while she was still trying to form sentences, her words melting into a sleepy hum. Ginger tucked her in. For a few minutes, she stood and watched her sleep.

Ginger is grateful that the nap spared Rachel the drama of the Lamms leaving their house with Paisley in a wheelchair. She hopes Rachel is still asleep now, as the couple returns after their tour of the neighborhood, both of them looking as if they aren't quite going to make it up the driveway.

Just as they reach the top, Paisley's eight-year-old, Melody, comes bounding out of the house, holding hands with Paisley's mother, Rita. The two of them help Paisley up and into the house while Mason wheels the empty chair into the garage. Melody, always an imp, jabbers all the time. Ginger imagines her saying, "Come on, Mom, you can do it. Remember the little engine that could. *I think I can, I think I can, I know I can.*"

Oh, the little engine! It was Paisley's mantra for her daughters, at races and softball games and difficult swim practices at the pool. Paisley had every mother in the neighborhood chanting to her children, I think I can, I know I can.

And mostly, they did.

Ginger is not so sure, today, if Paisley can

anymore. Melody will probably never share a day with Paisley like the one Ginger has just shared with Rachel. Melody, so guileless, is certain to be in for a shock when her wiry, athletic body starts to change. She could use a mother then. If she isn't going to have one, if Paisley isn't going to have the chance to share her younger daughter's adolescence . . . it seems such a senseless loss.

Having escorted her mother into the house, Melody comes out again, this time with her little dog, and plops down onto the grass, sitting almost motionless except for idly petting the dog. It's one of her rare moments of repose. The only other time Ginger ever saw the girl sit still like this was at a picnic last summer, when Melody lounged on the grass for at least five full minutes, allowing Paisley to fluff her hair with one hand while gesturing with the glass of wine she held in the other, to embellish a story she was telling. At one point Paisley had flashed Ginger a brilliant smile, revealing those teeth whose glistening whiteness Ginger was never aware of until Eddie mentioned them with such admiration and delight. Back then, Paisley had leaned toward Ginger and whispered something in her ear as if they were the best of friends.

Oh, it had been wonderful! Although Ginger has no memory of what Paisley told her, she remembers with the same shivery warmth she'd felt then how flattered she was that Paisley had chosen *her* ear, Ginger's ear, to whisper into.

And now.

What did Paisley do to deserve this?

What does anybody do?

She reruns the image of Paisley sitting in that lawn chair, one set of fingers tangled in Melody's hair, the other curled gracefully around that wineglass. She remembers the sun glinting off the glass; she recalls the radiant brilliance of the day.

The wine, she thinks. And with grim certainty, she knows there's a specific reason why this is happening to Paisley and not to someone else. All she needs to do is confirm it.

Later, dinner is ready but Ginger is reluctant to awaken Rachel from her nap. In the den, Eddie and Max are having one of their recent discussions—which is to say, arguments—about his driving. It sounds like they're going to be at it for a while. Ginger heads upstairs, figuring her daughter has slept so long because of the medicine she'd taken for the cramps. She shouldn't have any more pain for the rest of the night.

But Rachel isn't in her room. She's out in the yard, as usual. It's one of those nights when the stars seem like sharp pinpricks of light shining through the dark fabric of the sky, so bright there seems to be nothing but pure dazzle behind the curtain. For once, Rachel doesn't seem to be staring moodily at the Lamm house across the cul-de-sac. She's intent on the night sky, probably busy thinking, *I'm a woman now. A woman.* Ginger is astounded by this knowledge herself. She puts her guilt about Paisley's illness aside. Watching her daughter stare at the planes circling toward the airport and the stars whirring through the heavens, Ginger is amazed that Rachel herself—Rachel herself—is in the middle of the dance.

CHAPTER II

October 29

The MOLS started years and years ago, back when the women of Brightwood Trace were mostly housebound with toddlers and longing to get out. MOLS stood for Mothers Out to Lunch Sometimes, a title they came up with jointly during their first outing. The name appealed to them because it sounded like "molls," the girlfriends of mobsters, who no doubt lived lives far more exciting than they themselves had, or for that matter, wanted.

From that first meeting on, MOLS had met at noon on the third Wednesday of every month except December, always at Arnie's Plain and

Fancy, a diner where they could be sure of a table and decent food. Arnie's, third Wednesday, noon—easy enough to remember. No one had to be in charge; no one had to RSVP. If you could get a sitter and be there, fine; if you were at the doctor's office for little Joanne's third earache in a row, everyone understood. The "S" at the end of MOLS stood for "sometimes." Nobody could be expected to show up more than sometimes.

Everyone thought MOLS would wear itself out after the children went to school, but it didn't. It persisted through kindergarten and beyond; it persisted into the years when the mothers went out to work or took on heavy doses of volunteering. It turned a group of casual friends into something cohesive and lasting. Seven or eight women might still attend during the fine brisk days of fall and spring, dropping to just two or three in the heat of summer. Only once, during a blizzard, had no one shown up.

Julianne doesn't usually take a lunch hour. Normally she packs a carton of yogurt or a tuna sandwich and eats whenever there's a break at work. Like many busy medical practices, Peter Dunn's office is officially closed from twelve to two, but it's rarely empty or quiet. Julianne is at Arnie's today only because Ginger called her yesterday and, with some urgency, asked her to come.

"Can you get away at eleven thirty instead of

twelve? I have something I want to ask you about. You're way overdue for a long lunch anyway."

"Well, sure." Julianne knows this must be about Paisley. She and Ginger have never been close, except that in their younger years, when so many of their carpool friends were totally and happily tied up with domestic arrangements, each of them had wanted, in addition to their families, meaningful outside work. For Julianne, it was medicine; for Ginger it was not, Julianne knew, selling hot tubs in particular but running a business, being competent, being able to cope. During a recent encounter in the supermarket where Julianne and Ginger were both shopping for bag-lunch ingredients, Julianne had lamented the madhouse that was usually Peter's office at noon, and Ginger had complained about eating at her desk so she could fill in for the manager during his lunch break. "I'm too cheap to hire extra help," she'd said. "If it's an emergency, Eddie comes downstairs from his office." They are not ladies who lunch.

Now, waiting for Ginger at a table far too big for her in case more MOLS show up, Julianne sips hot tea in deference to the chilly rain outside and studies the truly awful Halloween decorations. A life-size, stuffed scarecrow sits atop a bale of hay by the front door. A selection of black cats and witches dangles by strings from the ceiling. There's a grinning paper pumpkin on each table. Anyone under five would either squeal with delight or go screaming out in terror. Has Arnie's always been this tacky? Didn't one of the MOLS once admire the decor for being tastefully understated, uniquely suitable for a diverse clientele ranging from the Brightwood Trace crowd to the mechanics at the Quickie Lube?

Ginger arrives in a trail of raindrops, slings her dripping slicker over the back of a chair, and pinches the pleats of her gray slacks back into place before sitting down. "I meant to be early, and here I am, late and drenched."

"You're not late. I'm here early because I took your words to heart about deserving a long lunch hour." Julianne hadn't expected the bristly irritation that had filled her at the thought of having to get permission to go out for a real lunch. Why shouldn't she go out more often? Why shut herself up with foot problems? Announcing that she needed two full hours away from the office in the middle of the day had pleased her, not just because she knew she had enough clout to make the demand, but because she was captivated—enthralled, even—by the idea of getting *out,* even in a pour-down rain.

A waitress appears almost instantly, and Ginger points to Julianne's tea. "The same. No lemon. No cream." The moment the waitress moves off, she says, "I wanted to ask you about Paisley"—wasting no time getting down to business. "She used to be healthier than any of us. Why do you think this happened?"

Although this is exactly what Julianne expected, now that she's here, away from a doctor's office, she feels as squeamish as Doug. She wants to talk about new movies, books, their kids, anything but illness. With a wan smile, she says, "Even working for Peter, I've seen enough patients to tell you that you never know why somebody gets sick and somebody else doesn't."

"But sometimes there are contributing factors. People get lung cancer from smoking," Ginger points out.

"Yes. Of course." Julianne lifts the thick, plastic-encased menus from the table and hands one to Ginger, who ignores it.

"I have this theory," Ginger says. "It's nothing that will help Paisley, but it makes sense to me. I wanted to run it by you because of your medical background." The words sound as businesslike as Ginger's gray slacks, but her tone is tentative. "Is it possible the cancer was caused by her drinking?"

"Her drinking?" Julianne arches an eyebrow.

"I know. I know." Ginger picks at a fraying corner of her menu. "A lot of people drink more than Paisley does. Not all of them get sick. A lot of old drunks live practically forever because the liquor serves as a preservative. But people have different levels of sensitivity, don't they? Paisley always seems to have a glass in her hand. Ever since I've known her."

"Yes, but I've never seen her sloppy, fall-down drunk," Julianne says.

"Me, either."

But Ginger holds Julianne's gaze so unblinkingly that Julianne feels compelled to offer something more. "You never know what role alcohol plays in a disease process. You usually don't know what role a whole laundry list of risk factors plays."

"She's jaundiced." Ginger makes this sound as if it proves something.

"You have to remember," Julianne says softly, "that the liver is only a secondary site for the cancer. The cancer originated in the pancreas." From the look on Ginger's face, Julianne feels she's delivering a whole new set of bad news.

Then Ginger puts on a brave, wry smile. "It's amazing what people will do to put sense to things that don't make sense, isn't it?"

"Amazing," Julianne agrees.

"If it made sense, then maybe I'd feel like I could *do* something. It drives me crazy not to be able to do something."

"You could go see her," Julianne says softly. "I think that's what she wants. I think that's probably all any of us can do."

Ginger studies the table. "I know. Every day I'm going to, and every day I don't." She lifts her eyes and regards Julianne questioningly. "Why is it so hard to go visit someone who's sick?"

"I don't know," Julianne says, though she does know. It's normal to shy away from illness and death. It's natural to gravitate toward laughter and life. What's not normal is to sense death in the tips of your fingers, to take it into your belly, into your blood. For all she knows, it's the break from sanity she's feared for many years. For all she knows, the next time, she might not come back.

Wrongheaded as it seems, she'd love to believe in Ginger's theory. Paisley *does* drink. The habit has never left her incapacitated, as far as Julianne knows, but it's always been part of who she is: Paisley Lamm, neighborhood beauty, mother of two, sweet as she can be but drinks too much. No one would dispute that.

She glances at her menu. The offerings haven't changed much in the past decade. Daily specials with meat and two veggies. Grilled cheese sandwiches, BLTs, burgers. Nothing as self-important as the simplest pasta dish at Caruso's. Doug would be appalled. From the middle of the table, the round paper pumpkin grins up at her with its yellow jack-o'-lantern eyes—merry enough, but devilish, too. In a quick, unexpected segue, her mind does a backward loop to a

Halloween years before, when Paisley had looked at her with the same gleeful expression the jack-o'-lantern is wearing, while taking Melody trick or treating on the streets of Brightwood Trace. Melody was dressed as Barney, the purple dinosaur on toddler TV, so she couldn't have been more than two or three. Watching Julianne dole out candy, Paisley had lifted her hand to toast Julianne with a beer she was holding. Conspiratorially, in a stage whisper, she'd said, "I brought a little adult treat along for myself." She'd taken a long, dramatic sip.

Julianne had pretended she was too busy dealing with the children to respond. With three young sons already fascinated by fast cars and alcohol, she'd thought Paisley was setting a bad example. It was one of the few times she hadn't admired Paisley, a moment so intense that even all these years later she can still call up the sharp sting of disenchantment she'd felt then. Couldn't the woman even walk around the block without some kind of drink in her hand?

Can drinking cause cancer? The medical literature says maybe yes, maybe no. Julianne does the rerun again: of Paisley sipping beer while Melody fills her trick-or-treat bag. Of Paisley sipping Painkillers while dancing to the oldies around her hot tub. Of Paisley sipping wine on New Year's Eve.

And when Paisley came into the pre-op exam

room complaining about her stomach, maybe Julianne had suspected something more than an ulcer because, subconsciously, she remembered all the liquor Paisley had consumed over the years. Cause and effect: Paisley drinks too much. Drinking has made her sick. The blackness that assaulted Julianne was only her own horror at touching Paisley's liver and having all her suspicions confirmed.

But no. Julianne has been horrified before. Horrified and shocked. This was different. Except for the day with Eudora Nestor, the leukemia victim, she had never felt like she was dying.

"Ready?" The waitress hovers above her.

"Oh, yes." She gulps back the queasy memory of that day in the examining room. "A cup of the New England clam chowder"—her standard order—"and a small Greek salad."

"What an international combination. I think I'll stick with England," Ginger says, and orders the fish 'n' chips.

"What a cholesterol buster!" Julianne retorts.

"Ah. What difference does it make? A little saturated fat every once in a while? How much can it matter?"

Andrea arrives seconds later, as dry from head to toe as Ginger had been wet. She touches Ginger's slicker on the spare chair—"What did you do, take a bath?"

"Tried to run for it between cloudbursts and didn't make it."

Andrea sets her umbrella next to the dripping coat and takes the seat as far as possible from the rain gear. "I don't think anyone else is coming. Too nasty outside." She picks up a menu. "Did you order already? I'm about starved."

When Andrea makes comments like this, Julianne usually thinks it might do Andrea good to starve a little more. Anyone who knew her back when Courtney was sick remembers her painful, twitchy scrawniness during that time. She'd looked like she needed a good meal. Now she looks like she's had it. Ever since Courtney got better, Andrea has been gaining weight, not so much that she's exactly fat, just chubby and lethargic. She dresses in unflattering styles and refuses to get a good haircut or put highlights in her mouse-colored hair. She speaks in flat, beige monotones that don't quite suppress an undercurrent of fear. Like the superstitious old wives who hide from the evil eye, Andrea seems to believe that if she doesn't make too much of herself, the evil spirits won't notice her or take aim. As long as she tries to erase herself, Courtney will stay healthy. She doesn't say this out loud, but everybody knows. Her life is dwarfed by the illness of a child who's been well for ten years.

But today Andrea seems perkier than usual. *Decidedly* perkier.

"How's Paisley?" Ginger asks. "My kids see you going in and out of her house all the time. They say you're the only one brave enough to visit her every day."

"Brave has nothing to do with it," Andrea says, sounding like someone coming awake after a long sleep. "She's my friend. Eleven years ago she got me through Courtney's surgery and chemo."

"Courtney's doing okay?" Julianne asks.

"She just had all her tests. We're waiting for the rest of the results. So far, so good."

"I'm glad." Julianne *is* glad, though Courtney has turned into such an unappealing creature that some of the younger kids call her "growly-face" because she looks like a dog who'd bite the first chance she got. Julianne has advised the children not to take this notion public. "Every year's a milestone," she tells Andrea.

"We were talking about Paisley just before," says Ginger, doggedly returning to the subject Julianne had thought they were moving away from, after meeting early to have this private discussion. "We were wondering—well, I was wondering—if Paisley's drinking could have something to do with her being sick."

Andrea goes expressionless. "Paisley's drinking?"

"You know what I mean. She always has a glass in her hand."

Andrea gives a short bark of a laugh. "Oh, *that*. Paisley hasn't had a drink for years."

152

"Be serious," Ginger says.

"I am. She doesn't drink at all. Not even wine. Paisley would just as soon no one knew about it, but I guess it doesn't really matter."

Julianne isn't buying this. She tries to remember the pre-op patient history sheet Paisley filled out. On the multiple-choice question about alcohol consumption, hadn't she marked "one or more drinks per day"? Julianne isn't sure she noticed.

"She stopped drinking six or seven years ago," Andrea says. "Brynne was in third or fourth grade. One day she came home from school and accused her mother of being an alcoholic. They'd been studying it in school, and the teacher had defined an alcoholic as someone who took a drink every day.

"It was really awful for Paisley. She was completely shocked. Completely taken aback." There's a brisk defensiveness in Andrea's tone. "It had never occurred to Paisley that she drank too much. She almost never got drunk. The last thing she wanted was to be labeled an alcoholic and embarrass her daughters. She told Brynne she was going to stop drinking then and there, and she did. She never had a drop of alcohol again."

"What about at the picnic last summer?" Ginger asks. "I sat in the lawn chair right next to her, and she was holding a glass of wine."

"Holding a glass, maybe. But not wine. Or if it *was* wine, she wasn't drinking it. She knew people were used to seeing her with a glass in her hand. She didn't want anyone to think she was making a big deal of going on the wagon. That would have gotten back to the kids, too. So she'd walk around with a glass of apple juice or seltzer, and people wouldn't know the difference. They still don't." Andrea's voice is infused with a kind of gentle admiration. A kind of love.

This makes Julianne feel foolish—no, *ashamed*—for wanting so badly to join Ginger in analyzing Paisley's illness into a neat equation. Over a period of years, too much liquor in an alcohol-sensitive person equals cancer. So simple. If that were the case, how would you explain Courtney? She got sick when she was three.

The soup comes, very hot, and with the spice wafting up. Julianne puts all her energy into shutting down her mind. She's lunching at a restaurant, away from sick people, and she intends to eat.

Julianne goes to the gym after work, then shares a pizza with one of the women, not in a hurry to get home. She doesn't want to feel there's plenty of time to stop by Paisley's. Toby is with Bill, their weekly dinner out.

They're back when she gets in, sitting of all

places in the living room, usually reserved for Christmas parties and the insurance guy. They're laughing. What do they talk about, a father and his seventeen-year-old son? At that age, the other two boys wanted nothing to do with their parents. Toby rises when she walks in, gives Bill an odd little salute. "Next week," he says and saunters into the den.

So that's it. He's leaving her with Bill in the living room. Trying, after all these years—despite Julianne's three years with Doug, despite Bill's happy marriage and seven-year-old daughter—to get his parents back together. Bill sees it, too. He raises his eyebrows. "I think he's matchmaking."

"Not going to happen." She feigns comic distaste.

He laughs, but she knows they both find it sort of sad—not their failure to kiss and make up, but Toby's hope.

She sits down on the other end of the couch. She never feels quite at ease with him. "We've been decent parents."

They share a moment of silent agreement before he speaks. "So how's it going?" he asks.

"Crappy."

"Crappy? Why?"

For a second Julianne thinks she'll make a joke, but then, like a tub of water overflowing, she confesses the whole business about her tingling fingers, about Paisley, the whole damned mess. If anybody ought to understand, it's Bill. He's a surgeon. He knows.

Bill hears her out, alert but noncommittal. "And this has happened twice?" he asks when she has finished.

"And it was just as awful each time. I thought I was dying."

He nods. As far as Julianne knows, this could be the prelude to his suggesting a psychiatric evaluation. "Maybe," he says after a time, "you felt that way because you didn't want someone else to die."

"Don't humor me, Bill."

"I'm not. You saw things wrong with these two women. You might not think you noticed anything different, but you did. It happens to me, too, sometimes, in surgery. I know when someone's in trouble before they are. Sometimes seconds before. It's not a case of ESP. It's a case of being a surgeon for a long time. Of subconsciously picking up subtle changes before anyone else does. It's not a negative thing."

"That's because you don't feel like someone's injected poison into your veins."

"It's meant to be uncomfortable. A jolt of adrenaline. Something that helps you act fast enough to help them."

"This is no jolt of adrenaline. I haven't helped anybody. I'm just the messenger."

"You don't know that. Not after just twice."

"Yes. Well. Kill the messenger. They say the third time's the charm. Next time I'll probably end up lying flatlined on the floor." She's serious, but she hears a thread of lightness in her voice and can't quite believe she's treating this dire subject with humor.

"You probably just have a gift for diagnosis."

"From which I'd prefer to be spared. It would be one thing if I had a gift for *healing*. But just to bring on the bad news—no."

"There can't be any healing until you know what the problem is."

"Well, I'm no good at that, either. I have no idea what the problem is. Just that there *is* a problem."

"Which is always step one, Jules."

Jules. *Don't call me Jules.* "I know it's step one, Bill. But let's drop it." She was foolish to confide in him. He hasn't a clue. Why would someone's fingers tingle to tell her *something* is going on, but not *what?* Why would they offer only a multiple-choice menu? The patient is healthy (no tingling), ailing a bit (tingling but not so much you'd want to run to a chiropractor), or terminally ill (the blackness). It's bizarre. Trying to understand it is like driving through fog with the brights on, only to discover that the more light you shine on it, the less you can see.

"You've known Paisley for a long time," Bill

persists. "You know her whole history. If something was wrong with her, it's not surprising that you picked up on it."

Wrong, she thinks. This is exactly the argument she rejected at lunch.

"Paisley was your friend," he says, as if this settles it. "And what about the other woman? Did you know her, too?"

"No."

"How old was she? Was she arthritic? Diabetic?"

"She was in her early fifties. Not diabetic. Normal blood pressure."

"And how did she look? I mean before you touched her?"

"I don't remember, Bill. I honestly don't."

"You've been working in this field for a long time. Maybe she was pale. Maybe there was something about her."

"*No,* Bill."

"Okay," he says softly. He always knows when to retreat. She hates that. "And how is Paisley doing now?" he asks. "Do you see her?"

You'd think she and Paisley were joined at the hip. Julianne keeps her tone clinical. "She's jaundiced, as you'd expect. She's getting weaker. Mason apparently took her outside for a ride in a wheelchair the other day. I missed it."

Bill nods.

"Brynne says she has a persistent backache that

Tylenol doesn't help." It's a relief to know that Bill knows what this means. The cancer is beginning to affect that huge plexus of nerves near her spine. Paisley will need stronger analgesics, eventually a morphine drip. The painkillers will make her nauseated. She won't eat. Everything can happen very fast. "The last time I saw her"—she had not thought of this until now; she doesn't even know how she knows—"I thought her abdomen was a little bit distended."

"See? You notice. You want to deny it, but it's what you're trained for and what you're good at. Not everybody has a talent for diagnosis. It's a gift." He gets serious. "As long as you're working for a podiatrist, you're wasting it."

Zap! Exit Bill the shoulder to cry on. Enter Bill the great sage. Now he'll badger her every time they meet. Always the control freak. "Ah, Bill. You're a font of good advice." She walks him into the foyer. It seems to her this is what they *do*: move toward a door, so he can leave.

At least she had the good sense not to confess how disgusted she is with herself for being less interested in Paisley's struggle than in her own traitorous fingers. That would have opened a whole other path of analysis she's not sure she can endure. The psychology of disgust. Come to think of it, she's disgusted with Ginger, too, for wanting to put sense to Paisley's illness so it will be easier for her to look across her cul-de-sac into the windows of a house of tragedy. She's disgusted with herself for buying into Ginger's theory. She's disgusted with Bill for being here, for being privy to her confession, for making himself so convenient.

But she's going to be nice to him, oh yes. If she's nice enough, maybe he'll stay away.

"Thanks for listening," she says.

"Anytime."

Julianne is smiling, smiling, smiling as she closes the door.

CHAPTER 12

Paisley—Drinking

The story is that I stopped drinking so as not to embarrass the girls. That was only part of it.

It was true that Brynne's third-grade teacher, Mrs. Rose, told the kids an alcoholic was someone who took at least one drink every day. Somehow the concept of the drink containing *alcohol* had dropped out of the equation. There wasn't a single student who hadn't seen their parents drinking. Orange juice, water, ginger ale. They went home, upset, anxious to sound the alarm. Some parent—not me—confronted Mrs. Rose in the principal's office the next morning, brandishing a dictionary. "*Alcoholic:* someone addicted to alcohol. How do we define 'addicted,' exactly? One drink a day? One *alcoholic* drink a day?" It went on from there.

A parents' meeting was called to allow Mrs. Rose to explain herself. She was in her sixties, a dour woman who could have used a few vials of Botox to soften her frown. "Ladies and gentlemen, I'm sorry you're so upset. I was only quoting statistics," she argued weakly. "I certainly didn't mean to confuse the children. I didn't mean to be unclear." She offered her sincere apology. Already, a substance abuse counselor had been called in to clarify the issue to the children. The meeting might have gone on longer and gotten louder if Mrs. Rose hadn't been so visibly shaken. She was out on sick leave the following week. She took early retirement.

Score: Alcohol, one. Abstinence, nothing.

I didn't drink every day. I rarely got drunk and never *looked* drunk, never acted drunk, even if I'd had quite a lot. I'd learned early to keep the sweet buzz a private pleasure except at a party when a little giddiness seemed the order of the evening.

Brynne was eight then, a calm, steady girl, never as wild as her two-year-old sister even when she'd been the same age; but smart, thoughtful, cloistered, and observant. She'd seen me pouring vodka into my orange juice; she knew what it was. "You shouldn't drink that every day, Mom," she said.

"Oh, I don't."

"It can make you sick."

"I know, honey. I'm very careful."

This was at least a month after the incident at school. Brynne was a worrier, easily troubled and then unable to let go. Rubbing the wounds deeper, sometimes for weeks, pulling off the scabs. Where did she get that? Not from *me*. Telling her I was careful only disturbed her. Sometimes when she was upset she'd ride her bike around and around Lindenwood Court until she calmed down.

That particular afternoon felt endless. Melody was taking a three-hour nap. There was no chance of getting out, though I'd been home all day. Outside, the air was chilly and the sky was gray and gritty. On days like that I allowed myself a shot or two, or at least a glass of wine. It was bourbon and ginger ale that day. I was careful to mix it while Brynne was upstairs changing clothes, but she knew. Maybe she smelled it on my breath.

Opening the garage door, she retrieved her helmet, got onto her bike. I came out onto the front porch, baby monitor in hand lest Melody wake up, and sat on the step to watch her. I clinked the ice around in my glass, though my hands were freezing. Brynne wore a pair of child-size biking shorts Mason had found in a sports store. They didn't come down farther than her knees. I should stop her, send her upstairs for warmer slacks. But no, the activity would keep her warm. I was a little dizzy.

Brynne was having a contest with herself. Around and around the court, faster and faster. An angry speed. She didn't look at me. I would talk to her later, assure her once again about the drinking. I put down the glass.

With every pass, she circled in a smaller arc, leaning a little more to the side each time to make the ever-more-narrow turn. On her face as she passed me, an expression of victory. She pedaled furiously. She leaned too far. At the end of the cul-de-sac, the bike tipped, skidded, came to a stop at the edge of our front yard. Brynne went with it, her bare calf scraping the street as she slid. It was already bleeding before she stopped moving.

Her helmet hit the pavement. She landed on her side, her foot still on the pedal. The sound she made was not a sob, not a scream, more like a roar.

Of pain? Anger? Or some unthinkable damage inside her brain?

At such a moment, you think the liquor will burn right out of you.

It doesn't.

"Brynne? *Brynne!*" I knelt at her side, lifted her head. She was crying now, unmistakably weeping. "Let me see your leg."

It was a bloody mess, scraped up and down. At such a moment, do you stay with the child, or run inside for the phone? My cell was sitting on the kitchen counter. The baby monitor was still in my hand. Melody was screaming.

Even sober, I might not have thought clearly. But this . . . this was paralysis. We sat there, doing nothing.

Ordinarily, someone else might come out of their house. But not today, this gray, grim afternoon.

"We need to call 911," I finally said.

"No." That quickly, she grew calm. Her face was streaked with tears, but her expression was entirely composed, as if she'd realized, irrefutably, that she needed to take care of me.

She was eight years old.

Pulling away from me, she took off her helmet and began to stand up. I offered my arm. "Let me help you."

"No."

On the monitor, Melody howled. "You need to get her," Brynne said.

"I'll drive you to the doctor's office. They can clean you up."

"You shouldn't drive."

"I'm okay."

"No. You should call Dad."

Even if we'd lived twenty miles out in the country with no phone, I don't believe she would have gotten in the car with me at the wheel that day.

Brynne didn't have a concussion. Even with the helmet, the doctor said it was a piece of luck. She had a scar just below her knee from where a piece of gravel had lodged in.

That night, I found my glass on the front step. I threw out the liquid.

I hadn't known Brynne was standing there. "Don't drink anymore, Mom," she said. "It's making you sick."

"I won't."

"You can't just say it. You have to promise."

She was only eight. She took my hand.

"I promise I won't drink anymore."

I never did.

CHAPTER 13

November 5

Two days after Courtney's tests all come back negative, Andrea insists on a family celebration featuring hot fudge sundaes with whipped cream, the treat Courtney most coveted when she was a child and which today she terms "an orgy of empty calories" but eats. They would have celebrated earlier, but John made a quick trip to California and returned with the final, revised copy of his job offer in his briefcase. Andrea supposes tonight's festivities are for more than Courtney's health—though to Andrea's shame, Courtney knows nothing about the job offer or the ongoing discussions John and Andrea have been having about whether to accept it.

Andrea thinks she might have told her if Courtney had shown the least bit of interest in her father's comings and goings. John rarely travels as much as he has this fall. Courtney hardly seems aware of this. She lumps his trips together as "business" and never asks a single question. Perhaps all adolescents are this way at fourteen. Perhaps she's been preoccupied with the hard task of waiting for her medical results, especially in the light of Paisley's far-more-dire condition, and all it portends. Whatever the reason, Andrea has welcomed her daughter's indifference. Breaking news to Courtney about anything unexpected is like risking a volcanic eruption. No point standing in its path unless you have to.

After what seems like several centuries, Courtney finally goes up to bed. Ten minutes later, John and Andrea are in their own room, Andrea sitting on the bed with a yellow legal pad in hand, listing the pros and cons of his job offer, John pacing the carpet in boxer shorts and a half-unbuttoned shirt, looking like some long-legged wading bird making its way slowly through the shallows. He rubs the bald top of his head, then lowers his hand, then lifts it again to tug at the fine fringe of black hair above his ears.

"Only two things in the 'No' column," Andrea says. "That can't be right."

"What two things?"

"Cost of Living and Moving Courtney."

"How many things in the 'Yes' column?"

"About ten."

John paces a little more. Andrea shifts on the bed. They're both about to pop from the fullness of what they know and what they still have to determine.

"They want you the first of January," Andrea suggests. "Less than two months. That could go in the 'No' column." John has tried to negotiate for June, but the position has to be filled.

"January isn't so bad. I can rent us a temporary place next time I fly out, and we can move at Christmas." Idly, he unbuttons the rest of his shirt, which flaps loosely against his bony chest. "Christmas is as good a time as any for Courtney to make the break. What do you think? It will be an adventure."

"The adventure might be *telling* Courtney."

John removes the shirt, drops it into the hamper. "Sometimes I think the inmate is running the asylum around here."

"Don't be too hard on her. We'll be taking the inmate to a whole new asylum. It's scary."

"Of course, it is." With great deliberation, he

picks up the trousers he laid earlier over a chair and folds them onto a hanger. "We'll tell her as soon as I sign my contract."

"Does that mean yes?" Andrea puts her pencil down. "Does that mean we've decided?"

They stare at each other. "I guess it does." For a moment he stands perfectly still, then opens the big walk-in closet and hangs up the pants. His I'm-not-going-to-crack-a-smile expression is so stern, he's probably in shock. With the most unexpected rush of affection, it occurs to Andrea that the man she has been married to all these years looks like an egret from the waist down and a medieval monk from the neck up, who ought to be wearing one of those scratchy brown robes.

"What?" he asks, aware of her eyes on him.

"Nothing."

"Tell me."

"I'm just amazed that we're actually going to do it." All her previous ambivalence vanishes. A sense of lightness begins to rise in her chest, then drops into a lump of dread as the enormity dawns on her of the tasks still before them. "It's not just Courtney," she whispers. "I have to tell Paisley."

John gathers himself then, propels his pale body across the room, and sits down next to Andrea, who is perched so stiffly on the edge of the mattress she might be in a good-posture class. He begins to massage her shoulders.

"Paisley will be happy for you. You know she will," he says. "There's no point thinking about it now. Not tonight." His fingers knead muscles she didn't even know she had. She closes her eyes and concentrates on relaxing. *Don't think about it now. Don't think.*

"And also," he says after a time, "if things with Paisley aren't resolved by Christmas"—*resolved* is such a loaded word—"if things aren't resolved by then, you could stay here awhile."

She focuses on her shoulders, mumbles a melodic *hmmm*.

"The house will be on the market, but it's not likely to sell until spring," John says. "There would be nothing wrong with renting a furnished place out there and leaving this house furnished until you were ready to move."

They both know this is impossible. If Andrea stayed behind, Courtney would stay, too. And Courtney, knowing her reprieve was only temporary, would be unmanageable. The three of them have to move together, as a family.

Wrenching herself out of her half-hypnotized state, Andrea says, "The way things are with Paisley, my being here wouldn't make any difference. She doesn't confide in me, so how can I help her? I can't even be a shoulder to cry on. We might be two middle-aged ladies who've just met at a tea party. It's awful."

"I know." In this new, off-balance world

they've stepped into, with the future at once promising and looming, Andrea thinks John *does* know. He glides his hands over her shoulders as gently as if she were made of porcelain. Back in her carefree, life-is-a-beach days, she would never have predicted a moment like this. She hadn't imagined, then, that he was capable of anything as powerful as empathy. It was enough that he was centered enough to keep her grounded—a man who, if you promised you wouldn't smoke pot anymore, would hold you to your word. A man so self-contained that even on a night like this, his head filled with a jumble of emotions, lets himself be guided by the rational decision that this is where they need to be. In bed. Settling down. Ordering their lives into a routine, not yielding to the chaos.

Of course, when Courtney got sick, Andrea had hated those same qualities of self-control—the smooth, unruffled surface John showed the world as everything began to unravel; his refusal to admit his fears, much less share them; his holding back tears until his mother, an outsider, arrived to receive them.

Andrea never thought she'd forgive any of that. Until these past three weeks, she believed she and John were lost to each other for good, except for the placid exterior they had managed to keep intact. But so much has happened, in such a short time. Nothing seems certain anymore. The whole world has shifted. Now she believes that the mammoth of grief and terror stalking the room during Courtney's illness was all either one of them could see. Their child's cancer had misted their vision of each other not just then but for years after, leaving them as wounded and isolated from each other as Andrea has been, lately, from Paisley. How did John stay for so long at a job he didn't care for, just so Courtney could have health benefits? The feat amazes her. He must have wanted his family—wanted Courtney, wanted *her*—more than he wanted to be free.

Now he *is* free. Happiness glows all over him. She wants this to happen.

"You know," she says after a while, "anytime you go into Paisley's, you always hear music playing. The same oldies as always. Sometimes Paisley even puts on that silly feather boa she used to wave around. You'd think it would be pathetic, but it's not. It's cheerful. I can't explain it."

"It's hopeful," John says.

"The house has the same party atmosphere as always. It doesn't feel like they're working at it, although they must be. People come out of there and say, well, whatever they're giving her, it must be working. It *is* hopeful. Everyone knows she has pancreatic cancer, everyone knows it's also in the liver, everyone knows it's a death sentence. You can find that out in two minutes online. And yet it doesn't seem to be happening. She seems to be . . . herself, I guess. Even though she's jaundiced. And so weak. And I think she's losing weight."

"People in treatment almost always lose weight."

"I know." Blankly, the two of them stare across the room at the big TV they never watch. The cocktail of emotions that swirls around them is intoxicating at first, then exhausting. Andrea is drained. She sees that John is, too. As if at a signal, they settle themselves under the covers. "I'll tell Paisley about the move tomorrow," she murmurs. And without expecting it they are asleep, deep in the animal warmth of each other, cuddled together like puppies.

Ten seconds after Courtney leaves for school the next day, Andrea begins cleaning out the attic, throwing away things she didn't even know were up there. She's nervous, panicked, elated, all at once. John's new employer will pay for their move, for extra insurance, for packers. If Andrea throws out twenty bags of accumulated miscellany once a day for the next ten years, she might be ready for them. Like a thief trying to hide her stash, she puts the trash bags into the back of the car in the closed garage, opens the garage doors just long enough to back down the driveway, and hauls the stuff to the Dumpster behind the supermarket. She's pretty sure this is illegal. She'd rather be arrested than have the neighbors see so many castoffs in front of her house on trash day—at least until she spreads the word.

On the way home, her mind feels at once sharper than it's been in years, and also less focused. Maybe she won't take all the furniture. Maybe on the West Coast her dark mahogany heirlooms won't fit. Will John's new salary allow them to buy one of those out-of-sight-expensive California houses? Will Andrea have to go to work to help pay the bills? The idea intrigues her. Imagine—having a *career*. Of course, if Andrea isn't home after school, God knows what will become of Courtney. Nothing good.

Courtney. Clueless Courtney. Andrea dreads—truly dreads—being there when her daughter learns about the move and has a fit.

She also hates the idea of facing Paisley for exactly the opposite reason—that Paisley will surely treat the news with her usual upbeat, and now so patently *false,* cheerfulness, as if her illness didn't also require examination or attention, wasn't an issue at all. But this is something she needs to deal with. She sets her jaw, drives to her friend's house, and pulls into the driveway.

Taped to the front door is a sign, crayoned in

large letters on white poster board: "Paisley Lamm is resting now, but she would love to see you. Please check back later." The handiwork is Melody's, a border of shapeless hearts and flowers around the clumsily lettered words, attesting to the fact that the child is an athlete and not an artist.

Check back. Well, she will. She'll give Paisley an hour for her nap, maybe a little longer. By then the sign will be gone. Neither she nor Paisley will mention it. They'll never mention it at all.

But she doesn't go back. She's consumed by the prospect of her own boundless and frightening future. She can't bring herself to share it. Sometimes there's a secret so momentous, so vast, that for a time, even just a day, you have to keep it to yourself.

She means to go early the next morning, to be in and out of there before Paisley feels the need for a nap. Somehow the day gets used up. There's so much to do. Collect more discards from the attic, carry sets of mismatched plates to Goodwill. Hardly a blink of an eye and it's four o'clock. John calls to say his contract is signed and in the mail. Courtney stomps in from school and up to her room. Another hour and Andrea will have to start supper. With an effort of will, she heads to Lindenwood Court. Even if the sign is up, she's going to knock. But Rita opens the door just as Andrea reaches for the bell. Always well groomed, always composed, all the same, Paisley's mother looks exhausted. No wonder. "Oh, good," she says. "I know Paisley wants to see you."

She does? *Why?* Andrea wonders if Rita can hear the thudding of her heart.

Paisley's in her usual place, wearing her usual smile, the feather boa slung around her neck like a scarf too flimsy to keep her warm. She seems a bit dwarfed by the big recliner. Was it always like that? Beside the chair looms a portable metal pole holding a familiar-looking bag of liquid that takes Andrea back to Courtney's hospital stay as if it had happened last week.

"A morphine drip," Andrea says, projecting accusation rather than the sympathy she intends. "I thought you weren't in pain."

"Just a backache. On and off." A bandage and a piece of gauze hold the IV needle in place on Paisley's arm. She indicates the plunger she can push for more medication. "This lets me control it."

"I see." Andrea's voice is a rasp, harsh as a wire brush.

Paisley struggles to sit straighter in the roomy leather chair. "I should have told you."

Out of habit, Andrea almost says it's okay, then bites the words back because it's not okay, not even close. Here they are, zero hour, and what's the point of lying? "I hate to think you're in pain," she says instead, and this is true. She hates it, hates it. "Does this mean—? What does this mean?"

"Did you ever notice how there's always a hair or two left in the bathroom, even right after somebody cleaned it?" Paisley asks.

Terrific. Now they're going to discuss *housekeeping?* "How is this relevant? Why are you telling me this?" Andrea doesn't try to disguise her anger.

"Because it's like the hair," Paisley says, barely audible.

"*What* is like the hair?"

"The cancer."

Too quickly, Andrea says, "I don't follow," though the bar of ice gliding down her back tells her she does.

"You can mop and wipe and then do it again, but it doesn't matter. There's always a hair lingering somewhere. It's the same with the cancer. They try, but they can never get rid of it, not really. Not when it's this far along. That's what they said."

"The cancer isn't going away?" Andrea's voice is dull.

"Not going away. Spreading like wildfire. Eating me up."

"Don't say that."

"You wanted to know. You've been polite about this, but I know you wanted to know."

Andrea nods, because she did. She wanted to hear from Paisley's mouth what she's known, and pretended to herself not to know, all along.

"I would have told you right away, but I didn't want to tell the children yet. I wanted a little normalcy for them to—I don't know. Maybe to get used to this." As if that were possible, getting used to their hyperactive mother sitting demurely in the family room with drugs dripping into her veins, wearing a feather boa and taking frequent naps. "It's not that I thought you'd tell anyone," Paisley adds. "I just felt it was only right for the children to know first. I wanted to put it off as long as I could. But I decided to get *this*"—she lifts the arm with the morphine drip—"I got it this morning. We talked to them last night." She shifts again in the chair, which seems determined to swallow her up.

"So the treatments—?"

"I know everybody has a theory about my treatments. I've heard about more treatments than you can think of," Paisley says. "Well, here's the scoop. There *are* no treatments. There never were."

"What?"

Paisley shakes her head.

"No chemo? No radiation? *Nothing?* Then why did you tell me—?" Andrea stops, because she realizes that Paisley didn't tell her anything. Evasion was the whole point of their overarching silence. Paisley didn't admit to anything at all.

"Well, there was Tylenol," Paisley says. Unthreatening Tylenol. Of course. Four times a day, the bottle always in plain view on the end table. "The cancer had already spread by the time they found it. There was really nothing they could do."

"I don't believe that." The research Andrea's done—and she hasn't done a lot, because she doesn't want to know much more than she's already found out—doesn't hold out *much* hope, but it offers some.

"They told me I'd be eligible for one of the clinical trials, but the experimental drugs have awful side effects and don't do much. The best one that's actually approved for metastatic pancreatic cancer—the *best*—can prolong your life, get this, two weeks. Two *weeks*." An angry blush of color tints Paisley's yellow cheeks for the briefest second, then disappears. "So we decided just to . . . to hang on as long as I could. To keep it peaceful around here and tell the children when we had to."

"And now you 'had to.' "

Paisley nods. "I didn't want to be moaning and groaning in front of the kids when I told them I was thinking of checking out." She lowers her voice. "So we called in hospice."

Tears swim to Andrea's eyes, which she furiously blinks back. She forces her attention to the bag of liquid. "Does it help?"

"Sure. Remember how much it helped Courtney? The painkillers are even better now."

"They made her throw up."

"They say they can give me something for nausea."

Andrea notes that she does not say she doesn't *have* nausea. Paisley looks at something in the corner of the room, but when Andrea follows her gaze, there's nothing there. Both of them study the empty corner. After a time Paisley says, perfectly cheerful, "It sucks, doesn't it?" The hint of a tiny, honest-to-goodness smile.

Andrea grimaces, not seeing the cause for merriment. "It *totally* sucks. And now you're in pain."

"The pain is only sometimes." Paisley's smile retreats. "The real problem is being so tired. I mean, *mega*tired. It was less a matter of telling the kids because I had to than a matter of telling them while I still had the energy. The hospice counselor said the sooner the better." She settles back into the recliner. "Anyway, it's done."

"And how did they take it?"

"They didn't burst into tears or jump off the roof or anything. I think Brynne already knew."

"And Melody?"

"She's a little confused."

"I bet."

"We went the 'angels you can't touch but who look out for you' route. Not a good plan."

"I have a little trouble with angels myself," Andrea says.

"Then we went the 'Mama won't be here anymore but she'll be looking down from heaven' route. I guess that's just a variation of the angel story." Paisley stops, thoughtful. "She doesn't quite grasp the idea of dying."

"Me, either."

A statement, Andrea notes, that Paisley ignores. She asks instead, quite earnestly, "Do you think we made a mistake, not taking them to church more?"

"Hell, no. I think Melody would have hated it."

"Me, too."

They sit for a while and say nothing, which is a relief. *Such* a relief. "You're brave," Andrea tells Paisley finally. "Braver than I would be."

"Everybody's brave when they don't have any choices. When Courtney was sick, *you* were brave."

"I just remember being scared."

"Nah. You were a champ. You were a rock."

The rock is about to roll, she thinks, and then blurts out the very words. "This rock is about to roll, Paisley. John took a new job. We're moving."

"Moving?" Paisley sits straighter, interested.

"Andrea Chess, born and bred not ten miles from here, *moving?*"

"I wanted you to know before we told Courtney." She feels guilty, wanting to tell Paisley first, while Paisley wanted to tell her children. "I didn't want you to hear from the grapevine," she says.

Paisley cocks her head. "You think the news would do me in before my time?"

"I was a little worried." She forces a smile.

"Moving where? How far? What kind of job?" They're just exchanging information now. This is better. They can do this. Andrea tells her everything.

"We're both going on a journey," Paisley says when she finishes. She makes it sound as if they're embarking on separate but equal adventures, as if moving to California were not, by comparison, as inconsequential as sand.

In the end, neither of them can sustain this. Andrea looks at Paisley through a shimmer of tears, then studies the floor because they're not sentimental sisters and she feels like she's breaking some kind of rule. Without thinking about it, she reaches over and takes Paisley's hand, and in the same motion Paisley grasps Andrea's other hand, and they both hang on. They sit there for a while, not talking, because Paisley is dying. It's out in the open now, so what else is there to say? They have been friends for so long. All friendships end, one way or the other. Andrea knows people usually feel superior when someone they know is dying. *You're finished, but look at me, I'm going strong.* Andrea doesn't feel that way at all. She doesn't want Paisley to go without her. She doesn't want Paisley to leave her behind.

"If you're not going to be here," she says, "I'm glad I'll be on the other side of the country."

"You'll love it there." Paisley squeezes her hand. "I'm glad for you, Andrea. I am."

Exactly what Andrea knew she would say.

Then Paisley adds quietly, "This could happen pretty fast." Her voice doesn't waver, but when Andrea looks up, she sees that Paisley's face, like her own, is lacquered with tears. "The hospice people tell it to you straight. When it gets to this point, it can go pretty fast."

Andrea nods. No point in offering platitudes. "Whatever you need," she says. "Whatever I can do for you, let me know."

"I will," Paisley says.

"I'm not going to California until there's nothing else you need from me."

"You might be sorry you offered."

"Not a chance. Promise that whatever it is, you'll ask."

"Well, you can make sure Max Logan stays away from Melody," Paisley quips, raising and lowering her eyebrows.

Max Logan. Ginger's boy. Not funny, Andrea

thinks, but she plays along. "Well, let's see. Max is fifteen. Melody is eight. I don't think there's any danger from that quarter."

But Paisley quickly moves on. "Actually I do have a couple of things to ask." Her voice is beginning to sound like there's no air behind it, weaker by the word. "Maybe next time."

"Sure. Next time." Andrea squeezes her hand again, then lets go.

Andrea is out the door before she realizes what was different in there today other than the morphine drip, maybe just as important. There wasn't any music coming from the speakers. Nothing at all.

At home John's in the kitchen, taking a frozen lasagna out of the oven for supper. The house is eerily quiet. He hasn't even turned on the news. "Where's Courtney?" she asks. He points upstairs. A reprieve. Good.

"Paisley isn't taking treatments," she says. "She was never taking them. It was too far along." She weeps then, allows herself the luxury of long choking sobs into John's shirt. He holds her and strokes her hair, she doesn't know for how long, as if both of them are waiting for her heart to shred itself and then re-form for the next task at hand, not to be avoided: taking on their daughter. "I promised Paisley I wouldn't go until it's over," she tells him.

"Of course not," John says. They both take a breath, and Andrea fixes her face, and they call Courtney down to dinner.

Sitting at the table, Andrea studies her daughter for the first time in—she's not even sure how long. Since before her last round of tests, and maybe the ones before that. If you don't look, you don't have to know. Now she can't stop staring.

What she sees is the hardness. A hard-bitten girl of fourteen, her body fully developed with small breasts and wiry, hard-muscled arms and legs, no softness anywhere and probably none to come. Dark shirt and jeans hugging the unwelcoming flesh. Bitten-to-the-quick finger-nails, painted almost black. Face as round as John's with features as small as Andrea's, saved only by the big gray eyes and thick dark brows, if she'll only leave them alone, not pluck them into angry thin arches, as Andrea fears she might. Hair erupting from her head in a frizzy black halo she tries to tame with gel that only makes it greasy—and that to Andrea seems especially unfair because when Courtney was three, before the chemo, she had a fine cap of silky dark hair like John's, and remarkably long lashes that grew back into short, spiky stubs above her eyes.

Andrea had never been good-looking, either, but she'd been so lighthearted it hadn't mattered—a trait Courtney either hadn't inherited or that had been pummeled out of her by her illness. In the hospital she'd been bewildered at first, then frightened and tearful, and finally sullen and ill natured. She scowled at the nurses. Once, she bit one of them. She wasn't charming. By the end of her treatments, she looked and acted like a nasty, wizened dwarf. She's just as angry now. It radiates from her like heat, punishment directed to the world that hurt her. But cured her, too. Black nail polish can be removed. Fingernails grow. The scowl is harder. And even worse: the mask of perpetual surliness, etched onto the small features like a tattoo.

One reason Andrea doesn't look at her daughter is because if she has to face Courtney's surliness straight-on, she might not be able to suppress her urge to strike her.

How can you love someone so much, how can you put so much energy into willing them to grow and thrive, only to find—despite your overwhelming gratefulness to have them there— that lately you don't like them at all?

John waits until the dishes are cleared before he speaks. He's thought about this a long time. Andrea trusts that. No hedging. Right to the point. "You know those trips I've been taking to California?"

"Yeah. So?"

"I gave a couple of seminars. They liked them so well they offered me a job."

Courtney freezes, halfway to the sink, serving plate in hand.

"I've accepted a position," John says. "It starts the first of January. We're going to find a house out there."

"And when were you going to spring this on me? Christmas morning?" Her tone is so calm, so placid that Andrea wonders if she already knew. How was it possible to live in this house the past week or so and *not* know? Yet she senses Courtney's surprise. Her horrified surprise.

"Not Christmas morning," John tells her, equally placid. "We'll be in the middle of moving then. I was going to tell you right now."

"I think you'll like it there," Andrea hears herself gush. "All that sunshine. It's one of the nicest places in the country."

Courtney stares at her, then at John, as if they are speaking different languages. She unlocks her frozen body, carries the plate to the sink, sets it down. Andrea half expected her to throw it. She braces for shouts, for tears. But Courtney, usually so full of snap and bristle, just turns and heads for her room.

Oh, this was wrong, this silence. This was cruel.

Is it possible that only a moment before Andrea thought she didn't even like her? Now she trembles with the intensity of her love. She feels every iota of Courtney's pain, every fear—everything—as if once again they have opened her daughter's body with a scalpel of the sharpest steel, the future before them like a sudden darkness, and no promise at all of a cure.

CHAPTER 14

Paisley—Eating

Something I'm ashamed of? That day the dark wind started blowing through my head. No excuses. The sun was shining, shining.

Mason's newspaper hosted a barbecue every year. A command performance, not optional. The whole staff was expected. Spouses, children, significant others, too.

That particular event was on a sweltering day at the beginning of June, far too early for such heat. A rented tent, green and white striped, in the center of the publisher's big backyard, with tables and chairs underneath. A long food table where servers dished out huge portions of meat and beans and slaw, and bowls of banana pudding sweet enough to make your teeth ache. The barbecue was messy, dripping in red sauce, but no one cared. There were soft drinks, bottles of wine, a keg.

Print news had not begun losing readers in a

serious way yet, so the younger reporters—a talented, ambitious group—saw themselves as future Bob Woodwards, not relics (soon to be castoffs) of a dying trade. They hoped to make their mark in a year or two and then move on to more prestigious papers: the *Charlotte Observer*; the *Philadelphia Inquirer* if they were lucky; or if they were really good, the *Washington Post*. Mason hoped for that, too. He had become managing editor; he was on his way. I suppose it was digital news that finally stopped us, kept us where we were. But that was later.

Brynne was three then and wouldn't touch the barbecue. Not just because of the sauce, which was daunting enough, but because she didn't like meat. She downed a bowl of banana pudding and went off to run through the sprinklers with some of the other kids. Herb Clay, the copy editor, sat next to me as always, chatty and devoted as a puppy, jumping up to get me more slaw, more beans, food I didn't really want but ate because he was so anxious to bring it. Mason said, year after year, if you want Herb gone, just say the word. But I didn't. It was so clear that all he wanted was that half hour of closeness, so easy to give. I usually knew what people wanted.

I waved to Mason, who was standing just outside the range of the sprinklers, holding his messy sandwich and talking to his little cluster of followers. The entourage of newly hired reporters had materialized months before, at his promotion party, and persisted at every social function since.

"Employees always suck up to the managing editor," he'd said with a lightness he didn't seem to feel. "Part of the job." He didn't mind the young men, who tried to outdo each other with their perceptiveness, their wit, their forward-thinking ideas. But the fawning women made him uneasy. He was a serious, private person. At one of the first parties after his promotion, I'd spotted him literally backed into a corner, frantically scanning the room to catch my eye so I could rescue him.

That day I realized he'd gotten accustomed to the attention. He didn't return my wave. Probably didn't see it. He looked perfectly comfortable, holding his sloppy, dripping sandwich above his flimsy paper plate, nodding alternately to the speakers who surrounded him, who appeared to be talking all at once. The king holding court. One of the new hires, Karin Branch—Karin with an "i," not an "e," as she would be quick to remind you—pushed her way to Mason's side and said something that set the entire crowd laughing, a chorus of merry voices. I felt, unaccountably, left out. Why should I care about newspaper gossip? Why care about some in-joke I wouldn't get even if I'd heard it, delivered by a not-very-attractive twenty-something reporter trying to impress her boss? I assessed Karin with a practiced eye: chin-length hair the color and texture of straw, mediocre figure, stubby, winter-pale legs that jutted from poorly advised shorts. A good reporter, she was the star of this year's crop. At that moment I disliked her intensely.

Herb kept droning on about the appalling spelling of the college interns. I kept pushing the unwanted baked beans around my plate. In other years, I'd been pleased with myself for sticking with Herb all the way through his monologue. Now all I wanted to do was escape. I'd eaten too much. I needed exercise. Watching Brynne negotiate arcs of water from the vacillating sprinklers—so composed, moving with such grace and ease among the mostly older children that I couldn't help but be proud of her—I was jealous, all the same, that she got to run around and I did not.

Lighthearted: that's how people usually described me. Cheerful. Upbeat. But not then. I was bored, irritated, working myself up to outright rage.

Eight months before, I'd had my first miscarriage. We hadn't wanted a baby. Mason's promotion hadn't come through. We wanted a bigger house. But while the mind says no, still the body grieves. "I'm so sorry, honey," my mother said, "but this happens to almost everyone. Before you know it, you'll have another baby. You'll be fine." Then, heartlessly, "Up until now you've had such an easy life."

I didn't forgive her, but she was right.

Now I was trying to get pregnant. I was thirty-five. I'd been trying for six months. After that last, unplanned pregnancy . . . nothing. My doctor said I had "old eggs." I scheduled sex the way I scheduled dentist appointments. Nothing flirtatious, nothing spontaneous. I was in a race against time.

The reporters laughed again, and the society editor touched Mason on the arm. She was fifty and motherly, but I resented the gesture. I thought, *Well,* no wonder *I'm not getting pregnant! Mason is having too much fun with his little circle of admirers! He's not paying attention to the task at hand!*

As if you had to be goal oriented in order to conceive! As we well knew! Mason was always eager for sex. Spur-of-the-moment sex, half-anticipated sex in front of the TV, planned sex marked in red on the calendar—Mason didn't care. He was normal in every way. Just look at him, surrounded by groupies! The problem was old eggs. The problem was me.

I looked up just in time to see Mason take a bite of his sandwich, the kind of too-generous bite designed to get it into his mouth before the soggy mess fell apart. Most of it hit its mark—

success!—except for one gooey glob of meat and red sauce that dripped from the bottom of the bun and splattered brightly, like a clump of blood and guts catapulted from a gunshot wound, onto the front of his yellow golf shirt.

"Yuk!" someone cried.

A nervous burst of laughter rose from the little crowd. This was different from reacting to a joke. This would be laughing at the boss. Then Karin Branch's throaty voice, proprietary and not at all nervous, said, "Mason, we can't take you anywhere!" And the laughter erupted full force.

Unself-conscious, Karin took hold of the front of Mason's shirt, pulled it away from his body, and brushed most of the offending mess onto the ground. "Hang on." She kicked off her sandals and ran toward the crowd of children, looking like a child herself, unfettered and carefree as she unscrewed the sprinkler and commandeered the hose that was supplying it with water. "Just a second, kids. I'll bring it right back!"

A gushing stream of water burst forth, glistening in the sun as she dragged the hose toward the cluster of reporters. I saw what she was about to do. Saw the faces of Mason's staff bright with merriment. Saw Mason grin and stand his ground.

Karin aimed in his direction but wasn't close enough to connect. The hose looked heavy in her arms. Mason moved back a step. He laughed.

"What's going on, Mama?" asked Brynne, who had appeared at my side.

"Just playing with the hose."

"She's trying to get Daddy wet."

"Yes."

"It looks like fun."

Fun! A year, two years ago, that would have been me. Pretty Paisley, having fun. Surrounded by men; a few women, too; a crowd every bit as big as Mason's—and me not even anyone's boss.

And now. Oh, we were big shots now. *He* was. Security. Prestige. The raise that went with the promotion.

But no second child.

A dark wind began to blow in my head.

"Here. Let me clean you off," Karin shouted, taking aim again. The few reporters who hadn't already fled gave Mason wide berth. Mason stopped moving back, giving Karin free access to his sauce-stained shirt.

But no! "Karin!" I yelled. She pivoted. I grabbed the hose and turned it on my husband full force.

"Whoa, girl!" Mason shouted. The dark wind howled. I imagined police aiming fire hoses at men cowering in front of them. I held tight.

Mason leaped forward, jerked the hose from my hand, turned the nozzle back in my direction. There wasn't enough water pressure to hurt. But it was cold. I ran away.

Mason followed—"Oh, no you don't!"—and kept me in the stream of water no matter how I tried to zigzag, until I was soaked head to feet, my clothes glued to my skin, my white bra clearly visible underneath my shirt. Everyone was watching.

"Daddy!" Brynne, ran up, already soaked from the sprinklers. All the same, Mason doused her. Delighted, she screamed.

The three of us ran until Brynne seemed about to give out. "Enough!" I shouted, collapsing onto the lawn. "I give up!"

"Me, too!" Brynne collapsed beside me.

Such drama!

Someone took the hose and reattached it to the sprinkler. The children jumped back in. Mason helped me to my feet. Karin Branch watched us, riveted. Herb Clay, too. A dozen others.

The dark wind abated. The sun was a little too bright.

We hadn't brought extra clothes, except for Brynne, of course. We laid towels across the seats of the car and headed home.

"What was that all about?" Mason asked after Brynne fell asleep two minutes into the drive.

"I'm not sure." *The dark wind,* I might have said. I might have said, *having fun.* "How could you let one of your newest employees chase you around like that, like she had a right to?"

"She didn't chase me. You did."

"You're supposed to act like the boss!"

"Karin is a jerk," he said. "A good reporter, but a jerk. You, on the other hand, are supposed to be the elegant and restrained wife of the managing editor."

"I've never been elegant and restrained."

His jaw worked. This was a company picnic. His show, not mine. I wanted to say: I couldn't have stopped.

Later, after we had showered and changed into dry clothes, I rubbed his shoulders and said, "If I was out of line, I'm sorry. I never meant to embarrass you."

"It's okay," he grumbled, not meaning it.

"Remember, we're Marines."

"I didn't forget." Before we got married, Mason's dad sat us both down and told us that Marines don't plan a retreat route because if they don't, there's no easy way out when the going gets rough. I was never sure if that was true, but it sounded convincing. "You move forward. You face up to your challenges. You don't retreat. You're young, and sometimes you'll wish you could. But don't."

No escape route, we promised. We brought up the Marines every time we fought.

"It won't happen again," I said, unbuttoning his shirt. "Never, never, never."

By the third *never,* he was smiling.

It was a dark wind, nothing more. The next time would be different, and so much, *so much* worse.

CHAPTER 15

November 12

Spare me, Iona thinks as Lori jabbers to her on the phone. *Spare me from Braxton Hicks.* Two months ago Iona had never heard of Braxton Hicks. But now. Oh, now. The English doctor who described "practice" labor contractions back in the 1870s might be living in the house with her. She's heard about him daily, and at the moment, nonstop.

Her stepdaughter-in-law does not spare her a single detail. Lori has been having Braxton Hicks contractions on and off—"but mostly *on,* Iona"—for the past week. Her belly contracts, relaxes; it doesn't seem to want to stop, though sometimes if she sits quite still, it will. Before long she'll be having the real thing.

"But it doesn't hurt? How can you have contractions that don't hurt?"

"Well, I certainly feel it, but I wouldn't call it painful. It's hard to describe."

Exactly. Iona makes what she hopes is a reassuring sound, but she can't imagine it at all. Doesn't Lori have some young friend to discuss this with? Some peer who's recently given birth and knows all about it? Apparently not. "When I go into the hospital," she tells Iona, "I hope you'll come, too."

"To the waiting room?"

"Into the labor room. You can stay for the whole birth."

Perish the thought. Iona has no wish to observe some slimy, not-even-kin child slither into the world, her head misshapen from the birth canal, face streaked with blood. She once watched a delivery on television. It was awful.

"I'm flattered, Lori," she says, "but it wouldn't be right. This is something you and Jeff should share, just the two of you." She gives herself an A for tact.

"It's different than it used to be, Iona. Whole families stay. It's not unusual."

I am not family, she refrains from saying. Her morning has already been sufficiently trying.

An hour ago, at Lowe's, where she was picking up hi-hat lighting frames for Jeff because he's supervising three different jobs and she felt sorry for him, a grizzled salesman paled—literally *paled*—when she asked where the lighting section was. With stiff politeness, he directed her to the proper aisle, his eyes fixed the whole time on the space above her right ear. Iona is accustomed to men not wanting to make eye contact with older women for fear the women might be coming on to them, but this guy was no young hunk to begin with, and so rude as to be insulting. She steamed her way to the checkout counter, where she received the same space-above-the-ear treatment from the female cashier. Only when she was ready to zip her sweatshirt to leave did she realize she'd unzipped it when she came in and also undid the top of her shirt, revealing her freckled chest and the upper portion of a favorite, tattered old bra.

She's not going to set foot in Lowe's for the next twenty years or until death, whichever comes first. She's not going to run any more errands for Jeff, period. If she doesn't put an end to this, he'll turn her into a regular gofer. She needs to make him manage his time more efficiently.

"Well, think about it," Lori says. "Jeff and I have talked about it. Both of us would like you with us for the delivery."

"Let's not decide until the time comes." Iona figures by the time Lori is having actual labor instead of Braxton Hicks contractions, she won't care if Iona is in the room or anywhere else on the planet.

She's just hung up and is wiping her slick-with-sweat hand on her slacks when she sees out of her office window that Marie Coleman is swaying up her walk once again, like one of those old Chinese women with the bound feet. Such a beatific expression lights her face that Iona knows they've gone from birth to death in the blink of an eye. This is about Paisley. This is about church. Iona is thinking of excuses even before she opens the door. "Don't ask me to go to some special service," she blurts before Marie has time to speak.

"Of course not. I know you're not religious." Marie's manner is as placid as Iona's is disturbed. "But I hope you'll do something for me anyway."

Bingo. "What?" Iona growls.

"I'm having a prayer meeting for Paisley tomorrow at my house. At ten. It'll probably take twenty minutes. You won't miss much work."

"A prayer meeting?" This is even worse than church. The last thing Iona wants is to go to a prayer meeting. Not only is she not religious, as Marie so accurately pointed out, she's not sure she believes in God at all. And certainly not a benevolent one you ought to pray to. People think this is because of her barrenness or Richard's cruel death, but it's more than that. Raised Catholic, Iona rejected organized religion early, hating the now-outdated idea of unbaptized babies being sent to limbo. Later, Richard sometimes took her to services at his synagogue, where Iona decided Judaism had no more appeal than Christianity. What kind of religion would celebrate its High Holidays by reading about a biblical figure as heartless as Abraham—a classic case of paranoid schizophrenia, in Iona's opinion—who nearly killed his son because he heard voices in his head and was rescued from the dirty deed only by other voices?

"Iona, what do you say?" Marie hugs herself into the spiffy tweed blazer she hasn't buttoned because it wouldn't be stylish. "How can it hurt to come? If there's a God and He's listening, praying for Paisley might do some good. If not, what have you lost? Half an hour?"

"Who knows, Marie, I swear."

Marie regards her coolly, as if she's committed some sin by using the word *swear.* "If you say no, you'll be the only one, Iona. Most people are actually *nice.*"

"Nice? People are cruel. People are selfish. People are thrill seekers. Even Dean, your own husband—didn't you tell me Dean goes to NASCAR races?"

"He went *once,* Iona. I think it was a fund-raiser for the college. What does NASCAR have to do with this?"

"You know why people go to those things? To see the crashes. They go hoping they'll see some driver be crumpled inside his metal cage and burn."

"You don't fool me for a minute with your cynicism, Iona. Not for a minute."

"Oh, yes, there's a delicious horror about watching some daredevil crash. Don't tell me there isn't. Remember when the Crocodile Hunter was killed? Didn't you wish they'd release the film of that stingray plunging its barb into his heart?"

"Of course not! I prayed for his wife and those two little children!"

The truth is, Marie probably did. The truth is, some people *are* nice, Marie among them. Iona would like nothing better than to send her away, but some vestige of Catholic guilt rises up like a traffic cop's hand to stop her. After all, she and Marie have such a difficult relationship already, why make it worse? A couple of years ago, after Marie adopted "have a blessed day" as her standard sign-off, Iona grew so annoyed that she finally snapped, "You know what, Marie? I think the last time I had a blessed day was in 1985." Marie had actually recoiled, as if Iona had slapped her. Iona can never tell if Marie is going to argue with her or simply back off, but she had not expected *that*. As far as Iona can tell, Marie has never told anyone to have a blessed day again. This is certainly an improvement. Yet Iona can't escape her awareness of Marie's delicate nature, or her responsibility for upsetting it that day, and probably so many other days she can no longer remember. Much as it maddens her to deal with someone so out of touch with reality, even so, she counts Marie as a friend. And the woman has a point. A prayer meeting might be useless, but after all, what's half an hour?

"Oh, all right. I'll be there. For Christ's sake!"

"Well, yes. For Christ's sake. Yes."

Touché, Iona thinks. This is the place in the script where Marie is supposed to march off. But Marie stays put. "I know you don't believe in divine intervention," she says. "But I do. I believe the more people who gather together to pray for something, the more good it does. So I appreciate your saying you'll come. It means a lot to me. Thank you."

Iona nods because what the hell else is she supposed to do? Why couldn't Marie have the good grace not to *thank* her?

The whole tawdry business makes her decide to go visit Paisley. Good deed for the day. Iona hasn't seen Paisley since the afternoon Mason wheeled her through the neighborhood in the wheelchair two weeks ago. If she doesn't go this minute, she won't. She grabs a pot of chrysanthemums off the kitchen table, the ones she bought for herself in the grocery store because they were such an unusual shade of orange fading to bronze. She hates to part with them, but oh well. Stuffing her cell phone in her pocket, she heads up the hill.

As usual, the Lamms' psycho little dog is running back and forth just out of shock range of the invisible fence that rings the property. The thing looks like a filthy gray mop with eyes. It doesn't greet her as she approaches the door, just keeps running its course. Rita answers and motions her in.

"Paisley will be so glad to see you. She's in the ladies' room. She'll be right out."

Iona waits in the den. Music drifts from the speakers: "Do you *love* me . . . Now that I can dance?" This is Iona-era music. She likes it, but it makes her want to shimmy around to the beat, which is probably inappropriate, under the circumstances.

She checks out the get-well cards instead, propped up on every surface as if they were celebrating some grand occasion. After half a dozen Iona realizes that only a few say anything meaningful and the rest have the standard cliché scribbled at the bottom saying, "You are in our thoughts and prayers." These are the exact words Iona remembers from the sympathy cards that arrived by the hundreds after Richard died. Thoughts and prayers, *bullshit.* Dead or alive, you *aren't* in most people's thoughts or prayers. Most people don't *have* prayers, and you're probably in their thoughts only long enough for them to sign the card and get it in the mail.

Now Iona is pacing. Actually pacing. Okay, she knows it's unfair to pass judgment on sympathy cards or get-well cards or any other kind of cards just because they mention thoughts and prayers. People don't know what else to say. What *do* you say when your youngish neighbor is battling terminal cancer or a guy like Richard gets stuck in a drainpipe and drowns? The most sincere thing Iona heard in the early days of her widowhood was from a workman who showed up to edge the lawn and said, while rubbing the whiskers on his chin, "Well, if that don't beat all."

She hears the toilet flush. Then there's Paisley coming across the hallway, smiling but jaundiced and thin, dragging an IV pole along toward the family room. "Do you *love* me?" the song asks again. Iona thinks maybe she doesn't. Her cell phone rings, a loud explosion of African drums downloaded from a website. She checks the number. Jeff. Probably wanting her to run another of his damned errands. She doesn't answer.

"Oh," she says, too loudly, holding up the phone as Paisley rearranges herself to sit down in the recliner. "I promised Jeff I'd check his job site. I thought I had a little time. I wanted to wish you . . ." Well, what the hell can she wish her? "I wanted to say I've been thinking about you." She thrusts the mums in Paisley's direction. "I brought you this. But I'm going to have to run."

"Of course." Paisley indicates a table for the flowerpot. "The mums are beautiful. Thanks."

Iona flees. She cringes at the memory of telling Marie that people are thrill seekers and gore seekers. She stands corrected. With Paisley there's none of that. Paisley's appearance is disturbing, not exciting, and Paisley's cheerfulness is a tender rebuke with a nasty punch. Everyone in Brightwood Trace feels like they've been kicked in the stomach. It's not fun. That's the truth.

She doesn't go home. The Lamms live at the top of the cul-de-sac, the highest point in Brightwood Trace. Beyond that, accessible through the Honeywells' backyard next door to the Lamms (the Honeywells both work, won't be home until later), there's a fallow field surrounded by trees. Everyone thought it would have been developed years ago, but it wasn't. Iona thinks of it as her private hiking grounds. She once saw Paisley back there, and a few other neighbors over the years, but not many. Heading into the open field, she hopes the trees in all their autumn glory will clear her head.

Big mistake. The first thing she sees is a trio of deer nibbling grass at the tree line. They give her one long, assessing look and then bound off, white tails bobbing. The sight takes her back to the year she and Richard lived out in the country—not a year she wants to remember—where the deer population far outnumbered the humans. The first thing Richard did was get Chance, so named because he was about to be euthanized the next day, if chance hadn't brought Richard to the animal shelter to rescue him. The dog, nearly grown but not quite, had been found sniffing around the trash cans in an outlying suburb—a pleasant-tempered creature, neutered and healthy, that the shelter workers believed had probably wandered away from a happy home. They were surprised no one had come to claim him. He was in his gangly stage, no longer an adoptable puppy, and after five days with no takers he was slated for the death chamber. Rules were rules.

Country life was supposed to strengthen the Feld family in a number of ways. Richard and Iona were still in the throes of trying to make a baby, or at least Iona was, ever more desperately because of her advancing age. The landscape was supposed to reacquaint her with the natural rhythms of things, which no doubt would include reproduction. Jeff, deep into his rebellious phase, was also supposed to find peace, throwing off his issues one by one as he wandered the surrounding woods and fields with his new dog.

As it turned out, Jeff was never at home. At fourteen, he was theoretically too young for a summer job, but he got one mowing lawns for a landscaping company, which took him into town where he could meet up with his buddies and get into as much trouble as ever. Iona was the one who ended up with Chance. Gentle as he was with people, the dog was not so kind to wildlife. He'd chase anything that ran from him, including deer at least four times his size. Iona often wondered what he'd do if he ever caught up with one.

His favorite prey that summer was woodchucks—chubby, guileless creatures Iona couldn't help liking, but too slow and stupid for Chance. They'd feed out in the open, far from shelter, and often didn't see the dog until he was practically upon them, poised to seize them by the scruff of the neck. The dog who loved everyone would spring swiftly, clamp his prey in his jaws, and shake it viciously, his gaze a picture of bloodlust until the creature was dead. Then he lost interest. No point trying to eat the woodchucks. Their hide was too thick for him to pierce.

The carnage went on against the backdrop of extravagant summer mornings and into the golden days of fall, a violent, senseless sport Iona grew to dread. Mercifully, the woodchucks disappeared for the winter. Maybe they hibernated. She didn't know. By the next spring, when the dormant grasses metamorphosed once more into thick green clumps, Iona had no desire to see the cycle of rural life repeat itself. The warmth that had teased the earth into fertility hadn't done the same for her. She was still barren. And Jeff, whose winter misery had settled into a quiet cloud of dislike, bristled again like Edward Scissorhands, ready to take a swipe at anything that got in his way. It was Richard who suggested that country living didn't really suit them. The place felt too isolated. Too dangerous. Who would have imagined, then, that Richard would meet his death not in some snake-infested field in the country, but in the manicured confines of a suburban park?

Nature. If they'd stayed in that house many years more, the woodchuck population would have been decimated entirely. It didn't escape Iona that the flood that claimed Richard was a natural occurrence, too. That was nature for you—trees in such a blaze of color that they took your breath away, and systematic genocide.

Compared to that, what could a bunch of pampered suburban women accomplish with a prayer meeting? As far as Iona was concerned, the cancer was as quick and deadly with its iron jaws as Chance had been. The cancer was the blood-crazed dog. And Paisley was the wood-chuck.

Her cell phone rings again. Jeff. No doubt still trying to get her to run another errand. She almost doesn't answer. Then she does.

"Iona?"

"Did you expect someone else?"

"We're on our way to the doctor," Jeff says.

"I didn't know today was the appointment."

"Lori thinks she might be in labor."

"No more Braxton Hicks?"

"She's not sure."

"Oh, my." Iona sounds like a tremulous old lady hearing news she's not quite sure she can handle.

"Lori wanted you to know, in case we have to go to the hospital. We'll check in, and then they'll put us in a birthing room and you can meet us there."

"Well, call me with the news as soon as there *is* news." This isn't the time to say she's not going. She's walking fast toward home, though why the sudden hurry she has no idea. "Good luck," she says. But Jeff has already hung up.

CHAPTER 16

November 13

On the morning of the prayer meeting, Ginger pulls on sweatpants and hauls the rug shampooer out of the closet. She'll clean the living room carpet, shower and dress before she goes to Marie's, and then head to work as soon as the prayer meeting is over.

"Playing hooky?" asks Max, who knows where she's going and why. "Since you don't need to be anywhere, a good plan would be to let me drive the car to school and then you can drive it back."

"Not a chance. The thought of being in a car with you at the wheel fills me with terror."

"So it's okay for me to crash with Dad in the car but not with you?"

"I didn't say that."

"It was implied." He slurps a spoonful of some multicolored cereal Ginger is sure she didn't buy. "I can't believe you're going to a prayer meeting," he says.

"Why?"

"It's not your style. You don't even go to church. Besides, everybody knows Mrs. Lamm is toast."

"*Toast* is something you can never know for sure."

"She has cancer. She's not taking treatments." Max sounds matter-of-fact, but he drops his spoon into the bowl with such force that pink-tinted milk splashes onto the table, which he does not wipe up. Instead, he rises from the table with jerky, work-in-progress movements so awkward that Ginger would feel sorry for him if he weren't so obnoxious. "Everyone says she'll be dead by Christmas," he says. "Maybe even Thanksgiving. They're taking bets on it at school."

"I hope you're not serious."

"Why wouldn't I be?"

"Well, let's see. Maybe because you're a decent person who knows the difference between good taste and a bad joke?"

"The odds for Christmas are around fifty to one,

Mom. Sorry to disappoint, but it's true." Then he's out of the room before Ginger can protest.

Eddie practically bumps shoulders with Max as he comes into the kitchen, briefcase in hand, dressed for a meeting. Blue-striped dress shirt, blue blazer, blue tie. Too much blue. She's not going to mention it.

"Max can't help it," Eddie says. "The teenaged brain isn't wired for empathy. It's designed to look forward."

"If you heard him, why didn't you say something?"

"Nothing to be gained. There are articles about it." Eddie pours himself a cup of coffee. "Think of Max as a butterfly emerging from his cocoon. At this point in its development, the butterfly is too busy to think of anything but emerging. It's an all-consuming task. It can't develop other skills until later. Max will learn sympathy later on."

"I see. He'll become a caring human being once he's stopped emerging?"

"Exactly."

"Or else he'll turn into a serial killer by the age of twenty."

"I don't think so." Eddie laces his coffee with real cream, high-fat cream, cream that's likely to kill him, and downs it in practically a single gulp. "Don't worry, you'll have your butterfly before you know it."

"I have trouble of thinking of Max as a butterfly."

"Trust me on this," Eddie says. He kisses her on the cheek and breezes out. Ginger is left standing there, thinking, *Where did Max learn to talk like this?*

Why, from Eddie, of course. He learned it from Eddie.

Then there is Rachel in the doorway, her delicate features unnaturally white. "Are you okay?" Maybe her blood sugar is low. "Here, drink some juice."

Rachel shakes her head. "Is it true? People are saying Mrs. Lamm will be dead by Christmas? Or even before?"

"Your brother is better at gossip than he is at tact." Ginger pictures her daughter standing on the staircase these past ten minutes, listening to everything, as invisible to Eddie and Max as if she'd been made of glass.

"But is it true?"

"Nobody knows." She pours Rachel a bowl of cereal she knows she won't touch. "Nobody can ever know something like that. All we know is, she's very sick."

"She's not in the hospital."

"No. She wants to stay at home. People will come in to help take care of her at home."

"If she dies, she'll die at home?"

"I'm not sure, Rachel."

"But it's possible."

"It's possible."

Rachel takes this in. She dips her head. "Just for the record," she says, "even when I'm a teenager, I'm not going to be a self-absorbed creep like Max."

"I know you won't, sweetie." Ginger is tempted to defend Max but decides against it. One self-absorbed caterpillar in the house is quite enough.

Then there Ginger is, standing in a circle with eight other women, holding hands in the middle of Marie Coleman's kitchen. It's an odd place to try to invoke some kind of holy moment, but after they finish their cake and coffee, it seems logical not to move into another room. And here's pretty, timid little Marie, good grief, sounding like she could be an evangelist.

"So we ask you, Father God . . . *we do not think it is too much to ask you . . .*"—she intones in forceful italics Ginger didn't think she was capable of—"for a *miracle,* on behalf of our neighbor and sister, Paisley Lamm, who is suffering such grievous pain . . ."

Ginger hopes this isn't true. Andrea insists Paisley is mainly just tired. Her back was hurting her last week, well, her stomach, too, but then she got the morphine drip and it helps so much. *So* much. She's uncomfortable, that's all.

"We ask this miracle on behalf of ourselves and on behalf of her loving family . . . yes, Father God, we ask a miracle on behalf of a devoted husband and two young daughters—*children, Father God, who need her so much*—"

Marie is beginning to sound as if she's gearing up for a revival where someone will speak in tongues or get saved. Ginger is a believer, or used to be, but she wishes Marie would settle down. As Max said, prayer meetings aren't her style. She took the kids to church when they were little, but it soon became clear Eddie was never going to join them, and after people began asking her to cook for potluck dinners and join committees, she quit. Eddie was running the store then. She was stuck with the kids full-time, restless for some out-in-the-world *adult* work of her own, not volunteer work, not child care. She hasn't thought about finding another church since. She hasn't missed it.

"We ask you, Father God," Marie concludes, "for this *MIRACLE* we all so earnestly desire for our friend. We ask you to make Paisley Lamm *WELL*. We ask this in your name, and the name of your son, Jesus Christ. Amen."

"Amen," everyone echoes. Ginger wonders what anyone can add after that, though somehow they do. They go around the circle, each one speaking if the spirit dictates—this was Marie's choice of words—and remaining silent if not.

Some newcomer to Brightwood Trace, a woman who has probably met Paisley once, drones on for at least five minutes. Ginger's mind wanders. The last time she saw Paisley before she got sick was not on the street or out in the yard but in Stein-Mart. Ginger had just found a pair of shoes for a wedding and was carrying them to the checkout. Paisley was standing in the aisle hugging a sleek black leather chair to her chest, which she was discussing with a salesclerk. When the clerk walked away, Paisley set the chair down with a clunk, looking miffed. She seemed a little embarrassed when she spotted Ginger. With a cocked head and comic face, she said in a joking, trying-not-to-show-her-frustration way, "These would be perfect in my dining room, wouldn't they? But they only have one. *One!*" She rolled her eyes toward the soundproofed ceiling. "The trials of shopping at outlet stores!"

That was what Paisley had been worrying about, less than two months ago. Chairs.

"Amen," everyone echoes. Then it is Ginger's turn, if she wants a turn, but she doesn't. Silently, she prays, "Show me what I can do for her. Let me help her if I can."

At first Julianne thought, *Why, this is going to be a coffee klatch, not a prayer meeting at all.* Good. She couldn't stand much more hocus-pocus right now. She exclaimed as loudly as anyone over Marie's delicious cinnamon/sour-cream coffee cake and groused with the others about the zoning changes Walmart is asking for. The only bad moment was when Andrea said Paisley had no pain, just discomfort. It wasn't exactly a lie. It just didn't account for Paisley's itching.

Brynne had showed up at Julianne's house only a couple of days ago to tell her about it. "I wanted to ask you something else about Mom. I won't stay long. I hope you don't mind."

"Of course I don't mind." Julianne had motioned her in.

"Mom's starting to scratch a lot. I thought you might know what to do. I got her some dry skin lotion, and then some allergy cream, but neither one helps." Standing in the front hall, apparently not wanting to venture farther, Brynne's voice was as coolly modulated as ever, but her eyes seemed haunted.

"I'm not surprised about the itching," Julianne said. "I'm not surprised the creams don't help, either. I think she probably needs a pill for it. It's probably coming from the inside."

"From the inside?"

"It's because her liver is failing," Julianne said softly. "The liver isn't removing the poisons from the body, so the skin gets itchy."

"Oh." Brynne nodded, such a serious, worried

gesture that Julianne could feel the girl's aura of peacefulness chipping away, bit by bit. She wanted to hug her, gather her in, offer comfort, but she sensed that touching would be like falling down the rabbit hole—and then who would the child come to for answers? She drew back.

Now she wishes Andrea had said something about the itching. Maybe Julianne should have said something when Andrea didn't. Itching can be a torment. It's not just a matter of discomfort. Everyone ought to know. Maybe what they ought to be praying for is a cessation of itching.

Well, too late. They're locked in a circle, holding hands, asking for a cure. Every one of them knows that Paisley's condition is terminal. Nothing that happens here can change that.

She hates the way Marie kept asking for a miracle. She doesn't like to think of God going against His own rules to intercede for someone. The idea of natural laws being interrupted, even for a good cause . . . well, isn't that what happened when the blackness ran through her those two times in the examining room? Didn't she know things no one was supposed to know? It was *wrong*. She can't get over this, even on Paisley's behalf. She was glad when Marie finished and they moved on.

She almost didn't come this morning. Maybe she shouldn't have. Until she got here, she was doing a little better. Doug and Bill are both out of town this week, Doug to a gift show with his sister and Bill to a medical conference. Such a relief! Bill isn't there to offer his theories about what happened to Julianne. Doug isn't there to hover and ask *What's wrong, honey,* until Julianne says, *Nothing, nothing,* in a sharp tone she doesn't intend.

Since the men left she's almost come to terms with her tingling fingers—admitting to herself that Bill is probably right (she'll never admit this to *him*) when he says she brings on the tingling herself, whenever she discovers some small clue, some pallor, some tremor, that signals illness in a patient she's examining. It's not an accident. Not the product of supernatural intervention. Not painful and not as mysterious as she feared . . . just the light of discovery inside her skin, illuminating it from within. It makes perfect sense.

The blackness is something else. It is the opposite of light. It is a sizzling darkness. She prays that it will leave her alone.

Andrea doesn't realize until she looks around the circle of women praying that she must have thought Courtney's illness was the last one she'd ever have to face. She'd believed that would be true whether Courtney got well or whether she died. In those days that was how her mind worked. Get through this and you'll never have to do it again. That idea seems childish now. Here she is—here they all are—dealing with an illness far more lethal than Courtney's turned out to be. Andrea is quite a different person from the one who told herself, *You will never have to do this again.* Now she believes she'll have to do whatever it is time after time. Now she's a person who believes everything is practice for something else. Everything. You just never know what it will be.

Iona hates this. She knew she would. If Lori's labor hadn't been a false alarm, Iona would have had an excuse to miss this. Well, no such luck. Braxton Hicks strikes again. Lori is only two centimeters dilated, not yet ready for action. Iona feels like an old fool, letting Marie con her into coming here and now holding hands with Andrea on one side and Mystery Woman on the other, as if they're some kind of human electrical cord trying to plug themselves into a higher power. It's one thing to pray for strength for the family, for forbearance, even for healing. But for miracles? She was glad when Marie finally shut up.

Nine years ago, when Iona was getting her remodeling business off the ground, she'd ended up in the hospital with an infection from a bite she got while feeding a neighbor's cat. When a clueless young doctor looked at her chart and said, "You could die from this," Iona had thought, *Good. Now I won't have to pay the estimated taxes.*

That was exactly what she had thought.

"We're treating this aggressively with IV antibiotics," the doctor had said, a kid half her age with what looked like the remains of teenaged acne. If he couldn't get rid of his own pimples, how did he expect to cure someone of a cat-borne bacteria?

An infection from a cat bite seemed almost too embarrassing to die for, but the drugs they gave her put her so far into la-la land that she didn't care.

Two days later she walked out of the hospital feeling pretty good. It was a miracle, the young doctor said.

"What? The miracle of antibiotics?"

"Antibiotics don't usually work on this."

"You shouldn't talk about miracles," Iona cautioned. "You're supposed to be a scientist."

The word *miracle* made her nervous. Where did the medicine stop and the miracle begin? Why waste the miracle on Iona? She had never really felt grateful.

She was relieved when Marie finally stopped shouting and being dramatic. Drama didn't suit Marie at all. Iona was glad the house did not immediately catch on fire and burn to the ground.

Now they've gone most of the way around the circle and Andrea is praying, far more softly than Marie, but clutching Iona's hand tighter as she says something about the immortal soul. As far as Iona is concerned, the jury is still out on immortal souls. Even after twelve years, she'd like to think of Richard floating around out there somewhere, stopping by to see her every once in a while. She wouldn't mind communing with his soul, if he had one.

They had been married ten years when he died. She's been a widow longer than she was a wife. Why is she still wishing they could be in contact? Some people really do mate for life, she supposes. *Mate for life.* It sounds like something animals do.

Well, of course, it's more than that; she'd be kidding herself to pretend otherwise. For the ten years she lived with Richard, everything else in her life played out against the background of his presence—their careers, their troubles with Jeff, even her barrenness, which in no way diminished their love or their desire for each other. Their lovemaking always left her basking in a glaze of pleasure. The fact that he'd chosen her for his wife made her feel, over and over again, that a veil had been drawn over her imperfections, leaving her worthy and necessary in a way she hasn't felt since. Even so, who would have imagined she'd remain monogamous all these years, after promising to love and obey only till death do us part?

She wonders if Mason will remarry. If he will be one of those men for whom one woman can quickly replace the other, providing she can cook and do laundry and offer sex.

She wonders if he will weep for Paisley, freely and honestly, right from the start. She doubts it. Too bad. She herself wasn't a touchy-feely person, either. She was as proud and as determined not to fall apart as Mason will probably be, especially with those girls to be strong for. Oh, Iona shed her share of tears, but never in public, not once. Instead, in the months after Richard's death she sometimes broke out into the most terrible sweat. People probably thought it was a hot flash, but Iona knew the difference. There was no heat, and her eyes stayed dry. She was the very picture of a stoic— no one could tell a thing—when all the time, from every pore, it was as if her skin was crying.

She had slept, too. Some widows didn't sleep. Maybe that was expected. But Iona did. Except during the fierce bursts of energy when she was looking for another house, she never felt fully awake. She took two or three naps just to get through the day. It wasn't fatigue, though. It was grief, masquerading as exhaustion. She was exhausted for a year.

These things—all these things, she fears—are

in store for Mason and the girls. She does not wish these for them. *Be gentle with them,* she thinks. She doesn't know where those words come from. It's not exactly a prayer.

Something begins to happen then—a sense of something moving among them that wasn't there before. It alarms Iona at first, lest it grow into one of those fall-down flop-around jolts she saw in a TV show about the Holiness Church, but it doesn't. This is different—a perception of the room being fuller than before, not with people but with a dignified sort of . . . not *affection,* exactly, but close. A bit like the way she felt when Richard lifted her hand to his lips and kissed the tip of her fingers. A lovingness. A warmth.

Looking around the circle, she wonders if everyone else feels it, too. The faces in front of her are no longer sharp, no longer tight with tension. They're relaxed, even dreamy, almost as if they've all been rendered in soft focus.

It must be the morning light making them look that way; mornings are so beautiful here. But mornings are beautiful everywhere, depending on where you want to be. The something moves among them. The power. Outside it is not nearly this warm. Here they are. Marie. Julianne. Everyone. To Iona, they no longer look troubled. They look serene.

The last amen is said. The women let go of

each other. Their palms are clammy; they seem a little embarrassed . . . yet comforted, too. What was it they shared, anyway? *Did* they share something? It must have had to do with all this holding hands. Some touchy-feely jolt of emotion. That must be all it was.

Yet there's a smoothness inside Iona. Something to take with her. A sense that this was nothing ordinary. Whatever it was that had moved through the room, Iona senses that it was meant not just for her, but for each of them. Solace. A gift.

Iona doesn't think it will do Paisley a bit of good.

That night, Ginger watches Rachel slam out of the house into the front yard, into a gusting wind that sweeps her hair viciously off her forehead. It's all she can do to resist offering her daughter a hat and coat. Even at twelve, she reminds herself, sometimes you need the clarity of the cold sky.

Moments before, Rachel had capped hours of steaming around the house by pounding her brother on the shoulder and yelling, "I can't believe you're taking bets on Mrs. Lamm being dead by Christmas! You're such a dickwad, Max!"

Max had opened his arms in a gesture of helplessness.

Now, Rachel stands in the wind, thinking God-knows-what thoughts. Once, years ago, she confessed that, out there in the yard, she contemplated "mainly stuff nobody else cares about, like how it would feel to be in somebody else's body." Tall enough to look down on the tops of other people's heads. Muscle-bound enough that you could hardly bend your arms. "After a while I *am* all those people." Rachel had giggled then. What she hadn't said, but Ginger knew, was that sometimes she was Brynne.

And now? Leaning against the tree with its battered-looking ribbon, Rachel is probably thinking, *Dead by Christmas. Fifty to one. Dead by Christmas.* She probably can't imagine Brynne's mother, or anybody's mother, dead by Christmas, not unwrapping packages, not preparing the meal. Rachel loves Christmas too much.

It's not even the presents she cares about. Mostly, Rachel loves to sit in the kitchen sectioning Clementine oranges for fruit salad while Ginger slices apples, and the aunts and grandmothers make stuffing and put the potatoes on to cook. To Ginger, Christmas always feels like the one time she can help make a meal without feeling rushed, so after she cuts the apples, she goes through the bowl and cuts them smaller, just the right size to put in your mouth. She slices grapes and removes all the dark parts from the bananas. At Christmas they feel as if they have all the time in the world. The child Rachel who didn't mind sharing her thoughts once said that, when they eat that fruit salad, it tastes like love.

Across the cul-de-sac, Brynne comes out of her house with Trinket. She takes off the dog's electric collar and attaches her leash. No one ever walked Trinket before now. They left her in the yard. Now they walk her all the time. Trinket is a way to escape the house.

Turning her back to the cul-de-sac, Rachel studies the sky, and Ginger knows she's doing this so she and Brynne can pretend they don't see each other. She's offering Brynne her privacy. It seems to Ginger a remarkably mature act for a child of twelve.

Then Rachel turns her attention, as usual, to the sky. There's lots of air traffic tonight, even more than the usual pageantry of planes and stars. Rachel watches intently, but Ginger suspects her daughter is distracted, listening for the jingle of Trinket's rabies tag against the leash to signal that Brynne has passed by.

Just then, one of the lights in the sky dips from its horizontal course and moves with a kind of celestial grace into a slow downward trajectory. Is it a falling star? A crashing plane? Ginger's heart ups its tempo. Out in the yard, Rachel seems to freeze. Both of them wait for the explosion, the blinding flash of light. Ginger yearns for it. This is not a voluntary thing. For long seconds there's no sound except the thudding of her heart. Then the arcing pinpoint of light fades and vanishes from its path without a sound.

It was just a falling star.

In the yard, Rachel turns and heads for the house.

Ginger wonders if she made a wish.

CHAPTER 17

November 17

The first thing Andrea sees when she walks into Paisley's family room is the hospital bed that now sits where the couch used to be. It's very white—white frame, white sheets, white coverlet—a patch of medicinal sterility in the warm-hued room that used to be all leather and honey. If not for the throw rugs and golden hardwood floors, the room would be unrecognizable. White is not Paisley's color.

"Don't worry, I haven't taken up residence there yet," says Paisley, indicating the bed but sitting, as always, in the recliner, the only piece of furniture that hasn't been moved out of the way. Notebook in hand, she bites on the end of her pen, then scribbles something on the paper.

The strains of "My Girl" blare from the speakers. She turns down the music. "It's easier to sleep down here at night than make Mason carry this IV doodad up and down the stairs. Don't look so upset, Andrea."

Andrea tells herself she isn't upset. She's steeled herself for this. It's been a month and three days since the ribbons went up. Given the circumstances, the hospital bed might well have been necessary before this. She turns from the bed and points to the notebook. "Shopping list?"

"Planning my funeral," Paisley says.

"Don't try to shock me. I'm unshockable." Andrea thinks this might actually be true—or if not unshockable, at least unflappable. At home, where Courtney continues to play the offended daughter sulking in frosty silence, Andrea goes about her business with remarkable calm, aware that Courtney's outburst—surely there will be an outburst?—looms like an approaching thunderstorm. Andrea sorts through her possessions, discards amazingly large numbers of items she's decided she doesn't need, and packs fragile valuables in Styrofoam peanuts. She brims with a sense of purpose. Nothing fazes her.

Each evening on her way to the Lamm house, Andrea is filled with this same steady resolve. She no longer tries to visit Paisley during the day, because this means she has to second-guess when Paisley will be napping or the hospice nurses will drop in. She keeps herself busy with packing and other moving arrangements. In the evening—it's dark before six now, but sometimes so oddly warm for this time of year that she has to remind herself it isn't later—she generally finds Paisley awake, having the brief burst of energy she rations out between now and bedtime, saving her best moments for Brynne and Melody, who come in after they do the homework Mason supervises while Rita washes the supper dishes. Paisley no longer takes meals with the family. She no longer takes meals at all.

In addition to the hospital bed, tonight Andrea notes that Paisley has cheekbones she's never seen before. Gorgeous as she's always been, Paisley has lacked the elegant facial architecture of the great beauties. Now she seems to have acquired it. She's lost that much weight. The cheekbones don't look half-bad. "You don't look ready for a funeral," Andrea says.

"I will be." She turns the notebook so Andrea can see the words, "Funeral Requests" penned at the top of the page. Below are a myriad of details, including the names of people who will speak and the topics they should consider taboo (alcohol, college antics—remember, children will be present!). The handwriting is scratchy, barely legible, suggestive of the effort it took to produce it, with little resemblance to Paisley's usual neat script.

"I hope I'm not on that list," Andrea says. "You know how I am about speaking in public."

"What you're really trying to say is you'll be too broken up. I bet you'll surprise yourself. Don't worry, the speakers are mostly aunts and uncles." Paisley shifts position. She can't get comfortable anymore, even with the IV, though she won't admit it when Andrea asks. "I've made arrangements with Andrews Mortuary," she says. "Don't let somebody screw up and send me to Tate's. Every time I go there I come out feeling awful."

"I think you're supposed to feel awful at a funeral."

"No. A funeral should be a celebration."

Tell that to your kids, Andrea thinks but doesn't say.

"I have a couple of things I want you to do for me, funeral-wise," Paisley says.

Andrea's stomach twists. "I've already said I'd do whatever you needed."

Paisley beckons Andrea closer, then closer yet, so she can whisper in her ear. Andrea listens. Her innards unknot enough to make her want to smile, but she holds back and, when Paisley finishes, frowns and tries to sound stern. "No!"

"I thought you were keen to do whatever I needed."

"There's a difference between need and want."

Just then Paisley does that presto-change-o

trick she's gotten so good at lately, not by choice. The energy drains out of her in a single whoosh. She sits where she sat before; she looks the way she did before, but she's a shell, a whisper. "Promise," she says.

Against her better judgment, Andrea does.

"And don't forget," Paisley adds, so low Andrea can hardly hear her, "wherever you are, you still have to keep an eye on Max."

"Done," Andrea says.

Paisley closes her eyes. The exhaustion that for so many weeks has seemed like a weight is something else now. It has become an escort, taking her somewhere Andrea can't follow.

But Andrea stays where she is; she can't bring herself to leave. Settling into the chair next to the recliner, she watches Paisley's features relax, throw off the tense, pleasant expression she'd worn while giving instructions for her funeral. How had she managed that? Andrea never could have—the expression or the directives, either one. Paisley won't nap for long, just enough to amass energy for the kids, to fortify herself for half an hour of quips and smiles and good cheer.

Go home, she tells herself, but tears spring to her eyes, and she can't bring herself to tiptoe out of the room just yet. She doesn't want to be away from Paisley, and she doesn't want to head home, not while John is still out at a meeting. Surely Courtney will have arrived home by now, and the atmosphere inside the house will be coated with ice. Andrea has tried to talk to her daughter, but with no luck. "I think we need to sit down and discuss this move," she'd said. "We probably should have told you while the negotiations were going on, but with all the uncertainty, there seemed no point. I'm as surprised as you are that it actually worked out."

"You couldn't possibly be as surprised as I am," Courtney had replied, with perfect, frigid calm.

Paisley shifts her weight, makes a small noise. Pain, Andrea thinks. Always now, a modicum of pain, impossible to hide when she's sleeping. It seems ludicrous, on top of that, to be worrying about something as unimportant as Max Logan, who is no danger to Paisley or her family or anyone else who doesn't get too close when he's at the wheel of a car. *Max.* A teenaged boy so nondescript that his salient feature is his inability to drive. A child who, for no reason other than Paisley's returning paranoia, is suddenly, *again,* the emblem of an act of despair. Why?

Andrea puzzles over this. In Paisley's place, Andrea would have put all that behind her. Having been a wild woman once, before her daughter's cancer tamed her, she knows there are some indiscretions—drunkenness on a night before an exam, an unfortunate pairing with a man—that have no consequences. There really are.

All the same, Andrea feels responsible for Paisley's troubled state of mind. Her memory drags her back once again to the months after Paisley's last miscarriage, the one they never talked about until months later, on the morning when Paisley leaped up from Andrea's kitchen table while they were drinking coffee and vomited violently into Andrea's sink.

"Okay, what's going on?" Andrea demanded after she wiped Paisley's face with a towel and helped her back to her seat. "Are you pregnant? Still sick from the miscarriage? *What?*"

Paisley set her elbows on the table and rested her head in her hands for long moments before she spoke. "After the miscarriage," she whispered, "the idiot doctor who did the D&C told me I'd never have children again. That's what I didn't want to talk about. I've never even told Mason."

"Good God." Andrea was stunned.

"I figured if I couldn't have other children, if I couldn't even do *that,* then what good was I?"

"What *good* are you? You're a good wife! A great mother! Pretty! *Nice.* People like just being *around* you."

Paisley nodded, as if she understood all this. "Good qualities don't count if you can't feel them inside." She put an index finger to her heart, then to her temple. "I should have told you," she said. "For a while the only thing that got me out of bed in the morning was having to get Brynne off to kindergarten. Even then I would have gone back and slept all day, but I promised I'd go for a walk first."

"Oh, Paisley."

"I didn't want anyone to see me. You know the overgrown field behind the Honeywells' house? There's hardly ever anybody back there. That's where I went." Paisley had grown calmer, almost detached. "Once, I saw Iona Feld, but we didn't speak to each other. The only other person I ever saw there was Eddie Logan."

"Eddie Logan?"

Paisley nodded. "It was a day when I didn't get out there till almost noon, which was unusual. There he was, all by himself, sitting on this blanket he'd spread out under a tree, with one of those thermal lunchboxes. Having a picnic like someone on vacation."

"I thought he ran that hot tub store."

"He said he was playing hooky—and he looked like it, too. He was wearing jeans and a lumber-jack shirt—imagine, a lumberjack shirt!—and chomping away on some kind of sandwich. He waved to me like his sitting there was the most normal thing in the world. I asked him if he did that often."

"And did he?"

"He said he did it anytime he could. Ginger and the children were at her sister's, so he'd left an employee in charge of the store and come home to work on a computer program he was developing. It was the beginning of what he hoped would become a business. Imagine—he felt like he could only work on his program if Ginger didn't find out."

Andrea nodded, puzzled that Paisley was telling her all this. "He'd sneak away from Ginger to work on his computer, and then he had a picnic?"

"He said being outdoors helped him think. Then he said, 'And how are *you?*' And like I always do, I said, 'Great! Great!' It doesn't mean anything. It comes out of my mouth before I have time to think about it. But that day, it seemed like such a lie. Such a lie."

She studied the remains of her coffee cup. "So I burst into tears. Not polite tears. Big, sobby tears. What else could he do but put his arm around me and pat my back? But you know, I just kept crying. I didn't feel bad about it. Finally he offered me his cup of iced tea. I drank it. I felt a little better."

Her face had an odd, waxy cast now, quite the opposite of feeling "better," and her tone grew even more detached. "I would have gone home if he'd asked me any questions. But he didn't. All he did was give me half of his sandwich. I ate it, too. Then he told me about this web-based program he was working on."

"The one he was hiding from Ginger?"

"He was developing it for elementary-school teachers, to make it easier for them to teach social studies. He said, 'Kids spout baseball statistics, right? They learn them because it's fun. If history were fun, they'd learn that, too.' He sounded so . . . well, excited."

At long last, Paisley looked Andrea in the eye. "I was pulled out of myself a little by that. You know what I mean?"

Andrea wasn't sure she did, but she nodded her encouragement.

"I mean, the dark mood didn't stop hanging over me, exactly, but it drifted a little to the side. Eddie was trying to think up a title for the program. We ran through a whole list of names. Educator's Educator. Ten-Minute Tutor. We finally settled on the Teacher Toolshed. It made me feel . . . useful, I guess. I think I knew right then that the name would stick, that he'd do something with it. Or at least that he ought to.

"So I asked him, why don't you go for it? And he said . . . well, you know the story. His father had died. He needed to run the store. He was supporting his mother as well as Ginger and the kids. Ginger's good ideas had made the store more profitable, but she only worked there part-time because she was staying home with Rachel. He was stuck.

"He sounded so serious, and so sad. I guess I

wanted to . . . I don't know. All I know is, the minute he stopped talking, I told him I'd had a miscarriage and couldn't have more children. I told him the whole sordid story.

"By the time I was finished, I was in tears again. But this time when Eddie put his arm around me, it felt like it belonged there." She stopped. She didn't look at Andrea, but at everything else, the table, the clock, her fingernails.

"What happened, Paisley? Did he hurt you?"

"No," Paisley said, but went on in a mechanical way, detached, as if she hadn't heard. "The afternoon was warm. It was a good day for a picnic. It was—" She stopped again and, after what seemed like an eternity, said, "We ended up having more than lunch."

Andrea breathed in, thinking, *Is that all?*

"It was the only time Eddie ever touched me," Paisley said, as if asking for absolution. "It was more an act of—I hardly know what to call it. We were both so unhappy. It had nothing to do with . . . Maybe we were trying to comfort each other, I don't know. But it was horrible. Both of us were horrified even before we got up from the blanket. What if someone found out? We could hardly look at each other, much less speak. The only thing we said to each other was that we'd never say a word to anyone so as not to hurt our families."

Andrea got up, moved around the table, set a hand on Paisley's shoulder. "It happens," Andrea said. "It's over. It's all right."

Almost savagely, Paisley shucked her off. "It's not all right!"

"But if no one . . ."

"Listen to me," Paisley hissed in a fierce whisper. "Not long after that, I began throwing up. I didn't think anything of it at first. I'd been nauseated even before that. The doctor said it was because of my out-of-sync hormones. I hadn't had a period since the miscarriage. But this was worse."

As if through a thick fog, Andrea was beginning to understand. "So . . ." She couldn't finish.

"So just in case, I bought a home pregnancy test kit the next day. Actually, I ended up buying three of them, each from a different manufacturer. All the results came out positive."

"Oh, God."

"That was a week ago," Paisley said. "At least it proves the damned dumb doctor was wrong when he pronounced me sterile."

Paisley's lip began to tremble. She spoke softly, ignoring the fat tears that ran down her cheeks. After all her yearning for a child, what if Eddie Logan, her nerdy neighbor, turned out to be the father? She couldn't possibly have an abortion. She *wouldn't*. She could only hope to carry the baby to term. It was her old hope, her only hope, skewed beyond recognition. Her face collapsed into a posture of pure misery. Andrea had never seen her so agitated, not even during the crisis with Courtney when Paisley had hotly insisted the girl was going to heal. Andrea was frightened at first, of what must be the almost incoherent tangle of Paisley's thoughts. Then she'd thought, almost with gratitude, *My turn to be strong.*

"First things first," Andrea said. "You haven't been to a different doctor?"

"I swore off doctors after the last one."

"I'll find you someone else." Andrea reached across the table and squeezed Paisley's hand. "Someone good."

They went together for the appointment. Paisley was a wreck. "Even if everything turns out to be all right, nothing is all right," she said. "How can I live with a new baby, and with Mason, knowing what I know? What if the kid looks like Eddie?"

"Eddie is so nondescript no one will notice," Andrea assured her.

"The kid will be related to Max and Rachel. The kid will be living across the street from its—"

"Half siblings," Andrea supplied, a concept so bizarre that both of them laughed, or coughed, it was hard to tell which. Andrea pulled into the doctor's parking lot. Paisley walked in as if at attention.

The new doctor examined Paisley and then ordered an ultrasound. Andrea was allowed to sit in and hold Paisley's hand.

Twenty minutes later, in the doctor's office again, he gave Paisley a due date.

"Are you sure?"

"The fetus is small, but the measurements are usually pretty accurate. Plenty of time to do more testing later."

The two women looked at each other, bewildered. According to the doctor, Paisley was nearly at the end of her first trimester of pregnancy. If that was true, it wasn't her out-of-sync hormones that had kept her from having periods after her miscarriage. It was the fact that she must have gotten pregnant right away, that first month after the miscarriage. "I didn't think there was any point using birth control if I wasn't going to conceive," she whispered to Andrea.

Back in the car she said, as if still in disbelief, "I was nauseated even before the afternoon with Eddie. Maybe that's because by then, I was already pregnant."

"Well, of course, you were," Andrea said.

But for a long while, Paisley didn't allow herself to believe the child was Mason's and not Eddie's. There was the slimmest possibility it wasn't. Tests could lie. More amazing yet, it seemed incredible she'd gotten through the perilous first trimester of a new pregnancy without knowing about it or having the slightest problem. She was in a constant state of apprehension for the next six months.

"All this worry isn't good for you," Andrea told her, fearing that what had started as clinical depression had now morphed into an equally debilitating anxiety.

"Relax, Paisley," Andrea kept insisting. But Paisley didn't, even after Melody made her appearance, a healthy full-term baby, several weeks too early to be Eddie's child. "But not *definitively* early," Paisley fretted.

But gradually the evidence began to seem irrefutable. Melody was born with Mason's deeply cleft chin and, right from the beginning, his chocolate-brown eyes. Paisley and Eddie were both blue eyed, two recessive genes. If Melody's chin and dark gaze weren't proof of her parentage, what was? She was an athletic daddy's girl right from the first. Even Mason's parents noticed it. Mason's mother pronounced Melody "a female clone of her father—if there *were* female clones." Overwhelmed by this statement, Paisley relaxed.

A year later Paisley confided to Andrea that Melody had made her understand the meaning of grace. The child was a gift. Paisley certainly didn't deserve her. Yet there she was.

Over time, the seriousness of the situation receded so much that Andrea and Paisley made the improbable meeting with Eddie into a joke. "You can't call it a one-night stand, considering that it had happened closer to noon," Paisley pointed out. "It was more an afternoon delight."

"Sounds like a trip to the Dairy Queen."

"One-*day* stand?"

"It only lasted an hour."

"*Lunch* stand, then."

"Well, we did have sandwiches."

They referred to it as the lunch stand from that point on, though the subject came up ever more rarely.

Years later, after a Lindenwood Court block party, Andrea watched Eddie go back into his house, his arm slung casually around Ginger's shoulder, the epitome of a pleasant neighbor, a good husband, a nice guy. Tossing a stack of used paper plates into a trash bag, she asked Paisley idly, "How do you live right across the street from him? How can you stand it?"

Paisley grew thoughtful, treating this as a serious question. "After a while you forget about it, don't you? Well, not really forget—I'd be lying if I said I didn't feel an occasional twinge. But life catches up with you, you're busy, you go about your business. And pretty soon it seems natural to wave when you see each other on the street. It's old history. It's not part of your life

242

anymore. Maybe it's that simple. People are pretty adaptable."

Andrea nodded but felt vaguely disturbed. Paisley was once again her playful self. The women in the neighborhood loved her but were jealous. Paisley charmed them back into her good graces. That's how Paisley was. That's how they all were.

Adaptable.

Yet every once in a while, Paisley would make some comment, not quite a joke, to suggest she still feared Melody's paternity was in question. "I'll have to make sure Max never romances her once they grow up," she'd say, "just in case it's incest." She punished herself with the possibility.

Trying to keep the mood light, Andrea would answer, "Well, he'd only be her half brother. Their kids might have six fingers, but probably not two heads." If Paisley didn't laugh, Andrea would add, "You're forgetting the Mark of Mason. The cleft chin. The dark eyes." Almost always, that would chase the haunted look away.

Now, listening to Paisley's even breathing, Andrea isn't sure why guilt has consumed her friend again when there is so much else to deal with, in this difficult task of letting go. Paisley means for Andrea to keep tabs on Max from California or anywhere else she goes. "Through your many reliable contacts," she says. She expects it. She trusts Andrea to do it. To keep

Melody from having a romantic liaison years from now with a boy who might turn out to be her half brother. And though Andrea doesn't believe for a minute that Max and Melody are related, Andrea will do exactly what Paisley asked.

Courtney still isn't home when Andrea walks into her house just before nine. She's put off her homecoming as long as possible. After she left Paisley's, she went to Barnes & Noble to pick up some of the empty boxes the staff aren't supposed to give away but do, to longtime customers like Andrea. She lingered there, not anxious to face her daughter, her torn-up house, John's absence at a meeting that always runs late. A pan of chicken enchiladas, Courtney's favorite, are still warming in the oven, untouched. Although covered with foil to keep them soft, after all these hours they're hard and unappetizing, the tortillas like charred poster paper folded over dried-out poultry. The anger that floods Andrea is, on the surface, entirely for the ruined meal.

Courtney has done this before. It's a school night. She'll be in just before her 9:30 curfew, claiming Andrea *knew* she wouldn't be home for dinner, doesn't Andrea remember? She had that project she was working on at the library with Jen or Jessica or one of the other *J*'s, all of her friends having *J* names, or so it seems. Picking up the phone, Andrea hits the speed-dial for Courtney's cell. The voice mail kicks in. Andrea hangs up.

John won't be here until after ten. Andrea stands in the kitchen for . . . she doesn't know how long.

From the front comes the slam of a door outside, the sound of a car moving off. Then, nothing. The silent taunt of Courtney standing in the yard, not moving, knowing Andrea is waiting for her. With her heart thundering in her ears, Andrea strides through the hallway, flings open the door.

On the lawn, beside the tree festooned with its white ribbon, Courtney sits with her legs splayed out in front of her, jacket and schoolbooks flung around her in a haphazard circle. "Hi, Mom." Her head bobs with silent laughter. She reeks of liquor and smoke.

"You're drunk." Andrea is visited by an image of her own drunken nights years before, her own sit-downs on various lawns, heedless of the books and sweaters and purses strewn on the grass or in the mud or atop the snow. At first, she can't manage anger.

Then she can. Anger seeps through her like white heat. She was much older than fourteen in her own dissolute days. Eighteen. Twenty. Old enough to know what she was doing. She forgives herself her youthful excesses. She does not forgive Courtney. She hauls her to her feet.

"Ouch!" Courtney yells as Andrea marches her toward the door. "Ouch, I'm not kidding!" Courtney inclines her head toward the arm Andrea holds in her grasp. The child is wearing a sleeveless tank. It's mid-November, not freezing, but cold enough. Looking down, Andrea expects goose bumps. What she sees, wrapped like a bracelet around the flesh of Courtney's left arm just below the shoulder, is a series of tattoos.

"Oh my God!" She drags Courtney through the doorway, through the hall, into the bright kitchen. Courtney squints. Andrea examines the outlines of purplish stars etched into her daughter's skin—purplish rather than blue because of the bloom of inflammation spreading out from each of the little lines.

"Jesus Christ, what a mess! This was done with a sewing needle and ink, wasn't it? Not regular tattoo ink. How long have you had this?"

"Not long," Courtney whispers, shaky. "I got it today."

"Got it where? Who did this to you?"

Courtney shakes her head.

"Don't play dumb with me, Courtney. You can't legally get a tattoo unless a guardian signs. Can't you see it's getting infected? *Who did this?*"

Although Andrea is no longer touching her daughter, Courtney flinches. "I don't know." Her breath is rank, more bourbony than beery, more cigarettes than liquor.

"Oh, I see. You had a couple of shots of liquor to get up your nerve and then got tattooed by some butcher with no license, no disinfectants, no . . . And now you *don't know* who it was?"

"Some guy Jessica's boyfriend knows."

"Some *guy?*" Andrea's circle of concern shifts. There's Neosporin in the medicine chest, antibiotics they can get tomorrow from the doctor. But some *guy?*

"Some guy who also gave you the liquor? Some guy who also drove you home? Did you sleep with him, too?"

Courtney stonewalls. Andrea stares her down. She senses Courtney is finally about to answer when, instead, the girl goes dead white. "Oh shit!" Courtney claps her hand over her mouth and sprints to the bathroom. Instead of following her to wet a washcloth and hold her daughter's forehead, for once Andrea sits at the table and listens to her daughter retch.

Courtney is still so ashen afterward that Andrea postpones the who-what-where inquisition for another time. Or never. What difference will it make, once they're in California?

"You had to do this *right now,* didn't you? Smoke a whole pack of cigarettes. Get drunk. Get a tattoo. Right now when we're getting ready to move."

Courtney says nothing.

"Well . . . does it make you feel better?"

Courtney seems puzzled. "When *am* I going to do it, if not *right now?* Did you forget? I was the kid who had cancer. For all anyone knows, it could be lurking in my blood right now, waiting to make a comeback." She sounds perfectly sober. "I could be dying right now and no one would know. Maybe not even me."

"Oh for God's sake. Don't be so dramatic."

"Don't be so dramatic," Courtney mocks. She goes to the sink and fills a glass with water. "Do you think I'm stupid? I know what the statistics are for getting sick again if you had a childhood cancer. When am I supposed to do anything, if not now?"

"When you grow up, that's when! You're *going* to grow up, too. All your tests were negative. Start acting like somebody with a future!"

"Huh!" Courtney clunks her glass down onto the counter and snaps her fingers. "It can happen that fast. Mrs. Lamm was fine a couple of months ago, and look at her now."

"Mrs. Lamm's condition has nothing to do with you!"

"Of course, it does!"

"Listen to me, Courtney." Andrea gets up, moves toward her. "You got better. Mrs. Lamm isn't going to." She pictures Paisley in the recliner, eyes closed above the jutting cheekbones, uttering the small, pathetic whine of a trapped animal—a suffering animal, this is what it comes to, isn't it? "Mrs. Lamm is going to die. *You*"—she jabs a finger at Courtney's chest— "are fine. And have a good chance of staying fine if you don't turn into a drunken, tattooed slob ruining her lungs with smoke!"

"Fine?" Courtney taunts. "Fine if I study hard? Eat my veggies? No boys. No cigarettes. No piercings, no tattoos. Fine so I can do all that when I grow up? *If* I grow up. If it doesn't come back to get me *for no reason* like it's got clean-living Mrs. Lamm right now!"

Andrea grabs Courtney's tattooed arm again and leans in close. "Exactly," she says, fury twisting through her. "If it doesn't come back for no reason, who knows, maybe you'll stay well for the next sixty years. Or you might get hit by a truck tomorrow. There are no guarantees. None. But that doesn't give you the right to be a little bitch!"

She lets go of Courtney's arm, flings her away, halfway across the kitchen.

Courtney regains her balance and stands there. She is stunned.

So is Andrea. She's never laid an angry hand on her daughter. She didn't think she ever would.

They stare at each other. It's Andrea, not Courtney, who leaves the room.

CHAPTER 18

Paisley—Walking

*I knew Eddie Logan would be out there that day.
I didn't run into him by chance.*

I'd been taking those long walks in the morning
for months by then. They say if you walk long
enough, you can sleep without dreaming. I
trudged through the deserted field behind the
Honeywells' house for an hour, sometimes more.
Wildflowers grew there, but nasty stuff, too: briars
and brambles, weeds as high as my knees. I kept
thinking, well, I could be bit by a snake. Good
riddance. All I wanted to do was sleep. When I got
home, I dropped into bed and sometimes stayed
there until Brynne came home from school.
Dreams? Always. But the beauty was that when I
woke up, for the first moment, I didn't remember.

The last night before my miscarriage, Mason
had put his hand on my belly and said, "Live and
thrive, little guy." He gave a sheepish grin. This
was odd for Mason, who was rarely sheepish. He
said, "Maybe this time it'll be a boy."

The next morning I started bleeding. It was not
a boy.

It was not anything.

It's no crime for a man to want a son. No crime
for him to touch his wife's belly and say so. But

Mason was a newspaperman. He knew that making a thing public was a way to invite trouble. He knew silence could be a shield over whatever you wanted to protect. He shouldn't have been euphoric just because I'd reached the end of my first trimester. He shouldn't have imagined we were out of the woods.

A month after the miscarriage, locked away in my little bubble of despair, I still hadn't told him the doctor's verdict. One night he cupped my chin in his hand so I couldn't look away and said, "I know what's bothering you."

"You do?"

"I know they don't consider you high risk until after the third miscarriage. I know you think they should have done it before."

"I'm thirty-seven," I said. He had no idea.

Waking up from those long naps, I clung to that first, brief, wakeful moment of oblivion. Then I opened my eyes to the emptiness, the great cavern of . . . nothing. I forced myself up, to dress, to clean, to watch, because Brynne was coming home from school.

Some mornings my stomach was so queasy after my walk that I couldn't sleep. Then, I sat at the bedroom window, staring out at the cul-de-sac below, my mind blank. I had a vague, ever-present sense that I was smothering. No matter how fervently I gulped air, I could never quite catch my breath.

There wasn't much to see on weekday mornings on Lindenwood Court. Occasionally someone went out and then returned with groceries or a bag from Walmart. The only mystery was Eddie Logan, who'd pull into his driveway once or twice a week and disappear into his house for a few hours. I'd always liked a mystery. And this one struck me because I knew he ought to be working in the store.

Around noon he'd emerge from the house again, carrying a thermal lunchbox and a blanket. He would have changed from dress shirts into flannel, from pressed khakis into jeans. He'd look around—furtively, I thought—to make sure no one saw him. Then he'd walk quickly across the cul-de-sac toward the field behind the Honeywells, the field I'd come to think of as my own. Eddie was normally a pleasant-looking man, but not then. Sneaking across the street, carrying his lunch, playing hooky from work, he was a clown.

I watched him for weeks before curiosity cut through my fog. Why on earth would a grown man with a job have lunch in the weedy undergrowth of a vacant lot? Such a simple thing, curiosity. A knife of light burning the dullness from my eyes. I put on my jacket and headed for the field.

Eddie was sitting on his blanket under a tree, exactly where I'd thought he'd be, eating his lunch. His face lit up at the sight of me. When he told me he was working on his computer program secretly, I knew at once—I always know; if I have a talent, this is it—that he needed to let Ginger run the store. You could see that she wanted to. He needed to go back to computing. It was the perfect solution for them. The kids would be okay. The words I'd say to each of them came to me at once. Putting them on the right track seemed so simple. So *normal*. Like the promise of a future that had nothing to do with childbearing. It was no small gift, this sense of being alive and awake after so many months of sleepwalking. When Eddie asked me to help him name his program, I was flattered, excited, like a child. And like a child, when I told him about the miscarriage and its aftermath, I wept.

So when he put his arm around me, it felt natural. And when it stopped feeling natural, I allowed it out of gratitude. I'd seen Eddie looking at me, many times. I knew what he wanted. I'd been in such situations before. In a minute we would stop. I'd learned to be diplomatic. No one's feelings would be hurt.

But that's not how it happened.

When I was seven years old, I was nearly swept out to sea by a riptide. My mother and I had been holding hands, jumping the breakers. We hadn't counted on the undertow. Without warning, a wave broke on the shore in front of us and rushed back with an angry, unexpected power. It pulled me under, pummeling me with pieces of debris it had collected from the ocean's floor, leaving me unable to surface as I struggled for air. I fought and thrashed, to no avail. My mother, fighting to keep her own balance, somehow managed to keep hold of my hand. The pull outward, oceanward was enormous. Once, the violent rush of water nearly dislodged me from her, but she held on, clinging to me, a great force. Then I understood. *She,* and not the water, was holding me under. She was larger, stronger, more powerful even than the sea! I couldn't fend her off. There was nothing I could do. *Nothing.* My lungs ached, then burned. My mother was making me drown! Then, suddenly, the sea lost its grip. Sputtering, I came up for air. My mother was still holding on to me. She had pulled me free.

What happened with Eddie was like that. Powerful and unexpected: inevitable, somehow. A drowning and a saving, all at once. Eddie clawed at my shirt, fumbled with my jeans, a hasty, harsh disrobing. A dark wind blew through my head. A tumbling into depths.

Then we were a tangle of bodies, him on top, me below, our rough, needy coupling more fever than passion, less an act of will than urgent necessity, a fanatic zeal. Yet I wouldn't have stopped it. Couldn't.

Suddenly he turned me over, and I was on top, his strong arms lifting me to sit astride him, his fingers digging into the flesh of my arms, holding me there. His face boiled up below me, and in it I saw the shadow of his unbidden joy, *unwanted* joy, and slicing through the dark wind in my head, one cogent thought: he must have wanted this for so long. A gust of breeze blew. Out in the world were tall trees, an immeasurable swath of sky. I heard birds singing. Why, it's not dawn and not sunset, I thought; birds shouldn't be singing right now. I saw a person walk by. It did not seem real. But yes . . . yes. In the sweeping rush of the moment, I might even have waved.

The onrushing sea. Dark wind. Birds. The sky. Then it was over.

Dazed, stunned, we sat up, half-conscious, who knows for how long. After a time I saw him next to me and recognized him not at all, not the longtime neighbor, not the rusty hair, the freckled skin. A stranger's face. A voice: "Oh my God. We shouldn't have . . . We shouldn't . . . ." It frightened me. Who *was* he?

Then his shame registered, and I knew.

"We can't tell them," he said.

"Of course not." An awkward, graveled voice I barely recognized as my own.

"We can't hurt them. It would make this . . . worse." He didn't look at me, nor I at him.

He dislodged his clothes from the pile and put them on. The crisp air smelled not of daylight or leaves, but of the rank musk of his shame.

For me, there was numbness instead of shame. No angst—at least not yet. He picked up his blanket, his picnic, his heap of belongings, and stumbled toward his house. I thought about the witness. What had the witness seen? Had I really waved? I told myself: no matter. This is someone who won't tell. Later, I was haunted by that.

We agreed we'd never tell anyone, hadn't we? Our families would never know.

Before that day, smarting from the fresh wound of hearing I wouldn't have more children, I sometimes thought, *I have done nothing wrong. If I'm going to be punished, I want to be punished for* something. But then, to find out I was pregnant.

I did not imagine *that*.

Despite the circumstances, I wanted the child. I worried I wouldn't carry it to term. I worried it would have rusty hair and Eddie's lopsided smile. I made myself sick with that worry. But a fist of purpose settled in my chest. Mason would never suspect. Nor would the child. Or Brynne. We were a family. Whatever I had to do, I would.

I wanted to avoid the Logans, at least at first, but I didn't. It had to be business as usual. I had one short talk with Eddie, during which I told him what I hoped was the truth: that I was pregnant, without knowing it, despite the doctor's verdict, even before our afternoon in the field. He seemed enormously relieved. *Embarrassingly* relieved. I convinced Ginger she ought to take over the store. It wasn't hard, talking her into doing what she wanted to do anyway. A good deed. Maybe it would be worth something.

Melody's birthdate was auspicious. So was the cleft in her chin, Mason's cleft, a vertical line with a deep indentation at the top, as if someone had taken the point of a pencil and pressed hard. Attractive, and certainly unusual. But not proof. It would have been easier to live somewhere else, not to have to face the other possibility just across the street.

Once, on what pretext I can't remember, I told Mason we ought to sell the house on Lindenwood Court and move to another neighborhood. He just laughed. "We already moved once. I thought we decided this house was perfect." He was right, of course.

Seeing Eddie, who'd been so relieved, *so* relieved, to hear he'd had nothing to do with my pregnancy—*that* was the hard part. I told Andrea the breezy hellos came easy after a while, but they never did. With every encounter, I remembered what was at stake. I remembered the witness. I waved to Eddie across the cul-de-sac and said, "How're you doing?" and responded when he asked the same, "Great! Great!" A pretense that went on for years and years.

You're always amazed what you're capable of. You swallow the lump in your throat, bite back the heart-pounding fear of discovery. If the rush of blood in your ears makes it impossible to hear what you're saying, you talk all the same.

You smile and move forward.

You don't retreat.

CHAPTER 19

November 20

It happens again the week before Thanksgiving.

The patient in question this time, Harold Fetterman, is seventy-three years old, a large, gregarious man scheduled for surgery on an ingrown toenail. Sitting on the examining table, unembarrassed by the unruly tufts of white hair that cover his chest and ample belly, he exchanges a few pleasantries with her, then grows quiet to let her listen to his heart. He's been through this before. Julianne's fingers begin to tingle the moment she touches him with her stethoscope.

This is a new phenomenon, the sensation running through an instrument instead of coming directly through contact with the skin. Her fingers begin to tingle, then burn. The blood thrumming in her ears is far too loud to let her listen to anyone's heartbeat but her own.

The blackness that swiftly follows seems to emanate from Mr. Fetterman's chest. It surges through her hands, into her arms.

Somehow, she allows it—the savage, coursing sizzle in her blood, the trembling weakness. The visceral knowledge of a failing body, crumbling toward death. The rape by something that does not and *should not* belong to her, entering all the same, claiming her, and then, satisfied, gone. Somehow, she manages not to flinch.

Though she can't escape the sense that she's going to faint, she also knows with deep certainty that she won't. Though she can't elude the pain, as wrenching as physical pain but *not* physical, and somehow worse because of that—yet even at its peak she stands a little apart from herself, watching. Analyzing. Trying to make sense.

When the weakness dissipates—after only a few seconds, though it feels like hours—she is aware, more than she was the other times, that if this is the Angel of Death calling, it is not calling for her. To that extent, she is free of it. She is free right now. It is calling for Harold Fetterman.

Without knowing any more than that, without having listened to his heart or been privy to any more of his medical history than what he's just told her, she excuses herself to tell Peter she thinks he's on the verge of a heart attack.

259

By the time Julianne returns to the examining room, Mr. Fetterman's color is a little gray. He hasn't complained or said a word, but his expression has grown uneasy. "My chest feels a bit tight," he tells her moments later, just before the ambulance screams up to the front door. "I'm having a bit of trouble breathing." Julianne is about to sound the alarm when the EMTs rush in, maneuvering their gurney, and Mr. Fetterman is whisked to the hospital less than a mile away.

Afterward, she stands rigid in the corridor, trembling. Denise, the other nurse who does physicals, puts her arm around Julianne and guides her to a chair in an empty examining room. "Sit down in here awhile, honey," she says. "It's a shock. Anyone would feel like you do." Denise brings her a glass of water. Julianne drinks it, then stares at the wall. She doesn't know how much time has passed before Peter comes in. "The hospital called," he says, "to say how fortunate Harold Fetterman was to have such a serious coronary event caught so early."

"He's still alive?"

"He's in intensive care." He tells her to go home for the rest of the day.

Inside her empty house, she flops on the couch in the den, turns on the TV, and is able to stay awake just long enough to pull an afghan over her shoulders before she falls into a deep, restless sleep. Now and then she hears the voices on television and tells herself she ought to wake up but can't. Two hours pass before she fully opens her eyes. Her head aches. Her tongue feels swollen and fuzzy. But the fear she's harbored all along, that the episodes of blackness signal a visitation of madness that will be harder to return from each time, is gone. There was no break from reality here. The invasion of blackness was real. Harold Fetterman's heart attack was real. Julianne is more grounded in reality now than she was during the other two episodes or during that fearful time years ago, when she was wrested from the brink of madness by Paisley. She is not insane, and she won't be. She'll be all right, even though sooner or later, probably before the end of the workday, someone will call to tell her that, despite the hospital's high-tech efforts, Harold Fetterman has died.

She forces herself up and into the kitchen. She's going to cook a meal for herself and for Toby. Meatloaf. Mashed potatoes. She can't remember the last time they had that. But there are no potatoes in the bin. She puts on her coat to go out to get some, just as the phone rings.

"How are you doing?" Denise asks. "Everybody at the office was worried about you."

"You called to tell me Mr. Fetterman died," Julianne says.

"No. I called to see how you are. Things are still dicey with him, but he's holding his own."

Julianne thinks she's heard wrong. "He's going to recover?"

"He's not out of the woods yet. You know how it goes. But at least he's in the hospital. At least he has a chance."

Julianne isn't so sure. Her fingers haven't lied yet. The dark lightning that runs through her signals decay and death, not recovery. If Mr. Fetterman has been granted a reprieve, what does that mean except that he'll be around long enough to let the gravity of his condition sink in: the ominous portent of the most innocent sensation in his chest, the slightest shortness of breath, the terror that comes with knowing his weakened heart must eventually give out, as Julianne knows it will. Her first experience, with Eudora Nestor, also foretold a death that didn't arrive until months later. Julianne doesn't like to think what those months might have been like. It's going to be the same for Paisley . . . although Julianne doesn't allow herself to think of Paisley in this context. She doesn't allow it because if she did, it would make her feel, not like the concerned neighbor she wants to be, tries to be, *intends* to be . . . but like the angel of death.

She means to turn away from these thoughts entirely. She needs to do this for simple self-preservation. Tonight, she's going to carry through with what she planned before Denise's phone call. Cook dinner for herself and her son.

She combs her hair, puts on a jacket, and drives to the supermarket for a five-pound sack of potatoes, pretending she has nothing else on her mind. Ignoring the dull, throbbing headache that's still with her, she drives home. Headache or not, she's going to share this meal with Toby, be grateful when he offers to help her clean up, then excuse herself to crawl into bed. But a shadowy figure is pacing in her driveway when she pulls in, half hidden by the hood of a sweatshirt. "Andrea?" she asks, trying to mask her resentment.

"Sorry if I scared you."

"I wasn't scared. I just didn't see your car."

"I walked."

Andrea never used to walk. Maybe this is her secret for losing weight. A walking regimen prescribed by one of those women's magazines? Not something she would have expected from Andrea, though she looks almost shapely. Julianne leads her in through the garage, shouts a quick hello up the steps to Toby, who must have come in while she was gone, and pours two large glasses of wine for them to carry into the den. If this is about Paisley, they're going to need it.

Settling into an armchair, Andrea takes a long sip, then stares into her wineglass as if she's spotted a piece of dirt. "Do you remember that night years ago when everybody got so drunk in Paisley's hot tub?" she finally asks.

Drunk as she'd been that night, Julianne remembers all too well. "My most vivid memory is of my hangover the next day," she says cautiously.

"Me, too. But I remember you told us you couldn't live with Bill. You also said you'd be the one we'd come to when our kids grew up and got a tattoo or needed an abortion."

"So which is it? Tattoo or abortion?" Julianne doesn't know the first thing about abortions.

Andrea sets her glass on the end table. "Courtney got a tattoo."

Ah, yes. Julianne can picture it, growly-faced Courtney scowling out at the world, camouflaged by tattoos from shoulders to toes.

"On her arm." Andrea points to a place just below her shoulder. "Sort of a bracelet of stars. I think some kid did it. It took about ten minutes to get infected."

Julianne isn't surprised.

"It's all right now. For the moment. It's half an inch deep in Neosporin," Andrea tells her.

"Yes. As long as you get it looked at later."

"You had a tattoo once," Andrea says

"Not on my arm." Julianne once thought the tattoo was her darkest secret, that tiny butterfly on the left cheek of her butt. It turned out most of her neighbors knew about it.

"You don't still have it," Andrea reminds her.

"No. I was afraid the boys would see it. I went

to a town far enough away that I figured Bill wouldn't hear about it through his medical buddies and had it lasered off." No point giving her sons an excuse to disfigure their own skin when they grew up. Rebellion was one thing; irresponsible motherhood was another

"You think you could recommend your personal out-of-town tattoo-removal doctor? One phone number, and I'll chug my wine and leave you alone." Andrea lifts her glass.

"It's been a long time," Julianne says, but she heads across the room toward the computer where she stores her address book. "I'm not sure I even have the number anymore."

"Thanks for checking, though."

"A tattoo is an easy fix," Julianne says. "Better than needing advice about abortion. Abortion isn't my area of expertise. Abortion, or robbing the liquor store, or any of that. And, of course, you were always the expert on drugs."

"Lucky to live to tell the tale, too." Andrea swirls her wine thoughtfully. "One time I smoked some extrastrong . . . hash, I think, but I'm not sure exactly what it was . . . and was high for three days. My roommate ended up in the hospital. Me, I slept it off and took my midterms the next week. I was so lucky, for such a long time." She stops abruptly, as if to remind both of them how quickly her luck ran out.

"You want to know what I remember about that

hot tub party?" Julianne asks as she scrolls through the addresses. "I remember thinking the only thing I was the expert on was having three kids in five years. I hated that." She lifts an eyebrow. "I pretended I was an expert on all kinds of sleaze, but it wasn't true. I was trying to make a break."

"Are you saying you were a fraud?"

Julianne laughs. "I guess so. Oh, look, the doctor is still in here. Benjamin Ziegler." She writes down the information. "If you don't find him, you could probably call any dermatologist or plastic surgeon."

Andrea tucks the doctor's number into her purse. "It's a start." Picking up her glass, she chugs her wine, exactly as promised, and stands to leave.

"You know, you never grew your hair long before that year Paisley invited us to her hot tub," she tells Julianne as she heads for the door. "You never drank much. You never had a belly button ring. If you were a fraud, you weren't a very good one. Everybody knew there was something going on."

"They did? Well, of course they did. I was such an idiot."

"No. You were restless. All of us were," Andrea says. "Then most of us reformed, and that was worse. Look at me, I went from party girl to little gray mouse at the first sight of a cancer cell. It wasn't a good way to live."

"So now you're turning back into a party girl?"

"Too late. Wild, wonderful California beckons, but I'm taking my kid. It's not party time, believe me. Courtney hates me. She hates John, too, just not as much."

"She doesn't hate you," Julianne says as she opens the door. "She's just upset."

"Yes, and no wonder. I spoiled her rotten from the minute she got sick. This is what I get. But I'll be damned if she's going to a new school on the other side of the country with a tattoo around her arm. I hope having it taken off hurts like hell."

"Oh, it will," Julianne assures her. "Unless they've changed things since I got mine taken off, you can be sure she'll feel the pain."

Andrea nods. "Good." Her small, nondescript features look, for once . . . rather fierce.

Julianne becomes aware of her headache again even before she waves goodbye to Andrea at the bottom of the driveway. *Solitude,* she thinks gratefully. Then a voice says, "Mrs. Havelock?" And though Julianne has grown accustomed to Brynne occasionally hanging out in her yard after dark, waiting for Doug to leave or Julianne to get home because she's been forbidden to be in a house alone with a boy, even Toby, she's startled when the girl calls her name.

"What's up?" Julianne asks, walking her toward the house.

"I wanted to ask you about something. I mean, since you work in a doctor's office . . ." It always begins like this.

"What, honey?" She opens the door again. In the warm light of the hallway, as usual, Brynne practically screeches to a halt.

"It's just that . . . She's not comfortable anymore."

"Well, we talked about that, didn't we?"

"I know. But this is all the time. Even when she's sleeping. I can tell."

"Do you want to come sit down?"

Brynne shakes her head no. She folds her arms over her chest, as if to brace herself. "She's never going to be comfortable, is she?"

"Probably not." Julianne is not going to lie.

Brynne drops her arms, sags a little. "It's even getting to Melody," she says. "Up till now she didn't really notice."

Julianne sighs. What child named Melody wouldn't be despondent, when the only music playing is a dirge? "Come on in," she says and leads the way into the kitchen before the girl can refuse. Julianne pours her a Coke and sits her down at the table.

"Has someone told Melody what's going on? Your father? Your grandmother?" Julianne asks.

"Everybody's told her. I think she just gets more confused. Or *did* get more confused. I think I straightened her out." She takes a drink and holds the fizzy liquid in her mouth a long time before she swallows. "When we were little, my mom used to read us *The Little Engine That Could*. I mean, all the time. So the other day I asked Melody if she remembered how Mom always told us how we should be like the little engine who said, *I think I can, I think I can.* Well, of course Melody did.

"So then I asked her, remember the other engine who can't help take the toys over the mountain because she's tired and just wants to go back to the roundhouse? Well, I think Mom is getting so tired she wants to go back to the roundhouse. That's what I told her." Brynne sets the Coke down onto the table. "I think she got it then."

Julianne's chest tightens at this notion of Brynne, age fourteen, having to mother her eight-year-old sister, maybe from now on. She puts her hand on top of the girl's only long enough to reassure but not embarrass her. This is what she learned from raising boys. "That's very brave," she says.

"I always knew she wasn't going to get better," Brynne says. "But for a while . . . it was actually okay. She seemed like she was resting. I hoped we'd go on like that. I didn't want anything to change."

"Of course you didn't."

"But now." Tears brim in the girl's eyes, and

her voice trembles with them. "I don't want her to have to go on like this. It's too hard for her. She's too tired."

"Yes." The beat of Julianne's headache is strong behind her eyes. How old do you have to be before you understand that the burst of energy that guides us through the world turns into the exhaustion that makes us loosen our hold, and finally the pain that teaches us to die? "Pretty soon she'll just be too tired."

Slumping once again on her couch after Brynne leaves, Julianne thinks she can't stay awake another moment. Then she recalls what Andrea said earlier, about Paisley's hot tub party all those years ago, and how everyone had noticed Julianne's unaccustomed long hair, and the enormous amount she was drinking, and the way she showed off her belly button ring, and knew something was going on.

Something dangerous.

But only Paisley knew that.

And soon, she would take it to her grave.

CHAPTER 20

Ten Years Earlier

Two weeks before Paisley's hot tub party, Julianne had been home alone with her seven-year-old son, Toby, when a Pandora's box opened inside her of murderous instincts she had not known she had.

It was evening, almost dark. Toby had obediently taken the dose of Tylenol she'd given him to control his fever and gone upstairs to get ready for bed. She was about to go up to say goodnight.

If not for the sudden summer virus that had laid Toby flat earlier that day, the whole family would have been at a baseball game at the stadium in the city. It was a perfect outing for them, far enough from home that Bill had to get someone to cover for him, which meant he would pay attention to his sons and not his medical practice; far enough from home to make Julianne feel, for a few hours, released from the burden of planning activities and hot-weather meals. The promise of that evening had muted, for weeks, not just Julianne's summer weariness, but even the restlessness that had haunted her for a year, the misery that pressed down on her like a weight, inexplicable and so disturbing she sometimes thought she was going crazy.

When Toby grew listless and spiked a fever, there was no question that Bill should go to the game with Joe and Will, and Julianne stay home with her son.

Not even a discussion.

Julianne had not, for some reason, done the dishes that day. It was unlike her. A jumble of glasses and plates and silverware rested in the sink, along with the large knife she'd used to cut watermelon and a smaller paring knife—a short, deadly length of steel that regularly took nicks out of her fingers.

"Mom, are you coming up?" Toby called down the stairs.

Julianne had the oddest sensation then—of herself, in some alternate reality, lifting the paring knife from the sink and slipping it into the pocket of her shorts. Quite clearly, she saw this other self going up the stairs and into Toby's room. After that, her vision clouded. She sensed, but could not quite imagine, the woman with the knife moving quickly and purposefully toward her son, intending to hurt him in some unspeakable way.

No!

Toby was her baby. Sometimes she thought she loved him best.

This is the power you have over a child who depends on you. You are the custodian of his innocence.

This is the power you have in the world.

If not for Toby, she could be at the ball game. She would not be in this house forever and ever, with Bill and his riches, till death do us part.

She could be free.

"Mom?" Toby called again, his voice gravelly with phlegm.

"In a minute." She grew aware, as if from a distance, of a tightness in her chest. A fog in her mind. A lapse that was not quite a total break from reality, but close. She said to herself, *Walk out of here*. Before you become that woman. Before you do anything, *walk out*.

Snatching a large, heavy serving platter from the sink, she dropped it over the paring knife so she couldn't see it. *Walk out,* she said to herself in the sane, cool back of her mind.

She did not walk out, though it was a pleasant evening. Instead, she ascended the stairs. She kissed her son goodnight. A wave of tenderness and love for him welled in her chest. She pulled his top sheet up to his shoulders. The air-conditioning cut on, purring through the vents. Already, she could tell, his fever was beginning to break.

Later that night, after Bill's breathing had grown deep and even, Julianne lay a little apart from him in their king-size bed, shivering. She did not turn to him for warmth. She hugged herself tight but couldn't stop shaking. Now and then she got up to check on Toby, who was sleeping as peacefully as his father. Back in bed, she huddled against herself: icy, solitary, unforgivable. She didn't think she slept, though in the morning she opened her eyes to the surprise of daylight and found her skin covered with sweat.

For the rest of that week and the next, she tried to hire babysitters every day. It was not easy, this late in the summer, to get caretakers for three active boys. Once when no one would come, she was so haunted by the memory of that imagined self lifting the paring knife (now inaccessible, relegated to the bottom of the trash) that she locked herself in the bathroom for a full twenty minutes before the horror of her vision yielded to her fear of letting the boys run wild in the yard.

All the other days, she fled as soon as the sitter arrived, devoted to less-than-lethal forms of personal destruction. She had her belly button pierced and adorned her flesh with a small silver hoop. Better to pierce her own midsection than a son's. She had a butterfly tattooed onto her butt. Every piercing, every mutilation she could devise for herself was one she would not imagine inflicting on her child. One day she considered piercing her eyebrow but decided against it because it would set a bad example for her sons. She did not really want to harm them. She loved them; she wanted them to live and thrive.

She had two more holes pierced above the existing ones in each ear. The cartilage must be thicker there, harder to penetrate, and the procedure hurt. Later, she removed the first set of earrings from the tender new piercings and never replaced them. She allowed the holes to close up.

In Home Depot, months before, Bill had introduced Julianne as his wife and the boys as "my children." *My* children, not "our children"— as if she were there merely to help with them, to be his servant.

For the past year she'd been jogging in the mornings after the boys left for school on the bus, hoping the exertion would suck up her restlessness. It hadn't worked, though it had helped her lose weight. Certainly it was better than nothing. In summer, when the children were home, she couldn't count on getting out. During the school year she'd lifted weights at the gym, another routine that fell before the shapeless morass of school vacations. It seemed to her that all she had left of her efforts to regain her balance was the hair she'd been growing for a year, at Paisley's suggestion.

"Haven't you ever worn it long?" Paisley had asked back then. "Not many women are natural blondes. If you ask me, the more blond hair the better. It would become you."

It didn't become her. Chin length or longer, it was too wavy to look anything but unkempt.

When it finally reached her shoulders, Paisley was too polite to say anything, but Bill suggested that she might want it shorter so it would dry faster, what with all the trips to the pool. Julianne, rebellious, told him she thought the wild and messy look suited her. She tossed her head whenever she sensed that anyone was looking. Sometimes she flirted. She was thirty-four years old, the mother of three. She was not a flirt.

For a year she had contemplated going back to school for a degree so substantial that it would trump her BA in nursing and demand she start a career, no matter that, for tax purposes, Bill didn't welcome more income. For a year she had feigned interest in kinky sex when all she really wanted was to avoid having another baby—although she might have reconsidered if she could have ordered a girl.

Before the advent of children, she had been a good nurse. Intuitive. Caring. A healer.

What had happened to her?

Then came Paisley's Hot Moms in the Hood party at the end of that fearsome two-week stretch. For a few hours, Paisley's powerful Painkillers muted Julianne's pain. In her drunken stupor in the hot tub, she pushed away the nightmarish evening of the knife just long enough for her problem to reduce itself to a simple truth. She could not live with Bill. She wanted to be free of him. She wanted a life of her own choosing.

The next day, thick tongued and thirsty, head throbbing and eyes rebelling against the light that poured into her kitchen as she poured Honey Nut Cheerios into bowls for the boys, she thought, *What a damned fool I made of myself.* She was too physically sick to dwell on her mental illness just then. Too sick to contemplate the different, single life she knew she was never going to have.

The following morning, Paisley called and said, "Get a babysitter tomorrow. We're going shopping."

"Shopping?"

"Wear decent clothes. I'm taking you to Novella."

Novella was a snottily upscale department store. A customer who arrived in jeans, even good designer jeans, would be ignored long enough to sense that she had been rebuked. Paisley and Julianne both wore good linen slacks, summery blouses, and jewelry that in this heat they normally would have saved strictly for an "occasion."

"What do you need?" Paisley asked as they rode up on the mirrored elevator. "Pants? Tops? A whole new fall wardrobe?"

"Fall? Is that another word for paradise? For nirvana? Isn't that a couple of centuries from now when the kids go back to school? Too far away to think about fall." Julianne marveled at how much she sounded like a normal, sane person, even though she stood so far from herself that she might have been watching on closed-circuit TV.

"Okay, no fall clothes," Paisley agreed, just as the elevator doors opened onto the sight of fully outfitted mannequins in rust-colored wool, standing among a sprinkling of colorful autumn leaves. "But I bet the summer stuff is marked way down." Grabbing Julianne by the hand, Paisley dragged her across the polished marble floor toward the sign reading Misses and Juniors and guided her to the sale racks.

"See, what did I tell you?" Flipping through the selections without apparent regard to anything except size, she seized an armful of hangers, a bright array of blouses, shorts, capri pants, and sundresses in every style and color.

An elderly saleswoman in a dark dress, shades of Julianne's great-grandmother, escorted them to the fitting room. Julianne assumed she and Paisley would divide up the clothes and take adjoining cubicles, but Paisley said, "Oh, these things are huge," and pulled Julianne in with her.

Huge was almost an understatement. The dressing room was as large as many bedrooms, fitted out with three-way mirrors, wall-hung pincushions for the alterations staff, and two plushly upholstered benches for children and friends. Paisley hung the clothes on what looked like jewel-encrusted hooks. "Okay, Julianne, take your pick."

Inside her miasma of confusion and self-loathing, the sight of the lush surroundings where they could pamper themselves by trying on overpriced clothing they wouldn't need for a year seemed almost obscene. A woman who could imagine herself intent on harm as she carried a knife to her child's room didn't deserve luxury. She deserved . . . what? For a moment, literally, she couldn't draw breath. She sat down on one of the benches, opened her mouth and closed it, like a fish pulled from water. Then, with a great gulp, she drew air into her lungs.

"Julianne, what's wrong?"

Embarrassed, Julianne shook her head. Her mouth was desert dry, her heartbeat a storm. "Nothing. Really. Nothing." She meant to defuse the awkward moment with some clever comment, but nothing came. Paisley did it for her. Shedding her slacks and blouse without embarrassment, she said, "Come on, then. We're here to *shop*." She grabbed a full-skirted sundress festooned with oversize flowers and ferns, pulled it over her head, and turned to Julianne with an exaggerated frown. "Not really me, is it?"

"Only if you go for the tourist-who-took-Hawaii look."

Paisley plucked another dress from its hanger and thrust it at Julianne. "Here, try this one."

Julianne wasn't sure she could. But somehow she did, her limbs leaden but obedient.

"That tattoo," Paisley said when Julianne undressed again, pointing to the tender, barely-scabbed-over butterfly. "I didn't know you had that."

"I only got it a week ago. It's still sore."

"You did it to shock Bill."

"Sort of." If only it were that simple.

Paisley had the grace to let it go.

Mechanically, Julianne followed Paisley's lead as they moved from dresses to shorts and tops, strutting and modeling in front of spangled mirrors that gave themselves to themselves from every angle: front, back, profile.

Julianne had no opinion either about their appearances or about the clothes. She was dimly aware of rejecting a pair of bright orange capris, a classic, form-fitting skirt, a pair of lightweight, slim-legged cotton slacks that would be in style for years. Once, she had enjoyed choosing clothes, had enjoyed letting her sensitive fingers trace the cool slide of cotton across her skin, judge the warmth of high-quality wool, the sturdiness of suede. She had a knack for finding garments that flattered her figure, which was always too plump before this past year. It was a pleasure she once thought she deserved.

Today, for all she cared, the clothes might have been made, uniformly, of shapeless, scratchy burlap in lackluster khaki, or equally of the smoothest, brightest silk. She could hardly tell the difference. She was a woman who had thought of hurting her most beloved child. She couldn't believe she had thought such a thing. And yet she had.

A long slice of time passed, or so it seemed. Slowly, in spite of everything, as if the scene were changing slowly from black and white to color, from two dimensions to three, a certain shade of pink would cut through her dullness for a second, or the nubby texture of seersucker, the filmy feel of chiffon. And still, there were more garments to try. Then came a moment when she looked at herself in a translucent blouse of the palest aqua, in a fabric so soft it felt like a caress, and said to her own surprise, "Oh, look at this. This is pretty."

"It is," Paisley agreed. "It's your color. You should get it."

"I'd never wear it."

"Sure you would. Dress it up with slinky slacks. Dress it down with cotton."

"No." The veil of guilt and despondency closed in, choking off her voice. She couldn't breathe. When she lowered herself onto the bench as she'd done before, she somehow ended up missing the seat, sitting on the floor instead.

Another time, it would have been comical. She stifled a strangled cry.

"Julianne! Don't tell me nothing's wrong! Are you sick?"

She opened her mouth to speak, but all that came was the cry again, frightening and raw.

Paisley sat down on the floor beside her. She put her arm around Julianne's shoulders and let her weep. Another span of time passed. Julianne could not have said how long they stayed like that.

Then Paisley said, in a voice like a song, "Tell me."

So Julianne did. The knife. The self-but-not-self woman ascending the stairs. The slim, sane thread of her mind saying, *Walk away. Walk away.*

"I could have hurt him," she said.

Paisley crooned, "Oh no, of course not. Not at all."

"It was . . . very nearly a break from sanity."

"No. No." Her voice sad as heartbreak. "You didn't hurt him at all. Beyond a certain point, you couldn't even imagine it."

"But in a way I must have. I'm his mother. I'm supposed to protect him. To think such a thing, even once . . ."

"Shh. Shh," Paisley whispered. "You're not really afraid you'll hurt him. You're afraid because you believe it was wrong even to think it. But having a thought, even an awful one, is different from acting on it. All the difference in the world. Can't you see that?"

Julianne was not sure she could.

Paisley pulled back a little. She fingered the shoulder of the beautiful blouse Julianne was wearing.

"You should take it," Paisley said.

"I'm not buying anything," Julianne said.

"I don't mean buy it. I mean take it."

"Pardon?"

"Take it off, roll it up, and put it in your purse. Your purse is big enough."

"You mean steal it?" The words began in the distance where Julianne's misery lurked, then inched forward into the ordinary, curious front of her mind. "You're saying shoplift a two-hundred-dollar blouse?"

"One hundred, on sale."

"That's crazy." Paisley, of all people, to suggest such a thing. Shock distracted her, lifted her out of her fog.

"Well?" Paisley said.

A joke? Julianne wondered.

Maybe not.

Temptation teased her then, an imagined smell of lemons, sharp with the promise of sweet. She could hide the blouse in the far corner of her closet. No need to hide it, but she would. She could wander her house, wander her life, always knowing it was there. A dark secret, but not so dark. She would take it out and look at it whenever the mood struck. She would . . .

But, no. She wouldn't.

Why not?

Well, because.

"I couldn't," she said.

"What difference would it make, if you already feel this bad?"

"No difference, probably." The smell of lemons fainter now. An icepack to her fevered brain. Disappointment, yes. But also this: *Walk away. Walk away.* She said without hesitation, "I can't. I won't." Her heart thundering in her chest.

"Something cheaper, then. Here, this." Paisley thrust a cream-colored tank top into Julianne's hand. "I'll take something, too. That blouse you have on. I'll even wear it out of the store."

"You wouldn't!"

The saleswoman knocked on their door, causing Julianne to jump. "Do you need help, ladies?"

"No, but thanks," Paisley said.

"I'll be back in a minute. I'll get the things you don't want out of your way." When the woman moved off, Paisley said urgently, "Take off the blouse. Let's get going."

Julianne thought she meant, take it off, let's get out of here, forget the nutty notion of wearing the blouse out of the store. She pulled the soft fabric over her head, set it on the bench. Watched, dumbstruck, while Paisley lifted the blouse and put it on. "Paisley, don't! It's risky. It makes no sense. It's . . ."

"It's *amazing,*" Paisley said. "Come on, Julianne. Put the tank top in your purse. Put it at the very bottom."

Glancing down, Julianne was surprised to see the garment still in her hand.

"Don't just stand there." Paisley's tone playful on the surface, serious underneath. "We don't have much time. *Do* it."

"I don't think . . ."

"Hurry up, Julianne." Beseeching now. "Do it before she comes back."

"I'm still not . . ."

"Well, *decide.*" Paisley smoothed down the front of the blouse, hoisted her purse to her shoulder, and started to open the door of the dressing room. "I'll wait for you out here."

"No!" Julianne pushed the door shut. "What if we get arrested?"

"We won't. I guarantee it." Her cheeks abloom with circles of excitement.

"*Think,* Paisley. We'd be the Brightwood Trace kleptomaniacs the rest of our days. Is that what you want? Fine! Then go on out of this dressing room wearing that blouse. Just go on."

To her shock, Paisley did.

Numbly, Julianne stood for a moment alone,

looking at the jumble of clothes askew on their hangers or dumped carelessly onto the benches. Shouldn't they fold them, hang them, make some kind of order? Paisley couldn't possibly . . . Couldn't possibly . . . *Decide.* In the mirror, a pulse jumped wildly in her neck. What should she do? Tell someone? Offer to pay? *What?* With a vicious flick of her wrist, she flung the tank top from her hand onto the pile of discarded clothing. She walked out the door.

"Well? Did you take it? Where is it?" Paisley patted Julianne's purse.

"It's in the dressing room. That blouse ought to be in there, too."

"Too late now." Paisley bent her head in the direction of the saleswoman, lumbering toward them in her dark dress.

"All finished, ladies?"

"All those clothes, they were lovely, but there was just too much to pick from." Paisley engaged her with a brilliant smile.

Julianne held her breath, waiting for the accusation.

"Well, maybe next time." The woman turned away, opened the door to the cluttered dressing room, and, at the sight of the mess, uttered what sounded like a snort of disgust.

Julianne meant to speak, meant to act, meant to . . . Her thoughts were jumbled. Certainly she didn't mean to accompany Paisley on the endless, terrifying trip to the elevator. But somehow her feet took her there. "Not too fast," Paisley cautioned, eyes front, head high. "I don't think she noticed the blouse. I think the eye contact took up all her attention."

Julianne wasn't so sure.

Down one level. Across the polished floor. The dazzling sun beckoning from outside the glass door like a promise impossible to fulfill.

They moved as normally as they could, Julianne full of dread, steps leaden, Paisley floating on a mad euphoria.

They almost made it out of the store.

"Miss. *Miss,*" a man's voice said.

Both of them turned.

"Are you talking to me?" Julianne asked.

He wasn't tall, but he loomed: the perfect plainclothes security guard, fiftysomething and graying, a bit of a belly above the belted khaki slacks. Short-sleeved button-down shirt but, considering the weather, no tie.

Blood pounded in her ears, so loud she could hardly hear his answer. "Not you," he said. "Her. Your friend." He pointed to Paisley.

With an expression of benign curiosity, Paisley cocked her head. "Yes?"

"Your blouse, miss." He looked at her hard then, and the sight must have muted his gruffness. He seemed slightly embarrassed. "I don't believe you purchased the blouse."

Julianne froze.

Paisley looked down at herself and registered surprise. "Oh, no! You're right!" She laughed. "Julianne, I bet you didn't notice, either. We were so wrapped up in Millie's divorce—one of our friends," she explained to the guard—"that I forgot to change back into my other shirt."

The guard watched this performance, skeptical. "You forgot?"

"I'm so sorry," Paisley said. "I bet my shirt is still up in that dressing room. I'm so, *so* sorry. I'll just go back up there and change."

"Miss, I'm afraid I'll have to . . . ." Then he seemed to reconsider. Pulling from his pocket what looked like an old-fashioned walkie-talkie, he mumbled into it, then shut it off. He herded them back to the elevator. "We'll just see," he told Paisley as he pushed the button. Watching her. Wanting her, Julianne suspected. "Lucky I found you before you left the store."

"Oh, Lord," Paisley told him. "This is such a terrible, terrible mistake."

"Let's hope so."

The elevator door groaned open and released them onto the second floor.

The saleswoman, sour-faced now, produced Paisley's shirt that, indeed, she'd found in the dressing room when she'd removed the clothes they'd tried on but hadn't bought. "You forgot the shirt you walked in with and nearly walked out *accidentally* with a blouse worth five times as much?" Her voice rang with irritation, disdain, disbelief.

"Yes, I guess that's exactly what I did," Paisley whispered. "I'm so, *so* sorry."

Once more, the woman escorted Paisley into the fitting area, gave her the shirt she'd worn into the store, and stood outside until Paisley emerged, appropriately clothed, holding out the not-stolen-after-all blouse like an offering.

"Thank you for being so understanding," she told the saleswoman, all contrition.

Minutes later, she repeated these words to the security guard, who was escorting them out of the store, all the while undressing Paisley with his eyes.

"Close call," Julianne said as they moved into sunlight, into a wall of heat. "Polished performance."

"It was."

A spike of anger surged up Julianne's spine. Had Paisley *no sense* of the danger they'd averted? They were halfway to the car, walking in the full ninety-degree sun, before she realized Paisley was pale and shivering. Noting Julianne noticing, Paisley said, "I'm okay. Just—a little shaken."

Well, you should be. But she couldn't make the fury carry to her voice. "For a while," she said, "I figured you lifted expensive clothing all the time. Now I'm not so sure."

Paisley attempted a carefree laugh that came out like the bark of a small dog. "The last time I shoplifted was when I was five. I had gotten a little purse for my birthday, and I took it everywhere. Whenever I was in the grocery store with my mother, I'd stand beside her while she was in the checkout line and put a few candy bars or gum into the purse while she was paying. Nobody ever noticed.

"Then one day I opened the purse while we were on our way to the car, and Mother saw my stash. She walked me back into the store and made me return the candy. I had to apologize to the manager. It was horrible. I had to tell him I'd never do it again. And I never did."

"You almost did today."

"Yes." Paisley tried another laugh, equally unconvincing. "I could see you didn't believe me when I said being afraid of what we're thinking is different from actually doing it. But I knew you wouldn't shoplift anything. For me, it's scary after all these years, but I thought it would also be kind of a rush. For you, it's as if thinking about the crime *is* the crime. Even *imagining* you'd take that blouse. Even *imagining* you'd hurt your child. You wouldn't. You couldn't. I wanted you to see that."

Julianne said nothing.

"And you didn't take that blouse, did you? Even when I dared you," Paisley pressed on.

"Even when I made it sound like fun. Even when I did it myself. You wouldn't steal a blouse from the store, and you wouldn't hurt Toby. Think of it, Julianne. That night you couldn't even *picture* what that witchy self in your mind would do to him. It was too horrible for you. You never lost sight of the bridges you didn't want to cross. Not once. Not then, and not today."

"So the shoplifting was a deliberate, preplanned act of crisis intervention, and not a spur-of-the-moment impulse?"

"No, of course not. I thought of it when I saw how upset you were. I wanted to help you." But Paisley's face went the color of chalk, and her voice was a thread. "I didn't take the tags off the blouse. I didn't think they could do anything. But when I saw that saleslady . . ."

"She would have liked to skewer you. *Us,*" Julianne corrected.

"Yes." A heavy silence, and then Paisley took a long breath that made her stand two inches taller, revived. "It got you out of yourself, didn't it?"

Well, it had. Julianne's spiky anger melted into something that felt more like gratitude. Not once, not for a millisecond during that danger-filled episode, had Julianne recalled the terrible night she'd imagined hurting her son.

By the time they reached the car, Paisley's shivering had stopped and color had returned to her face. "Do you have a plan?" she demanded the moment they were on the road.

"What?"

"A plan for leaving Bill. At my party you said you were leaving him. Was that for real? Or was it just . . . I don't know. Songs of a summer night?"

"A very drunken summer night."

"See? That's why you're drinking too much and imagining you're going crazy," Paisley said. "Because you feel helpless. You feel helpless because you don't have a plan."

"It's not that simple."

Paisley shook her head, impatient. "It is. You're despondent. You're depressed. You're not psychotic."

"Or so one hopes."

"Well, I thought we proved that."

It still seemed slim proof to Julianne, but she didn't object.

"What do you want to do with yourself?" Paisley asked.

Julianne wanted to be . . . not evil. Not scared. Not . . . things too ephemeral to discuss. She didn't say anything.

"Well?"

When her voice finally came, the cool surety of it surprised her. "I used to think that if I could go back to school and get another degree, I could get a job that paid a decent living wage," she admitted. "Then I could leave Bill and be independent. But when you have three kids and the oldest is only eleven, you realize that it's too long a haul. You're in a cage. There's no way out. The whole idea of leaving him was stupid."

"I don't think so," Paisley said. "If Bill is so rich, and if you really want to be rid of him, get a good divorce lawyer. Get a settlement. Make him pay alimony and child support. Make him give you the house. Then you can go back to school and pay for whatever you need."

"That sounds so brutal."

"Better than being brutal to your own body parts. I'll find you a lawyer, if you want."

Julianne hesitated.

"I'll take that as a yes," Paisley said. "And I'll find you a therapist."

"A therapist!"

"Julianne, you're a nurse. Didn't it ever occur to you that you need treatment?"

"No." The realization scared her.

"It wouldn't hurt to have someone to talk you through it. I know someone good. You can call her at midnight if you need to, and she'll come to the rescue. Of course, I'll come to the rescue, too, if you need me. I'm only next door. But it doesn't hurt to have a safety net."

Never did Paisley say, *You need this because you're crazy.*

The lawyer Paisley found was known as a

barracuda, though his sharp teeth wouldn't be necessary, considering how quickly Bill agreed to everything Julianne wanted. The therapist was good, too, though Paisley had to drive Julianne to the first appointment or she never would have gone. In the end, Julianne went to the woman's office once a week until after the divorce, after she'd returned to school. After she believed, for certain, that she'd really never hurt a child she loved and shouldn't hurt herself, either. And wouldn't.

It didn't occur to Julianne until months later what a risk Paisley had taken that summer afternoon at Novella. If they'd been arrested— and Julianne supposed she was, at the very least, an accessory—then she would have been humiliated, embarrassed, humbled. But given Bill's special talents, it wouldn't have affected his surgical practice, or his income. Paisley was more vulnerable. "Newspaper Editor's Wife Arrested for Shoplifting" the headline might have read. Mason wrote a popular editorial. He was a public figure. The rest of the press would have had a field day, bringing him down. No wonder Paisley had been pale and shaking when they'd left the store.

Sometimes Julianne wondered what other feats of benevolent daring Paisley had undertaken, given her penchant for sensing how to help even before people told her what was wrong. She'd practically assaulted Andrea's husband for his apathy when his daughter was sick. She'd courted arrest and humiliation for Julianne. She'd offered aid as startling and effective as electric shock, only better. Who else had received it? She supposed she'd never know.

When Paisley's house went on the market not many months after the shoplifting incident, Julianne briefly indulged a fantasy that Paisley was selling because of *her*. Maybe she was embarrassed about their afternoon of not-quite-crime. Maybe she couldn't bear to watch Julianne go in and out of her house day after day, knowing what she knew.

Later, she laughed at herself for thinking that. Paisley didn't go very far, only up to Lindenwood Court. And when Melody came along, it seemed clear that Paisley and Mason had moved simply because they were trying to have another child and wanted a bigger house for their family.

She and Paisley had gone back to their old ways by then—seeing each other at neighborhood functions, in the supermarket, at the mall.

But for one afternoon, they had been bound to each other in a way Julianne had never been bound to anyone before or after, in a way Julianne suspected Paisley never had been, either. As far as Julianne knew, no one else knew Paisley had ever shoplifted so much as a stick of gum. It was something only the two of them shared. It had carried Julianne all these years.

So when Paisley got sick, and came into that room for Julianne to examine, it was no wonder Julianne sensed something wrong, the moment they touched. She had a special bond with Paisley. If her fingers flew straight to the source of the trouble, it was no wonder.

CHAPTER 21

Thanksgiving

Thanksgiving morning dawns cold, just as Ginger thinks it should, a thin glaze of frost across the lawn, one of the first all season. She hasn't cooked Thanksgiving dinner for years, not since she took over the store and her sister, Sally, declared that even a person like Ginger didn't have the energy to host a big meal one day and spend long hours at work the next. In the retail business, an ad for a high-ticket item like a spa can bring in enough traffic to make the Friday after Thanksgiving chaotic, even if it doesn't result in a sale. Eating at Sally's has become a family tradition. Ginger is banished from the kitchen except during the cleanup. The only thing she is allowed to bring is their grandmother's pineapple cake for one of the desserts.

This year Ginger gets up early and bakes two cakes, thinking she'll take one to Paisley's—not that the Lamms need food, but she hasn't made the trip across the cul-de-sac for days, and at least it's a gesture, it's *something*.

She enjoys mixing the cream cheese icing, tasting it a bit more often than she should, slathering it onto the cakes. She enjoys the task because it's satisfying but mindless, allowing her to think about work. The economy being what it is, the Christmas season is going to be a challenge. She doesn't mind—as long as they don't go broke, and she doesn't think they will. She has some ideas. Lease to own. Lease, period. She's sure it's possible to repossess a hot tub and still make money, though she hasn't figured out all the details.

Once, when she was a stay-at-home mom caring for young children, she'd hated long weekends. They were more of the same: no workplace challenges to look forward to, no mail, just the endless need to think up activities and outings to relieve the boredom of being housebound for yet another day. Once she began running the store, she began to feel more balanced. She likes cooking; she even likes vacuuming. Just not in concentrated doses.

The cakes are lovely. Swirls of creamy, off-white icing. An artful design of candy corn sprinkled on top, to please the younger children.

She leaves the bowls in the sink, then goes upstairs to shower.

Max apparently finds his way into the kitchen the moment she leaves. True to form, he assumes one of the beautifully iced creations must be for him and cuts a hefty slice. Though it's not even nine in the morning, an hour when both children are usually asleep if they have the chance to be, Rachel soon joins him in the kitchen. When Ginger comes downstairs, there they are, sister and brother enjoying a rare moment of congeniality, as they devour Paisley's cake. Eddie is the only one who's sleeping.

"Good," Max tells his mother, his mouth full. His Adam's apple, never a visible body part until recently, bobs up and down as he chews and swallows and speaks.

"Last year you wouldn't even *taste* pineapple cake," Rachel reminds her brother, picking delicately at her own cake with a fork. "You said it was too sophisticated. You said you had to be at least thirty to eat it."

"Well, now he not only gets to eat it, he gets the privilege of making another cake for me to take to Paisley's."

"*Now?* It's Thanksgiving. Dad said he'd take me out to practice driving."

"Dad is asleep," Ginger reminds him.

"What about Rachel?"

"Who cut the cake first? Whose idea was it?"

Max doesn't defend himself. "Thanksgiving is a holiday," he says.

"Fine. You can bake another cake on Sunday." On Sunday she can supervise him. Sunday is a better day to bring food, after all. By then, people are tired of leftovers. "Good thing it's an easy recipe," she threatens.

Max ignores her. He assumes he won't really have to bake the extra cake. He's probably right. "What time is dinner at Aunt Sally's?" He scrapes a blob of cream cheese icing off the cake with his index finger and sticks his finger in his mouth to suck it off.

"Gross," Rachel says. "Use your fork."

"What time?" Max asks again.

"Two."

Sally's is always a mob scene. Her husband has three sisters, each with several children ranging in age from toddler to teen. Sally's son, Devon, becomes a whirling dervish in the presence of so much company. The noise will be deafening.

"You think Amy will be there?" Max asks.

"Probably." Amy is a year or two older than Max, a girl who spent part of last summer in rehab for anorexia. "I expect you to act normal with her, no matter what." Although Amy does not gorge herself at family functions and then leave the table to throw up, she pushes her food around on her plate, fooling no one, and then declares she's stuffed.

"Mom, of course, I'll act normal. I'll even flatter her a little. When she comes in, I'm gonna say, 'Hey, looking good, Amy. Looks like you're putting on a little.'"

"Why be subtle?" Rachel asks, dabbing her lips with a napkin. "Why not just say, 'Hi there, lardass'? That way you can probably get her to fast for a week."

"You won't say a single thing to upset or embarrass her," Ginger tells Max. And, of course, he won't, because whenever Amy actually walks into a room, with her skeleton arms sticking out of the sleeves of her shirt, it's so scary that for the first second the room is actually covered by thick silence, a hush as if everyone's tongues had swollen inside their mouths. At those times, Ginger always looks at her own children and thinks how glad she is that they're normal. In view of that, she's less irritated that they commandeered Paisley's cake.

Ginger opens the dishwasher and begins to load the utensils and bowl from the cake batter. Outside, the day is breezy and overcast, sending silvered light and chilled air through the ill-fitting window over the sink. Even with the oven on, the kitchen is never warm. Rachel, in a fuzzy pink bathrobe Ginger hasn't seen for a year, pushes her cake away. "This place is an ice cube," she says. On her feet she has a pair of fuzzy bedroom slippers with sewed-on buttons for eyes and an extra flap of fur for ears. Whether the slippers are supposed to be dogs or rabbits, Ginger can't tell.

At the same moment, both Rachel and Max rise from the table and carry their dishes to the sink. They never do this.

A few days later, when it is not so simple, Ginger will remember how the sight of her children made her happy that morning, in the most uncomplicated way.

CHAPTER 22

Paisley—Dancing

Oh, yes . . . and the feather boa.

It wasn't really a part of my cocktail waitress outfit. It was a memento of my class in modern dance. I was eleven or twelve. Miss Lindsay was ancient and looked frail, her white hair pulled back from a narrow, wrinkled face, and her long legs so skeletal you wondered how they held her up. But she was strong and graceful. She'd been dancing all her life. In class she'd swirl and twirl as she demonstrated every step, waving the feather boa in the air. She taught us less about dancing than about having fun. At the last session, she gave each of us a cheap feather boa to keep.

"Drape it across your shoulders, my dears, and all the cares of the world will go away."

That original feather boa . . . well, who knows where it ended up. I used to fling it about while in my room at night, overloaded with hormones and restless, all alone but imagining otherwise, dancing to old rock 'n' roll tunes until the wild energy was doused by exhaustion, and I could finally drop into my bed and off to sleep.

Many years later I saw a feather boa in a costume shop and bought it. I've kept it all this time. I remembered the old lesson, even taught it to my daughters. I close my eyes and will it to be true.

"Drape it across your shoulders and dance, girls, and all the cares of the world will go away."

CHAPTER 23

November 28

As far as Iona is concerned, Lori could have done her a favor by going to the hospital on Thanksgiving instead of the day after. Then she would have had an excuse to tell the Amoias she couldn't eat with them. But she'd painted herself into a corner. Lori, despite her iffy pregnancy situation, had practically insisted on cooking a big meal for the holiday. "It's easy enough to make a turkey. Put it in the oven and take it out. You can bring the mashed potatoes."

"Bend over to put a turkey in, and you'll land in the oven yourself," Iona said. "Too risky. I'll make the turkey. I'll make everything."

"Absolutely not," Lori countered.

"What you really want to do," Jeff finally said to his wife, "is stay home in your pjs and take a nap. You know I don't like turkey anyway."

This was a surprise to Iona, and from the look on her face, to Lori, too.

"Besides, I have an obligation to the Amoias," Iona added, settling the situation. She was grateful to Hugh Amoia for buying three of her rehabbed properties in the past three years. She even liked his wife, Shirley. She accepted their invitation, figuring the couple would use the holiday to cement some of their business connections. But she knew immediately, from the odd assortment of relatives and elderly friends milling around the Amoias' living room when she arrived, that she'd been invited as a charity case. The Amoias didn't think she had anywhere else to go.

Iona brought the Amoias a nice bottle of wine. She drank most of it.

Now, when Jeff calls, she can barely open her eyes enough to see the numbers on the digital clock that say it's 5:04 in the morning. Outside, the sky is dead dark. The bedroom is cold. Iona's mouth is so dry from the aftermath of wine that when she picks up the phone, her hello comes out as a rasp.

"We're on our way to the hospital," Jeff says. "I know it's early, but I thought you'd want to know."

Yes, well, certainly, but did she need to know right now? Does he think the kid is going to pop out on the spot? "Lori's in labor?" she grunts.

"Yes. We'll be at the hospital in about ten minutes. You can meet us there."

"How do you know it isn't Braxton Hicks? How do you know it isn't another false alarm?" she asks, waking up a little.

"Her water broke," Jeff says.

"Oh." Iona's heart does a little flip-flop, which she tells herself is the result of the wine.

"It was a mess."

"You know, Jeff, I could have done without that particular piece of information."

"So you'll come? To the hospital?"

"Of course," she says, because what else do you say to someone driving across town at five in the morning with a laboring wife? "Are the labor pains . . . how are the labor pains?"

"Okay, but not too close together yet. So far, so good." Jeff sounds unnaturally hearty, as if he's trying to reassure himself. He sounds very young.

"Okay. Drive safely. Good luck." Iona hangs up the phone, shuffles into the bathroom, and drinks about a gallon of water.

No point hurrying to get dressed. She'll

probably end up sitting in the waiting room all day. Still, she's out the door before she knows it. There's no traffic yet. A couple of hours and the streets will be full of Christmas shoppers. Christmas tree stands adorn every corner, though why some families feel compelled to put up a tree the moment Thanksgiving is over, Iona doesn't know. Why give the thing a chance to dry out, shed its needles, and spark into flames the first time someone lights a match? She and Richard never got a tree before the middle of December—though who knows, if they'd had kids, it might have been different. By the time Jeff came to her, he wasn't little enough for it to matter.

Nobody stops her as she walks into the hospital and takes the elevator to the fourth floor. She could be a terrorist carrying a bomb. The waiting room at the end of the hall is empty. Inside, she dials Jeff's cell to tell him she's arrived. "Is Lori settled? What's going on?"

"Come down the hall to 3-B and see for yourself." He sounds maniacally jolly.

"I'll wait here." The last thing she plans to do is watch Jeff's wife huff and puff and pant her way through labor while Jeff tries to humor her. "Tell Lori hello. If something happens, call me." Iona supposes it's more a matter of *when* than *if.*

The nondescript brown couch is more comfortable than it looks. She forgot to bring a book. As she leafs through the magazines on the coffee table, a man who resembles Jeff comes through the swinging doors.

It *is* Jeff. Or is it? She stares at him a moment longer. "You got your hair cut."

Jeff grins.

"I hardly recognized you," Iona tells him.

"What do you think?" Jeff's ponytail, his signature fashion statement since he was fifteen, is gone. The new style is neither long nor short, just . . . ordinary. Except that his newly shorn hair seems thicker than it did pulled back in a rubber band, Jeff looks like a thousand other nice-looking, brown-haired young men with white-collar jobs. He could manage a clothing store. He could be a banker.

"You look—" Iona is at a loss to complete the sentence.

"Handsome. Impressive. I know." Jeff turns his head, models for her.

"But why now?"

"Because Lori was sure that if I didn't, she was going to have Braxton Hicks contractions until the end of time. She said the baby wasn't going to make an appearance until I looked like a father."

"Very sensible," Iona says. "She was probably right."

"Now come in and tell her hello."

"Into the labor room?"

"Really, it's all right." Without giving her a chance to protest, Jeff takes Iona's arm like someone escorting her onto a dance floor. "This part of the building is a birthing center, not a hospital. It has its own set of rules. You can come in. You can stay the whole time."

The notion of this, along with the wine Iona is sure is still active in her body, makes her light-headed. She lets Jeff guide her down the hall. "I tried to get you to cut that hair for years," she says. "You never listened to me."

"Sure I did. Not about the hair, but certainly about the earring."

"Earring?"

"Don't you remember? When I first got my ear pierced, I had that long, dangling earring?" He indicates a spot at his jawline to show the length of the offending jewelry. Yes, of course. It was appalling.

"Do you remember what you told me?" he asks.

"What?"

"You said anyone with something dangling between their legs doesn't need something dangling from their earlobes."

"Did I?" Iona laughs. She had. She'd said exactly that.

"Did you ever see me wear long earrings again?"

"Now that you mention it . . . no."

"Well, I listened to you, didn't I?"

Without her noticing until it is too late, Jeff guides her into the birthing room, where Lori is propped up in a hospital bed attached to an alarming number of monitors. Iona wants to flee but knows she'd look like an elderly, scampering rat. "Is there something wrong?" she asks, indicating the equipment.

"No, this is how they do it," Lori says. "Welcome to the modern birthing experience."

"Doesn't it hurt?"

"Not at all. They gave me an epidural." She sounds perfectly normal. "What do you think of Jeff's haircut?"

"It was a shock."

"He got to the barber on Wednesday just before the stores closed. I think we would have been here sooner except that it took the baby an extra day to realize the bum who'd been living with me had turned into a father figure. But at long last, here we are."

"Well, you do look more like a father," Iona tells Jeff. "Though I can't quite imagine it. *You.*"

Jeff motions Iona to a chair. She's too dazed to do anything but sit.

Lori points to what looks like an EKG graph being made by a pencil held by a robotic arm. The device is attached to a sensor on Lori's belly, and to a monitor with numbers that go up and down. "It measures the contractions."

Iona finds herself mesmerized by this. Over the next few hours, she watches Lori's contractions on the monitor and the pencil sketches of their mountains and valleys on the graph. At regular intervals a nurse comes in, or a doctor wanting to check the dilation of Lori's cervix, while Iona and Jeff wait behind a curtain the nurse pulls around the bed. Iona and Jeff take turns going down to the cafeteria for breakfast and later, lunch. They don't want to eat in front of Lori, who can't have anything but ice chips.

Iona buys a newspaper but doesn't read it. She watches the graph instead. It hypnotizes her. Most of the day passes in this manner. Once in a while, Lori dozes off, even as her contractions rise and peak and fall. Jeff, sitting on the opposite side of the bed, also dozes, clutching his wife's hand the whole time as if to ensure that she won't escape.

Once, while Jeff's eyes are closed, Iona registers that her stepson has rather nice, thick eyelashes. Probably she never noticed this before because she was too distracted by the ponytail. Maybe the baby will inherit them. She hopes so. Without makeup, Lori seems to have no eyelashes at all.

On her next visit, the doctor—a woman who can't possibly be old enough to deliver a baby—mumbles an unintelligible sentence containing the words *dilated* and *effaced*. She gives Lori a beatific smile. Lori and Jeff exchange glances. "Let's get this show on the road," the doctor says. "Time to push."

Iona's heart leaps like a flight animal into her throat. "I'll be in the waiting room," she says. Jeff forces his gaze from his wife's. "Why not stay?" he says.

"Three's a crowd." Of course, it's the doctor who makes three and Iona would be four, but this seems irrelevant. Iona flees to the waiting room in a broth of emotion, feeling at once excluded, relieved, and anxious. Her stomach is in a knot. She can't sit. This is why expectant fathers pace. She follows their example, pacing for fifty-seven minutes (she times it), until Jeff comes in and says, "Well, you're a grandma now"—not true, but at the moment, not the primary concern— "Come on. Let me introduce you to Rosalie."

"Rosalie." Iona tests the name. Jeff and Lori chose it months ago but wouldn't tell anyone, lest they'd have to hear negative opinions. Their secrecy had made her imagine the worst: Hepzebah, Imogene, Penelope. By contrast, Rosalie . . . who could object to Rosalie?

Iona means to be polite no matter how awful the infant looks. And, of course, the child does look awful, what little Iona can see of her, wrapped in a blanket like a taco and set in the middle of a portable—well, a portable *box* with see-through sides—a red, wrinkly creature topped by a pink cap that clashes with her complexion, and a smashed-in nose and small, lashless eyes of no particular color. She seems alert, though. Half an hour old, and looking around.

"Seven pounds four ounces," Lori says. "Not a bruiser, but a decent weight. She got a ten on her Apgar."

"Her Apgar?"

"A newborn strength and vitality test," Lori says. "Ten's the highest score."

"Oh." Why it makes sense to measure strength and vitality in a creature less capable than newly hatched poultry, Iona has no idea.

"Here. You can hold her."

"But I'm not—"

Before Iona has time to demur, Jeff has loosened the blankct to free the baby's hands, lifted her from her box, and set her in Iona's arms.

Support the neck, she reminds herself as blood drums in her ears. It isn't difficult. There's not much neck, or anything else, to support.

"Rosalie," she says, for lack of anything better to say to the child. As if she recognizes the sound, the baby grows perfectly still. She opens her eyes and regards Iona's face. They study each other for a long moment.

Iona dangles a finger at Rosalie's hand, perfectly formed down to the fingernails, which appear to need cutting. She touches the tiny palm. The baby clutches Iona's finger in her rosebud fist. Iona knows babies do this, she knows it's just a reflex, but it seems remarkable all the same. Not an hour old and holding on. Godawful to look at, but strong.

"You did good," she tells Jeff. "You, too," she assures Lori. The two of them seem to bask in her praise. Jeff turns to his wife and they gaze at each other adoringly, apparently love struck all over again.

Embarrassed, Iona keeps her attention on Rosalie. "Good thing you didn't have to see the ponytail," she whispers. Rosalie smiles. This is not possible, but there it is. A smile. All along, without meaning to, Iona has been trembling on the brink of loving her. The smile pushes her over the edge.

With that a fait accompli, she allows herself to note that the child's forehead, which she has been aware of all along, is higher and more intelligent looking than either of her parents'. It is exactly like Richard's. She had not expected that—Richard appearing not in the form of a ghostly visitation, but in a forehead.

Jeff's voice brings her up short. "You're boo-hooing, aren't you?" Jeff says. "Don't say you're not."

"I never boo-hoo about anything." But Iona watches a tear—her own tear?—fall onto the receiving blanket. "It's just that she's so perfect," she says. "Considering who her father is, I'm sort of astonished."

"I'm sort of astonished myself," Jeff tells her, while in the gentlest possible motion, he lifts his daughter into his fatherly arms.

It's nearly dark by the time Iona gets home. Her headlights sweep across her front yard, which looks fairly dismal in the twilight. The white ribbon hugging the willow oak is getting scraggly, and the effect is accentuated by the ragged circle of needlelike leaves that have now fallen onto the lawn like so much litter and still need to be raked. Iona notices in the distance that someone is out for a walk—she can't tell who— so instead of leaving her car in the driveway like she normally would, she opens the automatic garage door and pulls in, closing it behind her. Before long she'll be anxious to share her good news, but right now she wants to mull over her day in silence. Her life seems too momentous to share, just yet. What is it going to mean, after all? This birth?

Later, she thinks it would have been a perfect day, if she'd had the sense not to check her answering machine. The single message is from Paisley. "Do you think you could stop over?" Her voice sounds a little breathy, either excited or weak. Under the circumstances, Iona can't say no. It's like being summoned by a queen.

It's just early evening, not late enough to convince herself the matter can wait until morning. She gets back into her car and drives up to Lindenwood Court, hoping the "Paisley is resting" sign will be out and get her off the hook. But it isn't.

"Iona, good," Paisley says, as if this were a long-arranged business meeting. "Close the door, will you?" Before Paisley goes any further, Iona knows exactly what she wants. "About that time I saw you back there in the field . . ."

Iona pretends not to follow. "I go back there sometimes to walk," she says, noncommittal, just in case.

"This was a long time ago. Back . . . back when I was pregnant with Melody."

Iona pauses, as if she's struggling to remember. She shakes her head.

"Please, Iona. I don't have much time for this. Much energy."

Iona can see that. Paisley's voice that two sentences ago was as strong as ever is now a thread. "Why, yes, I do remember now," she says. "You were there with Eddie Logan. The two of you were having a picnic. Yes. We waved to each other"—they didn't, of course, considering—"and then I walked home. That's all I remember, Paisley. Was it important?"

"Not at all," Paisley says. Iona can see the weight lifting from her, as if it were a physical thing.

"You rest now," Iona tells her.

"In a minute." Paisley touches her hand, beckons her close, whispers in her ear.

Under any other circumstances, Iona would refuse. But what's the choice? "Honest to God, Paisley, you think of the oddest things."

"Then you'll do it."

"Sure. It's completely inappropriate. But why not?"

"Thanks, Iona."

"It's nothing," Iona says.

"I mean, thanks for . . . what you remember. And what you don't. It's not nothing. It's a lot."

CHAPTER 24

November 30

Ginger bakes the extra pineapple cake on Sunday morning before the rest of the house is up. She knew she wouldn't actually ask Max to help. She shouldn't have threatened him in the first place. Bad policy not to follow through. If Max and Rachel hadn't devoured the first cake . . . well, they had. And Ginger has been obsessing about it all weekend. She'd had the cake on her mind all Thanksgiving Day, even after they got home from Sally's, too sleepy from overeating to bake or do anything else before dropping into bed. She had it in the back of her mind all day Friday, a busy day at the store, and all day Saturday, which was equally busy. She'd sold two spas, more than she'd expected. She wasn't complaining. She just wishes she could have taken the cake to Paisley's before now and had it over with.

Slathering the last of the rich cream cheese icing onto the cake, she vows that Max isn't going to get within ten feet of it—not that he'll be up for hours. All the same, she sets the finished cake on a disposable serving tray and carries it with her, safe from attack, as she walks into her living room to peer across the cul-de-sac toward Paisley's. The "Paisley is resting" sign is gone from its perch beside the front door. This is the signal that she's ready for visitors. Good. A cake isn't much, and it's not particularly appropriate, but it's better than not doing anything at all.

Ginger's house holds last night's cold, but outside it's unseasonably warm again as she heads across the cul-de-sac. It's unsettling. Not good for Christmas sales. Heading toward Paisley's, she holds the cake in front of her like a shield.

There is a certain point—she has known this since her father-in-law's long battle with heart disease—when a person begins to die in earnest.

There is a hollowness about them. They begin to retreat. She has seen this, and she knows. When she walks into the den where the CD player sends the strains of "Unchained Melody" floating around the room like a cloud, Paisley sits up in a rented hospital bed, regarding her with that detached look that makes her seem as if she's already left, but making a great effort to smile. Ginger thinks, *This will be over soon.*

"I guess you aren't in the cake-eating mood," she says as she holds out her offering. It doesn't look like Paisley has eaten for weeks. So when Paisley speaks, Ginger is startled to find her still so present, so *there.*

"I'm not up for cake right now, but I'm sure the kids are. And Mason. He has an awful sweet tooth." With her right arm, the arm not encumbered by the needle for the morphine drip, Paisley gestures toward the folding chairs set around the room in a neat rectangle that reminds Ginger of funeral parlors. "Sit down for a minute." Then, exhausted by the effort, she lets her impossibly thin arm drop onto her covers.

"I wish I could do more for you," Ginger says. "When I made the cake . . . I know it's Thanksgiving weekend and everybody is up to their ears in food. I thought maybe you could freeze it. I just didn't know what else to do."

"You've done more than you know."

What, exactly? Ginger wonders. It seems an

odd time for flattery. "And I want to ask you one other thing," Paisley says.

"Sure," Ginger says. "What?"

Without lifting her tired arm from the bed, she beckons Ginger closer and whispers in her ear.

"Seriously?"

"Seriously."

It seems an odd request, but Ginger nods, because what else can she do? Discreetly, Paisley pushes the pump on her morphine drip, to give herself a little more painkiller. Her eyes drift shut, then open halfway. "Thanks." She gives Ginger a lazy smile. Ginger feels she's been rewarded.

She's glad that, although Paisley has become a shadow, dusky yellow and thin, the transformation hasn't made her skeletal, like most people at the end of their lives, but simply more ethereal—the blue eyes swimmy rather than snappy, enormous above the hollowed cheeks, the hair a dark cushion against the too-golden skin. Paisley will be beautiful even on the last day of her life. Her beauty will be a gift, a kind of blessing, for everyone around her.

Paisley has almost drifted off again, when suddenly she shifts positions and winces.

"Anything I can do?" Ginger asks and feels truly bereft when Paisley shakes her head no.

"I'm just creaky," Paisley says. "Everything's creaky." She stops to gather energy, stops for quite a long time, and when she speaks again, Ginger realizes she was trying to call up her old sense of humor. "You know what I could use right now?" she quips. "I could use a dip in that hot tub we had in the other house."

"Done," Ginger says, pretending to joke back. But adrenaline is already coursing through her in a joyful jab that catapults her out of her chair. Setting down the cake that will probably go into the trash, she begins making calculations.

How long will it take to get a spa over here and install it in the yard? Where should it go? What about the power line?

Here, finally, is something she can do.

She finds Mason on the screened porch, going through the Sunday paper. "Circulation's down," he says. "Circulation goes down, advertising goes down. It's a vicious circle. Daily newspapers are dropping like flies." He folds the paper and sets it on the table. A muscle works in his jaw. "What's up, Ginger?" he whispers hoarsely.

"She said she wishes she could sit in a hot tub like the one you used to have at the house down on Dogwood Terrace. What if she had one? Wouldn't it make her more comfortable? Those nice, warm jets of water beating on her back? I bet I could get one in as soon as tomorrow afternoon or Tuesday."

Mason sits motionless for a moment, his dark

eyes misted. "What about today?" he says. "She's hanging on by a thread."

Ginger stares at him. The Sunday after Thanksgiving? Deliver and install a spa on the Sunday after Thanksgiving? "Let me work on it. It might take some doing."

From here on the screened porch, she looks out into the yard and sees the exact spot, close to the house, where the spa ought to go. Well, why not? Labor will be hard to hire, but most of the neighbors are home. If she buys the patio blocks for the foundation at Home Depot, someone with a truck can pick them up. It doesn't take much skill to lay patio blocks. If necessary, she'll get Eddie to show them how. She heads across the cul-de-sac to her house, her mind racing. She phones Andrea, who phones everyone else.

One of the great selling points of the spas Ginger carries is that they can be installed without a plumber. Basically, they can be filled with a garden hose. That feature seems especially attractive today. "Eddie, come help me," she calls when she gets into the house. "Rachel and Max, you too." Already she's mentally running through the inventory of spas stacked in the storage yard behind the store. Already she's selecting a small one that needs only a regular outlet, not a 220.

"You think you'll be able to rouse Donny from in front of the TV?" Eddie asks when she tells him what she's up to. Even with the smaller outlet, a spa requires its own dedicated line. Donny, their electrician for years, is skilled but a bit lazy. Getting him out on a holiday Sunday, a football Sunday, is going to require tact, cajolery, maybe even bribery. Trying to find someone else would be impossible.

"I'll go to his house, if necessary," Ginger says. "If necessary, I'll pay him an outrageous Christmas bonus right now, on the spot."

"Show me where you want the trench to bury the power line, and the kids and I will start digging it," Eddie tells her. Max might be helpful, but the idea of Rachel wielding a pickax to break up the hard dirt is so ludicrous, both of them smile.

Ginger phones Skip Carson, who drives their forklift to move the spas around and operates the special trailer they use for delivery. He's not happy to hear from her. "This is for my neighbor who's dying. Waiting isn't an option. Please, Skip." She has no qualms about guilt-tripping him into it.

"No way you're going to get Trip or Butch today. I can't lift those things myself," he growls.

"I'll find you the muscle power." She'll recruit the husbands from the neighborhood. She'll promise them a fine workout without even going to the gym.

Before the morning is over, Ginger feels she's called in every favor anyone has ever owed her. Normally she doesn't like to get too far behind on favors, but instead of feeling bereft, today she's filled with an unfamiliar sense of exhilaration. Much as she enjoys her work, until now she hasn't realized how dry and dusty it sometimes gets, too familiar, too routine. Today, everything is easy, years of skills reaching this culmination, this impossible task.

Pick up supplies from the showroom, stop at Home Depot, check in with Skip. Usually she would jot down a list; it's part of what keeps her organized, but she doesn't need one. The tasks are etched neatly, indelibly, in her brain.

When she gets back to Paisley's just after noon, the yard is full of neighbors laying the patio blocks that have just been delivered. Mason, who has changed into a T-shirt and shorts, works among them with feverish energy, his summery outfit optimistic even for this unseasonable warmth, but beads of sweat dotting his upper lip, a satisfied intensity in his expression that makes Ginger think he's as grateful as she is for something do. So many of them look this way, thankful for the weight of stone in their hands, the feel of soil in a shovel. Even Iona Feld, swinging a pickax alongside Eddie in the trench for the power line, looks like she's enjoying herself.

The younger generation is out in force: Brynne; Max; Rachel; Julianne's son, Toby; even Courtney Chess with her shirtsleeves rolled up over a bandage that circles her arm like an honor badge. Andrea emerges from the house with a pitcher of lemonade, Julianne just behind her with a tray of sandwiches. The event is like a springtime barn raising, full of good fellowship and warmth. There is no sadness to this. Is that wrong, somehow? The only one missing from this picnic is Paisley.

All the same, aware of herself as the catalyst that set all this into motion, Ginger feels as if a heavy burden has been lifted from her shoulders. The burden of helplessness. She is infused with a sense of wonder. This is happening exactly as she envisioned it. It is not something she thought she could do.

The spa is in place before suppertime. It's dark, but so warm that Ginger knows Paisley will be able to use it, once it is filled.

Always when she sells a spa, Ginger likes to visit the customer personally to bring a supply of chemicals as a gift and answer questions about how everything operates, though it's simple enough. For cleaning, push the button, add a teaspoon of Clorox or other sanitizer. The pumps will run for ten minutes, then shut off. Under the circumstances, it seems ludicrous to go through this routine, but old habit demands it.

She'll remind Mason to be careful about children in the spa. No babies under two, and keep an eye on the older ones like Melody. Too much time in the hot water and their blood pressure can go up. He doesn't need these warnings. He's a careful man.

The Lamm house is quiet now. Trinket, the dog, lies prostrate on the back lawn beside the spa, exhausted from the day's commotion. Paisley is already in the water, shoulder deep as she sits on the ledge, Mason beside her, discreetly holding her up. Her eyes are glazed partly with morphine and partly with pleasure as the water jets beat against her back.

"Thank you, Ginger," she says. "This is heaven."

She flashes her white, white teeth. They *are* lovely, just as Eddie once said.

What a waste, Ginger thinks.

She doesn't wish this for Paisley. For herself, she's glad she's had the chance to do what she could.

Hours later, the treacherous warmth vanishes, just as everyone knew it must. The temperature plummets. Ice crystals coat the lawns. Ginger doesn't know why she startles awake in the predawn darkness. Maybe because the house is so cold. She goes to turn up the heat and spots Rachel, in jeans and a heavy sweater, tiptoeing downstairs and opening the front door. Outside, all traces of summer are gone, and there is a sense in the congealing, frigid air that there will be no more of it for many months. On such a night, even the most tenacious tropical flower knows there is no point trying not to freeze. Ginger knows—and certainly Rachel knows—that Paisley is dead.

Outside, Brynne moves like a shadow beneath the streetlights, going from house to house, removing the ribbons still tied to the trees. Rachel spots her, runs back inside to grab a scissors from the kitchen, and sprints out to join Brynne.

Ginger watches as the two girls walk down the block, then separate so that Brynne is on one side of the street and Rachel on the other. In each front yard, they cut the ribbons carefully from the trees. By now the bows are soiled and ragged. The girls cradle them gently against their chests. When they disappear at the end of the street, Ginger knows they'll continue until every ribbon is removed on every street in Brightwood Trace. When the neighborhood awakens, everyone will know.

Ginger sits at the window until they return. It's dawn by then, and very cold. As the girls climb the hill onto Lindenwood Court, they are faced with the oddest sight. Ginger sees it, too. Except for a few threads of dark-blue clouds, the lightening sky is streaked entirely with pink. The whole vista of frigid air arcs above them in the warmest, most vivid pink any of them have ever seen. Neither girl says a word. It is as if the sky is smiling.

CHAPTER 25

Paisley—Climbing

We went to the Rockies once. When people asked how we liked it, we said, "Great! Great!" But there was more to it than that.

We rented a car at the Denver airport and headed straight for the mountains, planning to see the city on the way back. On the steep, winding road, ascending toward those spectacular jagged peaks, the sky was so blue, the trees so green, the snowcaps so unlikely that we might have been moving through a dreamscape.

"Before this day is over, we'll be having a snowball fight," I told Mason. "Look." A peak had come into view, topped with snow as white as fine porcelain. "That can be our destination."

"Maybe we should stop for a noonie first."

"You'd be too worn out to do another thing."

"Wanna bet?"

I unfolded our topo map. "We started out at practically sea level this morning. We were at fifty-two hundred feet in Denver, and now we're

326

at eighty-six hundred and still going up. The highest we've ever been before was six thousand on that hike near Mount Mitchell."

I pointed upward to the tree line, an actual line almost straight around the mountain, forested below, bare above. "It's as if all the trees got together and decided they weren't going to grow one inch higher."

"As if in protest."

"Or else they unionized."

At the campsite, we set up our tent, gathered firewood for later, stuffed sweatshirts into our packs. Mason checked his watch. "Ten to three. Plenty of time to get up and down before dark." He slung two canteens of water over his shoulder.

The trail began with a footbridge over a stream of water, shallow and fast moving and so clear that the smooth oval stones beneath it seemed almost magnified. "The Laramie River," Mason announced.

"Looks like a creek. Too small for a river."

"In the West, this *is* a river." Ever the newspaperman, he'd done his research. "The water all looks clean out here, but you can't drink it. There's some kind of invisible parasite in the streams that makes you sick."

"What parasite? I never heard of a parasite."

"Giardia."

Poisoned water! Adventure! We'd been so

bored, SO bored. And now, keyed up, flying west, gaining two hours, embarking on our first vacation without the kids, we were unstoppable. More than twenty years together and still sizzling!

The trail we'd chosen led through a field of wildflowers, then up the mountain, a path of hard-packed dirt and rocks. At first it was wide enough to walk two abreast. When the trail steepened and narrowed, I fell behind, watching our canteens bob on Mason's back, his sturdy, muscular arms swinging, his legs covered with dense brown hairs above his running shoes. He wouldn't wear hiking boots. In his scouting days he'd gotten an infected blister from hiking boots and was convinced it could happen again. "Okay, be stupid," I'd told him.

He'd grinned. Now, though skeptical about his choice of footwear, I enjoyed the vista of his strong back, his strong legs, his hair curling at his neck beneath his baseball cap. Without the children, we'd be able to have sex anytime we wanted.

We didn't talk much because walking began to occupy us. Despite the switchbacks, the path was steep. Despite a summer playing tennis, I was winded. Thirsty, too. I would have taken a quick drink, but Mason had both canteens and I wasn't going to ask. I pictured the drinking fountain beside the tennis court, water coursing out in a thick silver arc. The air had grown cool as we ascended. What was odd was being so thirsty when it wasn't hot.

"Take it easy the first couple days," my mother had warned. "People need time to adjust to altitude. Don't go on one of your Olympic marathons."

Where she got the idea of marathons, I didn't know.

Just then Mason stopped, shrugged the canteens off his shoulder, and held one out to me. We'd come around a bend, in full view of a nearby mountain. The snow seemed not so far above us. We sat on a flat-topped rock that hunkered about four feet above the trail. I drank for a long time. Afterward, I slipped the strap of the canteen over my own shoulder.

"Tired?"

His asking made me realize that I was. "Hell, yes, I could use a little snooze right now."

He raised his eyebrows.

"Just kidding."

Mason jumped down from the rock to the trail. I felt obligated to do the same. My hiking boots had no spring in them. I hit the dirt trail hard.

We started off again. For a while thick trees on either side blocked our view of anything beyond them. Where there were breaks in the trees, we could see dark clouds gathering behind the peaks. "Let's hope we get up there before it rains. It almost always rains in the afternoon at this time of year. Thunderstorms, sometimes. They say if it's going to storm, stay below the tree line."

Why are we doing this if it's going to rain? I bit back the words. It was my fault. Mason would have settled for the noonie. The after-noonie. He was getting ahead of me. My boots weighed me down, made me sluggish and slow.

Not ten minutes after our stop for water, I was thirsty again. Still walking, I took a swig from my canteen. Moving while drinking was a bad idea. It added to my shortness of breath but failed to satisfy my thirst. My mouth stayed dry. I didn't like this.

A laughing couple passed, coming down the trail. Descending toward the shush of the Laramie River, soon they'd be dipping cupped hands into the clear water, marveling at each oval rock highlighted on the riverbed underneath. No one would believe anything toxic could grow in such clear water. It would taste cool, delicious. False.

What a thought!

I concentrated on rocks embedded in the packed dirt of the trail. The pale leaves of aspen trees, their white trunks. The sound of my own breath. Anything except the dryness in my mouth.

As we'd expected, the temperature kept dropping as we moved higher. I would have liked to stop to put my sweatshirt on and drink more water, but Mason was walking fast, light, in those damned running shoes.

We came to another shallow stream. Above the water, the air shivered. Mason barely glanced back at me before starting across, balancing on the flat, wet rocks. Once, his insubstantial shoe began to slip, and I was glad of it—glad!—but he caught himself. My clunky boots held to the rocks like magnets. On the other side, we waved to a Scout troop that had pitched tents and built a fire. A corner of a red plaid flannel sleeping bag protruded from one of the tents, a reminder of warm blankets, deep breaths, ordinary comforts.

Mason walked so fast, we might have been in a race. Maybe this was what my mother meant by Olympic marathons. I wasn't just winded anymore; now I was also sick to my stomach. I was light-headed. My nose was running. When I wiped it with my fingers, they came away red. I'd never had a nosebleed in my life. Rubbing the blood onto my shirt, I fought down nausea and made myself move faster, determined that if Mason expected me to compete in a marathon, at least he should see *this*. Dappled light fell onto the path with the movement of the clouds. From the distance came the rumble of thunder.

Mason turned to face me as I got close. "Doing okay?"

"Fine." He showed no alarm that I was hemorrhaging. Showed no sign of noticing at all. We'd been on the trail—how long? Over an hour. Two? He was the one with the watch. I squinted at the sky, trying to assess the angle of the sun. I was still on Eastern time, confused by the foreign pattern of clouds and brightness.

My hiking boots were heavier than they'd been at sea level. My nose kept dripping, but not enough to make an issue of it. Mason had no idea! My stomach roiled. My hands began to tingle. Maybe I was having a stroke! Any minute I was going to throw up.

Abruptly, Mason stopped. He froze and stared at something in front of him. Sick as I was, I caught up. Ahead of where he stood, the trail was gone. Instead, there stretched a huge, steep clearing completely covered by downed trees. Mason shook his head. "This is remarkable. An avalanche must have come through."

Before us lay a forest of slender, whitish trunks, not aspen trees but some kind of fir. Every tree for a hundred yards across had been uprooted in the avalanche's path. The expanse of downed trees went up the slope for perhaps the length of a football field, all the way to the tree line. After that the slope was bare except for some rock outcroppings, a thin covering of grass, and eventually, patches of snow well below the looming, white-capped summit. Behind the mountain, the clouds were the ominous purple of a new bruise. A few raindrops splattered down. Mason sat on one of the tree trunks and patted a spot for me. He opened his canteen and drank. I was too sick to be thirsty "Your nose is bleeding," he said.

"Thanks for noticing."

"It happens sometimes. From the altitude. Thins the blood."

"Thanks for warning me."

"Are you all right?"

"Fine."

"I can see you're not all right."

Well, no shit. "I'm all right," I said, hands tingling, stomach doing somersaults, head in a fog.

Mason eyed the wreckage in front of us. "We should call it a day."

Together, we stared at the trees. It was clear that the downed trunks provided hundreds of footholds along the slope. We didn't need a trail. It seemed a shame to get this far, only to turn back. The snow was *right there.*

"We could go across the trees," I suggested.

"You sure you're all right?" he asked.

"Fine," I lied.

The thin air made my lungs burn. I swallowed to keep my lunch down. We stood up.

Mason began to make his way across the tree trunks, graceful, as if the long day and the altitude had affected him not a whit. I followed, slow as a slug, boots heavy, stomach sour. Drizzle misted my face and hair. Not a lot of rain, but cold.

The tree trunks were wet and slippery. Sometimes they were so close together we had to step on top of them, one after another, flapping our arms like balance-beam walkers. Other places the trunks were farther apart and we found footholds on the ground, torn and furrowed by the violence of the avalanche. Every step was a challenge.

Then Mason looked up. He was drawn by the sight of the snow, the siren song of white in the middle of July. It could have happened to anyone. He lost his balance. First he pitched forward slightly, then back. He seemed to sit rather than fall. His stupid, flimsy shoe had gotten caught between two tree trunks. "Shit," Mason said. Sitting on the wet ground, knee bent, he wrapped his arms around the hurt leg, resting his head on his knee. "Shit," he said again. Gingerly, he dislodged his foot from where it was trapped.

"How bad?" I asked when I reached him.

"Not sure." Mason pulled down his sock. The ankle looked the way it always looked. "I think it's just twisted."

If it was broken, I would get the Boy Scouts we'd seen by the stream. I would bring them up before dark. I would will away any thunderstorms that were thinking about developing above the tree line. I helped him up.

"I'm all right," Mason said. He leaned on me and tried to walk. "Hurts a little, but not terrible." He tried to smile.

"Are you okay, really?"

"Sure." He sat down again. "Give me a minute."

We sat together on the cold, wet tree trunks. He massaged his leg. I fought the nausea that had retreated, briefly, during the excitement. I took a drink so there would be some moisture in my mouth. I swallowed two or three times.

From our position, the landscape beyond the fallen trunks looked steep but unthreateningly bare, and not so terribly far to the first patches of snow. "I wouldn't mind sitting here for a while," Mason said. "We have plenty of time. You should go ahead."

I might have said I was sick, but already this decision, this insane, altitude-sickness decision, seemed irrevocable. I said, stupidly, illogically, "I'll be right back."

He said, equally stupidly, "I'll wait."

The air stabbed at my lungs as I ascended slowly across the remaining tree trunks. My lunch and my heartbeat were in my throat. If I didn't do this and get back, who would take Mason down the mountain?

The trees gave way to bare ground. I moved across patches of thin grass and over outcroppings of rock. A steady rain had replaced the drizzle. I slipped a few times on the wet rocks but didn't fall.

The incline grew steeper. I wasn't really walking anymore—more like crawling. Leaning forward, clutching the grass and anything else that protruded from the ground.

A dizzying movement took over my stomach. My head. My lungs filled with hot metal points of air.

I clung to a rock. Red drops of blood dripped from my nose.

Chest on fire. Head whirling.

Then a wave of weakness. I couldn't move. My mother said take it easy, but she never said altitude would light candles in my lungs, turn my stomach, force blood from my nose. If she had, would I have believed it?

The rock was cool beneath my cheek. I turned my head to the side and threw up.

In front of me, a dandelion bloomed. *Dandelions grow above the tree line,* I thought.

I would concentrate on that, on things outside the sickness. I imagined the hiss of air on the plane, hissing from the overhead nozzle, thick and luxurious, whole milk after a diet of skim. I breathed that air.

Squiggling along on my belly, I lifted my gaze just enough to see, above me, snow. Glistening, even in the rain.

Strength trickled back into me. I rose to my knees, my feet. Hard shoes digging into the hillside. I held on as if to the side of a building. A wall.

Up. Inch by inch. Foothold to foothold. Up.

Mason was a speck among the fallen trees below.

I plastered my belly to a raw, wet rock, convinced it wouldn't let me fall. At the end, I didn't know it would be so simple. Reaching up, higher than I'd ever been before, I opened my hand to whatever it might grasp, and came away with a tiny sliver of snow.

I wished Mason could see it. He'd be clapping, jubilant, thumbs-up. I would have taken him with me if I could. I loved him. The girls, too. But some climbs you have to make alone.

CHAPTER 26

Early December

Paisley Lockhart Lamm, 46, wife, mother, and dear friend to all, died peacefully on November 30. She was diagnosed with pancreatic cancer 47 days earlier, on October 14.

An avid music lover and tennis player, Paisley's real and abiding passions were her family and friends. Paisley sought to instill in her children a zest for life, a commitment to family and friends, and the power of a smile.

Paisley is survived by her husband of 18 years, Mason Lamm; their daughters, Brynne and Melody; and her mother, Rita Lockhart.

The family asks that you spend time with your children, take a walk in the park with your loved ones, and make a toast to enduring friendship—lifelong and beyond. This is what Paisley would wish for you.

The low moan of grief that spills from Julianne's lips when she reads the obituary is the polar opposite of the wave of blackness that signaled Paisley's illness. Through misted eyes, she rereads the words and then sheds the tears that have been building since yesterday when she learned of Paisley's death.

"Come with me," she says to Toby, who hovers at the edge of the room, looking worried.

"Where?"

"To take a walk in the park." She hands him the obituary to read.

"She was always nice to me," he says, his deep young voice rough.

"She was nice to everyone."

To honor Paisley's memory, they do, indeed, take a walk in the cold park, clouds gathering, the trees spookily bare. Julianne brings along a bag of stale bread, which they feed to the ducks in the little lake. The tall, brawny Toby throwing crusts into the water echoes the smaller one, three or four years old, standing here, eyes alight at the sight of the scrambling, quacking creatures waddling up the bank toward him for their treat. She is so lucky. He is so large, so healthy. So kind.

This is what Paisley would wish for you. Yes.

The walk, done at Paisley's instruction, makes her feel slightly less of a traitor for owning the fingers that discovered Paisley's illness. But it does nothing to rid her of the sense that it is no favor just to *discover* someone's illness if you can do nothing to cure it.

Back at home, she goes on foot to Lindenwood Court, knowing the cul-de-sac will be full of cars. She cuts through the crowd directly to Mason. "It was a lovely obituary," she says.

"The girls helped me write it."

"I knew they must have. It was perfect." She squeezes his hand even as someone else comes up to claim him. When she turns, she comes face-to-face with Brynne, who must have trailed her through the room—and who is, she realizes, the one she came here to see.

"Your dad says you helped write the obituary," she says.

"Do you think she would have liked it?"

"She would have been very proud of you. Very touched."

"Thanks." The girl's eyes are swollen, but her face is as composed and implacable as the moon.

Julianne has tried to be strong for Brynne. She contained the tears she wanted to shed, at least while they were together. The one time she finally broke down, it wasn't until Brynne went home. This was during the first of Paisley's itching, when Brynne brought over a jar of skin cream she hoped would help, a pure and unexpected luxury the child surely couldn't afford—this was what made her cry.

Now Julianne fears for her. She thinks the word *orphan,* though that's not strictly true. *Motherless,* then. Fourteen, and a whole life to face. "I hope you'll still drop by sometimes," she says, aware that Brynne won't, but not wanting to shut off the possibility.

She hopes the girl is tougher than she looks.

On the morning of the funeral, Andrea is in the spare bedroom ironing her dress when Courtney shuffles in, still wearing the shabby sweatpants and old flannel shirt she sleeps in. Her fuzzy hair is all over the place, stiff from gel but shapeless, as if she's tossed her way through a night of bad dreams.

"We're leaving in an hour," Andrea says. "I want you to eat something and then get dressed." She speaks in the precise, clipped tone she's used ever since their confrontation over the tattoo. She used it when she explained that she would pick up Courtney from school early in order to keep an appointment with a doctor who removes dye from the skin. She used it to explain that this might be the first of several visits. If necessary, they'll continue the treatments in California after they move, until the offending ring of tattooed stars is gone.

In the doctor's office, Courtney leafed through a magazine in the waiting room, then endured the procedure with the silent stoicism she'd perfected when she was a cancer patient of three. Andrea was spared the dull, sinking feeling that usually accompanied her daughter's medical treatments. She could have watched a spinal tap or lumbar puncture without flinching. The flame of anger that had burned ever since she found Courtney slumped drunkenly on the lawn had not abated. It hasn't abated now.

"I'm sick," Courtney says, hugging herself into the oversize shirt.

"You're not sick." Andrea keeps her tone cool, though it's true Courtney is pale. "Even if you were sick, you'd have to go to this funeral. It isn't optional."

"I have cramps."

Courtney does not have cramps. She never has cramps. "If you were twenty-five years old with a new job, would you call in sick just because you had cramps?" Andrea lifts the dress from the ironing board and shakes it out.

"You're wearing *that* frumpy thing?"

"Yes. I told you." It's a perfectly respectable navy blue sheath.

"Well, don't wear it to *my* funeral."

Andrea struggles for clarity against the band that begins to tighten around her chest. "I don't plan to be at your funeral. I plan to be in the ground in Mount Olive cemetery, lying peacefully next to Dad, where by that time both of us have been resting for many years."

"The best-laid plans of mice and men," Courtney says.

"What's that supposed to mean?"

". . . oft do go awry."

"I guess I should be gratified to hear you quoting poetry."

"Robert Browning," Courtney says defiantly.

"Robert Burns," Andrea corrects.

"Yeah. Well. You never know who's going to be in that cemetery."

"No. You never do." With effort, Andrea moves to the closet, arranges her dress on a hanger, hooks it over the door.

"Anything can happen."

"We've had this discussion. We can have it again if you want to, but not now."

Courtney's lip begins to tremble.

"Anything can happen," Andrea says, more gently this time, "but I don't think it will." She unplugs the iron, sets it upright on the windowsill to cool. "I think the only thing that will happen to us in the near future is that we'll go to California." She begins to fold up the ironing board.

"I can't go," Courtney says flatly.

"It isn't optional any more than the funeral is."

"What if I get sick?"

"California isn't a third world country. They have doctors."

Courtney's face hovers on the edge of composure, then crumples. She sinks onto the bed. "You act like you don't even care," she says in a voice that grows higher pitched with each new syllable.

Abandoning her efforts to fold up the ironing board, Andrea goes to the bed, sits beside her daughter, reaches for her. Courtney shucks her off. Andrea tries again. This time she gathers Courtney in and shifts her weight so her daughter can lean on her. She strokes her gel-slicked hair.

Courtney weeps for a while. "It's scary," she whispers, and Andrea knows she means by this not just having the sword of Damocles hanging over her own head, or watching it slice off someone else's, but the entire specter of the unknown, which to a fourteen-year-old must be enormous.

"Scary, yes, but it could also be exciting. It could be like that"—Andrea struggles to think of something—"like that horrible roller coaster you like."

"The Dive of Death."

"Even if it's not *that* great, it could be . . ." Andrea waves her free arm to indicate the room, the neighborhood, their world. "It could be better."

Courtney leans into Andrea, buries her face in Andrea's shoulder. Andrea pats her daughter's back. Courtney blubbers. Courtney sobs. Courtney wails. It is the best thing that has happened in months.

When the sobbing slows, Andrea says, "You're okay, Courtney. You really are."

Courtney sniffs and sits up. She looks awful. "Yeah," she says. "Well."

And this is where John finds them a few minutes later, clinging to each other, faces red and blotchy, having said all they need to, for now, about life and death and California.

When Ginger and Eddie arrive at Andrews Mortuary, the parking lot is overflowing, as everyone knew it would be. They drop Rachel and Max at the door and then search for a space.

Paisley wouldn't allow a visitation and has given instructions that there be no lunch back at the house after the funeral. "One bash in the funeral parlor, and that's it," she'd told Andrea, who had passed the word.

Getting out of the car, clutching her coat to her chest, Ginger is glum and silent. Eddie is silent, too. Under these circumstances, he usually tries to tease her out of it.

"Sad?" she asks him.

"Just thinking."

"About Paisley?"

"Did I ever tell you she was the one who named the Teacher Toolshed?"

"She did?" This is a surprise to Ginger. "I didn't know you ever even had a conversation with her."

"That was the only one. I ran into her one day not long after they moved up to Lindenwood Court. She was upset because she'd had a miscarriage not long before."

"She had a miscarriage?"

"Yes, and when I mentioned the software, she seemed interested. I think it distracted her. I let her critique the names I'd thought up. She told me Teacher Tools sounded obscene. Teacher Gold Mine sounded like a game. Teacher Toolbox sounded too masculine."

"I could have told you that." Ginger hears the pettiness in her voice but is stung that she wasn't consulted, no matter that years have passed and she never gave this a thought until today.

"We went through Teacher Treasures, Educator's—Educator's something or other, I can't remember. And we ended up with the Teacher Toolshed."

"How many elementary-school teachers do you know who have a toolshed? Most of them are women. If you rejected Teacher Toolbox as too masculine, why was Teacher Toolshed any better?"

"I can't remember." Eddie takes hold of her elbow. They become part of a subdued parade from parking lot to mortuary, a hum of muttered good mornings.

"Teacher Toolshed," Ginger mutters. "I thought it was a product of your own bright mind."

"The software was," Eddie tells her. "Your brilliant husband went entirely solo on the software."

"And how long did it take you and Paisley to come up with the name?"

"Just that one afternoon."

"You were home in the afternoon? When you were still running the store?"

Eddie shrugs, too casual. "Maybe it was an evening. Maybe it was a weekend."

Ginger says to herself, *Don't*. Paisley was your friend. Paisley is dead. "And that was all you did? Talk?"

Eddie stops, allowing the crowd to flow around them like water around a stone. "What do you mean?"

"Did you sleep with her, too?"

The couple beside them slows, curious. Eddie starts walking again. In the cold gray morning, his face is slick with sweat. "What do you take me for?" he whispers.

Ginger knows then that he did. "All you had to do," she says quietly, "was say no."

His face locks into an expression so guarded that it's impossible to tell if he's disgusted with her for the accusation, or admitting the lie.

Ginger feels numb as they approach the entryway, hardly cognizant of her own hands as she signs the guestbook. "Go on. I'm supposed to wait for Andrea and Julianne and Iona." She's relieved she won't have to sit with Eddie. She couldn't bear right now to be inside the familiar circle of him: the scent of his aftershave, her arm brushing against the dark fabric of his suit, his wedding ring tight on his finger. She couldn't bear it.

There's a great deal of hushed conversation echoing through the hall as Ginger takes her seat over to the side, near the sound system. Julianne's son, Toby, is beside her, and then Julianne and Doug, who is either Julianne's friend or fiancé, Ginger isn't sure which. Then

Iona and Andrea's family. All according to plan. She wishes this would start. From her position, she can see Eddie and the children clearly, though they'd have to turn around to see her. Eddie's face is blotchy, not as if he's been weeping, but as if he's been running and has gotten out of breath. She wishes this would start. Finally a large man in a black suit—not a preacher—walks up to the podium. The crowd quiets.

"This," he says in a voice that sounds rehearsed and false, "is going to be the celebration of a life."

Ginger doesn't hear much of the service after that, only the occasional laughter and frequent muted sobs. She's glad she's on the aisle because if worse comes to worst and she has to throw up, at least she can get out.

She didn't expect this kind of physical reaction to Eddie's admission, or lack of it. She isn't seething. She doesn't even feel, outwardly, particularly upset. She just feels sick.

She knows when it happened and why. She knows her own part in it.

Eddie had been running the store for two years by then. He had not complained, but it was such an obvious struggle that Ginger had put aside her snotty disdain for hot tubs and started going in two days a week to help out. She didn't expect to like it as much as she did—not just getting away from the children for a couple of hours, but having this other . . . well, *purpose*. She saw right away that they ought to stop selling swimming pools and devote themselves to hot tubs and the pool chemicals that provided repeat business. Pools were expensive and risky. When she told Eddie, he was embarrassed that he hadn't thought of this himself. The fact of his ineptness made him even more somber and boring and careful than before. The only place he showed any enthusiasm at all was in bed.

Two months after her father-in-law died, Ginger found Eddie at his computer, working on the web-based program that became the Teacher Toolshed, a pack of lesson plans and activities elementary teachers could use to make social studies fun. The spark of excitement and enjoyment in Eddie's eyes had shocked her, it had been so long since she'd seen it.

She's been over the rest of it a million times. The way Paisley had asked, that same week, at exactly the right moment, "Don't you ever get bored?"

The way she had answered, with a lightness that masked the weighty truth of her reply, "Bored? Oh, yes. If I didn't work in the store part-time, I'd be eating bonbons all day."

"Now's your chance, girl," Paisley had said, almost joking. "With all due respect, now that your father-in-law is gone, you and Eddie can do anything you want with the store. I bet Eddie would go back to computers if you'd tell him you'd take over."

Ginger had already thought of this, secretly. But the idea was made so concrete, so *possible,* by the fact of its coming from Paisley's lips, that it had hit her with something like physical force. "There's nothing I'd like better," she'd heard herself uttering. "But I'm going to wait until Rachel's in school all day."

"Wait that long and your hair will turn gray and you'll be living on antidepressants."

"It's only two years," she'd argued weakly.

"Gray hair and antidepressants," Paisley had repeated.

And with that, Paisley had somehow tapped into not only Ginger's secret desire but also her primal fears: age and anxiety. Gray hair and prescription drugs. Three months later, Eddie was working full-time on the Teacher Toolshed, and Ginger had become what Paisley referred to as the Hot Tub Goddess. It was as if Paisley had given her permission to live her life, her *intended* life, and not some paler version of it she had fallen into by mistake.

Paisley had tried to help, Ginger supposes now, because Eddie was her lover.

More than eight years ago.

Eddie had slept with her. He had been unfaithful.

Does the fact that Paisley is dead make this beside the point, somehow?

Or does the fact of Eddie's betrayal, years before, spoil everything?

Ever since she and Eddie shifted jobs, their lives have been better, not worse.

Ginger can almost feel the soft breath caressing her when Paisley whispered in her ear her explicit, secret request for the funeral.

Such sweet, warm breath. Now all she feels is acid, and it is consuming her heart.

Julianne sees how white Ginger's face has gone. Nausea, she diagnoses.

Today, maybe they're all sick. Maybe they ought to be.

Doug takes her hand. Toby, looking down, observes. She unlatches her hand, pats Doug's knuckle lightly, sets her hand in her lap. She allowed Doug to escort her here because she knew Bill would be coming with his wife. She didn't want to be alone. Originally, Toby planned to drive separately and sit with the other neighborhood kids. If she'd known he'd change his mind, she would have told Doug to go ahead to work.

She wishes she had.

The man in front of Andrea shifts slightly, and all of a sudden she can see everything. The closed casket sits at the front of the room, on what looks like a little stage behind the podium. Flower arrangements are everywhere, except on the casket itself, which is decorated with the ribbons Rachel and Brynne took down from the trees. They've been cleaned off and made into a bouquet. Against the glossy surface of the casket, they look elegant and innocent. Andrea casts a sidelong glance at Courtney, sitting between her and John, and sees the unshed tears glistening in her daughter's eyes.

For a moment, Andrea can't bear to think the casket actually contains Paisley's body. It's too sad to imagine her locked into something so confining. In her mind, Andrea transforms the polished wood into an enormous tree, far more beautiful than the rough trees in the front yards of Brightwood Trace, huge and expansive, its branches reaching out, its majestic trunk covered with bows and streamers—one, single, ribbon tree, a gift, wrapped for Paisley, to send her off with all their love.

Iona can barely listen to the elderly aunts and uncles telling their stories in shaking voices. They seem to have loved Paisley so much, far more than most aunts and uncles do. Every now and then a funny anecdote evokes a small ripple of laughter, but not often. A funeral is not a celebration, no matter who says it will be; it is a memorial to lives that have been changed forever, and changed in the direction of loss.

She notices that, through it all, Mason and the girls are dry eyed. Only Paisley's mother occasionally dabs at her eyes with a tissue, then seems to decide she shouldn't and sits up very straight. They have spent all that time and energy loving Paisley, and now will have to live with the dark hollow of her absence the rest of their lives. When the last speaker finishes, it is as if the room is holding its breath.

A mournful final hymn begins, a recorded instrumental that wafts softly from the speakers amid the sound of sniffles, of noses being blown, dresses rustling as people stand up. This is the funeral director's standard closing hymn. The muted, doleful melody almost makes the underlying silence more profound.

That's when Iona and Julianne and Ginger and Andrea head toward the sound booth as Paisley asked them to do. At her instruction, they've done their research. They know they're dealing with an antiquated sound system, requiring a technician to change the CDs. Julianne—"because you're the prettiest," Paisley had told her—gets the man's attention and asks a question about the music. As they speak, Ginger and Iona crowd around as if to listen, blocking his view of the equipment. A foot away, Andrea plucks a CD from her purse and pops it into the player in place of the hymn. She turns up the volume as far as it will go.

And then—a blast of sound! "IF THERE'S A ROCK 'N' ROLL HEAVEN . . ." Roaring from the loudspeakers! Eliciting a communal gasp! The EMTs might have arrived and jolted the entire crowd back to life. Shocked, palpitating hearts send a burst of laughter up dry throats, over parched lips and tongues.

If there's a rock 'n' roll heaven, they have a hell of a band. The crowd can't help but pay attention. Iona knows the song well. The Righteous Brothers, not one of their biggest hits, but exactly the one Paisley would choose. A roll call of rock stars who died young. Roy Orbison, "who introduced us to his pretty woman." Elvis, who loved us tender. John Lennon, who "cried give peace a chance."

Paisley Lamm.

"Everyone's a star," the lyrics trill. Paisley always knew she was a star. It was a position she mostly tried not to abuse. She'd be perfectly comfortable, envisioning herself up there in that band.

If you believe in forever, the Righteous Brothers croon, *then life is just a one-night stand.*

A few people begin to move down the aisles, but most of them stay put, listening as the lyrics repeat.

If you believe in forever, then life is just a one-night stand.

Maybe so, Iona thinks. Maybe so.

CHAPTER 27

Christmas Vacation

In the weeks between the funeral and her departure for California, Andrea endures such a roller coaster of emotions that she comes to understand what it must be like to be manic-depressive. She's excited! She's hopeful! Imagine—a whole new world at the age of forty-six!

Then she's so exhausted she can barely drag herself out of bed. Maybe she's sick. She gets up primarily to set an example for Courtney, whose anxiety and fear are subdued but so close to the surface they almost shiver off her skin. Courtney leaves for school. Andrea sits on the living room floor, on the cold hardwood where the Oriental carpet used to be. She stares at the holes in the wall where the paintings have been taken down. The nearly empty house feels somehow . . . violated. Frightened. Sad. As if it senses that Andrea is abandoning it, which of course she is. The chill from the floor seeps through her. She feels frozen. Paralyzed. And no wonder. When she checks her watch, she sees that a full hour has passed.

With a colossal effort of will, she gets up from the floor, shakes out the numbness in her legs.

There is no choice here. She reminds herself how gracefully Paisley embarked on her own journey, much farther and more daunting than this one. She begins once more to dismantle her old world, the *known* world, and pack it up. She can do this. It's what Paisley would want. Paisley will hold her hand.

On the day the movers come, Andrea walks through her house and says goodbye to each empty room. The rooms of Courtney's cancer. The rooms holding the chasm that separated her from John. She tells herself there is nothing here to regret.

And so here they are, three days before Christmas, on the road. Christmas was going to be strange, no matter where they spent it. So why not in the car?

Andrea alternately dozes and watches the scenery while John drives. She's been doing this all the way across the country. John is so antsy, he won't relinquish the wheel. Just as well, because Andrea is overcome with fatigue. Today she falls into a dead sleep somewhere in eastern Colorado and wakes up to the sight of a cloudless blue sky and a huge, craggy, snow-capped mountain that appears to be rising in the distance out of the perfectly flat road they are traveling.

"Welcome to the Rockies," John says.

Andrea blinks. The landscape is completely foreign to her, sharp edged and treeless, not at all like the forested East Coast, with its gently mounded peaks that change colors with the seasons. This rockscape has the look of permanence, baking in the brilliance of an unforgiving winter sun. Stunning, but brutal.

"What do you think, Mom?" asks Courtney, from the cubbyhole she's tunneled in the backseat, wedged between computers and sound equipment and other treasures they didn't want to send on the truck.

John regards Andrea, too, out of the corner of his eye.

She doesn't try to speak over the drumroll of her heart, but she's sure they know. They're a chain, mentally holding hands, practically reading one another's thoughts. The scene before them is stark—a harsh, harsh beauty—and yet Andrea can feel the smiles tugging at the corners of their mouths.

This is completely new, they are thinking. This is entirely new.

"I hated to ask you, Iona, but I have about three thousand things to get at Target," Lori says two days before Christmas. She hands over a pink diaper bag overflowing with enough supplies to stock a nursery for a year. "She doesn't need to eat for two more hours, but here's a bottle just in case. I know you have to work. I really appreciate . . ."

"Relax, Lori. My schedule is clear. I live to babysit."

Secretly, Iona thinks this may be true. This is her fear. But when Lori closes the door behind her, leaving the baby a solid sleeping lump in Iona's arms, her concern turns darker. Why did she volunteer? Think of all the things that might befall the baby while Lori is away. Rosalie could choke on her milk. She could come down with one of those terrible, racing viruses that reduce an infant to a feverish blob in the space of an hour. She could succumb to SIDS. Iona could trip and drop her.

The baby stirs, makes a sound like a cat mewing, then settles peacefully against Iona's chest. A bubble of milk escapes from between her rosebud lips. A powdery aroma drifts up from her cap of hair. She is not even a month old. Iona is filled with dread.

Enough, Iona thinks. *Nothing bad is going to happen to her on my watch.*

A fierce protectiveness gradually replaces her terror. She is the lioness, protecting her cub. She is the mama bear.

Good grief.

Bending to kiss the perfect, smooth new skin of her granddaughter's cheek, she sits down in the new rocker/recliner she bought for herself as a Christmas/Chanukah present. She turns the baby so that when Rosalie wakes up, she can see the lights of the Christmas tree—an item Iona believed was a waste of money even before she married Richard and decided to forgo trees in deference to his Jewish religion. Then she couldn't forgo them because Richard wanted a tree for Jeff. But she had never liked them. They were messy. They were work. This year she changed her mind. Children enjoy lights and decorations. Life will be hard enough later on. They say tiny infants can't see much. Maybe the colorful globes and twinkling bulbs are a waste of money, but who knows? Iona reaches over to switch on the Christmas CD she put in place earlier. She settles in. In her sleep, Rosalie smiles and frowns and tests various other facial maneuvers before she decides on an expression Iona recognizes at once. In repose, she looks exactly like Richard.

On Christmas night after all the company is finally gone, Ginger watches Rachel go outside to look at the sky. She doesn't do this much anymore. It's cold, and apparently they've changed the landing pattern for the airport, which means lots of stars but not so many of the planes Rachel likes so much.

Across the cul-de-sac, there are still cars in front of the Lamm house. Visitors have been coming and going all day. Sympathy callers. Brynne comes out onto her lawn not long after

Rachel does, probably to get away from the crowd.

The two girls ignore each other, no doubt glad their houses are far enough apart that they don't have to feel impolite. After what they've been through, Ginger doesn't think they'll ever speak to each other much. There's too much between them for small talk. Yet in an odd way, they'll always be friends. A paradox. Ginger doesn't think either of them understands it.

Rachel turns her attention to the heavens, so intent and thoughtful she might just have figured out what's behind the curtain of darkness that hangs over the yard. Sheets of unseen light. Unknowable light. Ginger's heart contracts at the sight of her daughter contemplating a vastness she'll always long for but never see.

Turning from the window, she goes into the kitchen to help Eddie put away the last of the dishes. It seems the only place to go.

"How much damage do you think Amy's done to herself?" she asks, referring to the anorexic niece who fled from the table in the middle of today's elaborate dinner and didn't come out of the bathroom for half an hour. She's never done that before. Pathetic as the girl always looks, she's usually careful not to create any drama.

"Eating disorders are hard to control," Eddie says noncommittally as he drops a fork into the velvet-lined box that holds the good silver. He doesn't look up. Neither of them really care about the stricken girl, except to make conversation.

"Where's Max?" Ginger asks. "Why isn't he helping with this?"

Eddie shrugs.

Ginger's discussions with Eddie are full of such spikes and lulls these days. Gone is the easy, loose-tongued talk of the long married. They search for safe topics (Did you get something for Larry for Christmas? What about bonuses at the store?). They choose their words, they don't relax. It's worse than not having sex, which they haven't done, either, since the day of Paisley's funeral, a day when—Ginger reminds herself—*nothing happened*. Eddie mentioned that Paisley helped him name the Teacher Toolshed. Ginger suggested . . . well.

Who is the more injured? Eddie has pretended to be maniacally busy, which takes some doing in the weeks before the holidays when his business dwindles to practically nothing. Ginger really was maniacally busy, but that didn't shut off her thoughts.

Is she going to forgive him?

Both of them know what happened. Does it matter? Ginger feels wronged, yet is plagued by a quote from Christopher Marlowe: *But that was in another country, and besides the wench is dead.*

A terrible way to phrase it.

Putting the last of the serving platters in the china closet, Ginger turns to look through the dining room to the lit tree in the living room beyond, with its overstuffed chairs and what Max terms the world's most comfortable sofa and the piles of gifts they opened this morning and then replaced in boxes to sit under the tree where, by old tradition, they will remain on display until tomorrow. The house—an ordinary, dependable block of a place she rarely notices—through the screen of her current turmoil looks precious indeed. The lights, the old nativity scene and angels, the chipped porcelain squirrel on the mantel that Rachel bought for Ginger's birthday years ago, the mahogany secretary with Max's name scratched into the writing surface—each glows with its silvered patina of care.

It has been such a strange Christmas. Max is even more oblivious than usual, wanting only for Eddie to take him out to drive, demanding it no matter what else has to be done, totally selfish. Rachel has been an enigma, more poised than she was even a few weeks ago, yet subdued and even clingy, obsessed with homey detail. This morning when Ginger was making her traditional Christmas fruit salad, Rachel observed the operation with such close attention that she might have been trying to memorize the way Ginger chopped and cut. Ginger's sister and sisters-in-law, even some of the cousins, were chattering, working, steaming up the already-steamy kitchen, but Rachel didn't take part, didn't talk, didn't work, just watched.

At dinner she said, "You know what your fruit salad tastes like, Mom?"

"Like bananas and apples," Max answered for her.

Rachel glared at him. "You're so clever, Max." To Ginger she said, "It tastes like love."

"Well, thank you, Rachel." Rachel hadn't made this assertion for years, not since she was a babbling child. She would have died from embarrassment. And what an odd thing to say in front of the whole extended family, though most of them were too busy with their own small conversations to hear.

A fruit salad that tastes like love? What kind of love? The love of a family that still has a mother? She isn't sure what effect Paisley's death has had on Rachel. All she knows is, whenever Ginger is home, Rachel *hangs around*. It's not normal.

Ginger worries because she's seen events like Paisley's passing, and even some of her friends' divorces, pull their adolescent children back into childhood in the most annoying way, making them hold on to whatever adult is available the way a toddler clutches its mother's legs so she can't leave for work. She doesn't want to be held on to. She doesn't want Rachel to want it. When

363

you're twelve or fourteen or eighteen, *you're* supposed to be the one who leaves. Not your parent. Ginger has seen children who never grow out of that regressive phase, even ten or twelve years later. Children who at thirty still demand their mother's fruit salad at every meal.

Or—and this makes Ginger more uncomfortable yet—was Rachel referring to a fruit salad made by a mother contentedly married to a father, going about her business as usual? Ever since the funeral she and Eddie have thought they were quite clever, the way they've carried on so normally. Well, maybe not. What, actually, does Rachel know?

That was in another country, she thinks. Nearly nine years ago; it might as well have been a century. *And besides, the wench is dead.*

She's aware, then, of the tears in her eyes as she stares unseeing at the Christmas tree. Of the sting of humiliation because once, however far in the past, someone who had promised to desire only her—someone she *believed* desired only her—had not only wanted someone else instead, but taken action on it. Taken action. There's the crime.

She feels foolish, now, for finding Eddie's fascination with Paisley so titillating, so thrilling. For being so proud that she, Ginger, would be going home with Eddie that night, making love to him, asserting her pride of ownership. By morning, she was always sure, he had forgotten Paisley. Too satisfied. Too tired. Too content.

Has anything really changed? Did Eddie and Paisley run off together? Of course not. Has anything been hurt but Ginger's pride? She even has the luxury of not knowing for sure, because Eddie is never going to tell her the facts of what really happened back then. Whatever the facts are, she'll never be able to confirm them.

She remembers once again how Paisley suggested she take over the store, making it somehow *all right* to live what has been, ever since, such a satisfactory life. She has been drifting through so much ephemeral happiness she's barely been aware of it until now.

And less than a month ago, when she had stood in Paisley's yard, watching the strong jets of the hot tub send waves of water and comfort and solace onto Paisley's aching skin, she had thought, *I have done what I set out to do. I have done something good for her.* And that, too, had made her happy.

Looking at the room it has taken her so long to see, she is aware of the tears on her cheeks—part anger, part humiliation—but part, after all, tears for a lost friend.

It is too much to hold on to. What she wants, after all, is not this truth—if it is a truth—but the life she had before.

After a time she feels Eddie's arm around her shoulders. She doesn't shrug it off. Rachel rushes back into the house as if on cue, in a cloud of frostbitten air. "It's freezing out there. *Freezing.*" When the door slams behind her, it takes with it the passing breath of something cold. Ginger lets it go.

They're so fragile. Anything that happens to them can only make it worse.

They've had each other all these years. They have each other now.

How many families are ever this happy?

"Are you all right?" Eddie asks.

"I think so. Yes. Better."

If not for Paisley, how would they know?

The day after Christmas is always disorganized and scattered, but to Julianne, this one seems worse than usual. The sky is clotted with clouds, and a cold rain spits down every once in a while, thoroughly unpleasant stuff that keeps everyone in the house. Will has brought a girlfriend, Elise, who is apparently also his roommate, a fact Julianne didn't discover until now. Julianne hopes the girl is disease-free and vigilant about birth control, because she doesn't think the roommate situation is going to last. Elise exhibits her insecurity by pretending to feel all too at home, pouring orange juice into the wrong glasses, setting out napkins when Julianne always leaves them in the napkin holder, calling everyone in for bacon and eggs as if she's the cohostess who's been doing this forever. In the end Elise is far less helpful than the boys, and when she realizes this, she begins to pout.

"Are you going to your dad's today?" Julianne asks when they've finished eating. "Has he met Elise yet?"

Will raises his eyebrows because Julianne never suggests it's a good idea to see Bill, even when it is.

She's annoyed because none of them will *leave*. Joe has been on the phone all morning with other friends also home from college, but somehow none of them have managed to make concrete plans. Toby is glued to the television, overwhelmed not by the presence of his brothers, which he always enjoys, but by the intrusion of a girl into the mix. Doug will be coming over soon. Julianne is grateful that at least he wasn't there for Christmas dinner. His sister had invited him and he was obligated. Now he'll arrive in a burst of goodwill, bringing bagels or pastries or some other unneeded foodstuff, hoping to ingratiate himself with her sons, who don't like him and never will. They don't like Bill's wife of many years, either.

When the doorbell rings, everyone backs off, allowing Julianne to get it so they won't have to be the first to tell Doug hello. But it's not Doug at the door, it's a large, older man, a stranger, bundled into an expensive-looking overcoat. Or—no, not a stranger.

"Harold Fetterman," he says. "The guy who had the heart attack?"

Julianne remembers; of course she does. You don't forget a patient who sends the black horrors sizzling into your bloodstream through the medium of a stethoscope. What he's doing on her doorstep, she can't fathom.

"Well, come in," she says. "You look pretty healthy now." He must have lost ten pounds in the past month. Mortal fear will do that to you.

He holds out a large box of something frozen. "Steaks," he says. "I did a little research. I heard you had grown sons. Carnivores."

"But you shouldn't—"

He holds up a hand. "Of course I should. You saved my life. Besides, I own the company." He indicates the wrapping on the package: Fetterman's Frozen Meats.

"Well, in that case. But I don't think I saved your life."

"Oh, absolutely. I didn't even have chest pains. Just, all of a sudden I didn't feel so well. I would have had no idea. They said in the hospital that the quick treatment was critical."

Julianne takes the proffered package. "Come on in," she says again. "Come have a cup of coffee."

Harold Fetterman demurs. "No. I just wanted to thank you in person."

"You're welcome," she says.

When she closes the door, all the boys are standing in the entryway, watching. She holds her arms out at her sides to give them a better look. "Your mother the savior," she tells them.

They applaud. The show of adoration gives her strength. "How about going to a movie?" she says.

It turns out this is just the right suggestion. They want to be together, three brothers, once close, now not so close, especially with Elise tagging along. But a movie—yes. They're at such unsettled ages right now. In ten years, twenty, they'll be close again, in some new paradigm that includes wives and children. She can imagine them at Christmas in that distant future, in a room where all the other faces are, to Julianne, strangers. She doesn't see herself in that scene. They won't need her. In the largest sense, they don't need her now.

She calls Doug and tells him she's going to bed with a headache. This is not, she realizes, the way to treat a man you once thought you would marry. But he sounds relieved.

The empty house feels unsettled when the boys leave, the air still vibrating with the morning's pent-up energy. Julianne walks through the rooms, planning to pick up whatever scraps of wrapping paper and ribbon and other detritus that may still be lurking, but the house is amazingly clean. Someone has even vacuumed. Probably Will.

When the phone rings, she almost snatches it up without checking the caller ID, just to have something to distract her. She sees Bill's number just as her hand touches the receiver, and pulls it back as if it is hot. "Just wanted to see how everyone's doing," Bill says on the machine. He sounds lonely, though he has a wife and daughter to keep him company.

Uncharacteristically, Julianne is tempted to call back and say the boys are at a movie. Her real motive, she supposes, would be to tell him about Harold Fetterman's visit. There's no hostility in that, or neediness, either—though it occurs to her that the reason she could never have married Doug is because it would have been torture to live with a man from whom she has to keep secret the deepest part of her life.

Bill is the one, after all, who thinks she ought to seek a job where she can use her skills more fully. Maybe she will. His passive-aggressive approach always makes her wary, but for now, his suggestion seems less like an effort to get control of her than advice from someone who's trying to be a friend.

After two or three circuits of the house, she is at last calm enough to sit down. Harold

Fetterman believes she saved his life. Who knows? Maybe she did. At the very least, her sensitive fingers bought him some time, which he seems to be enjoying. She was wrong, the day he got sick, to think his survival meant only a few brief months of pain and fear when ignorance might have been better. Clearly, the man is glad to be alive.

It comes to her then that she also gave Paisley the gift of time. Not a pleasant or happy time, but immeasurably valuable all the same, in ways she hasn't understood until now.

Another nurse might not have asked Paisley the right questions. Might have noticed how healthy Paisley looked and never felt her diseased liver at all. Julianne has seen that happen. If not for Julianne, it might have been weeks before Paisley's condition was diagnosed. She would have been much sicker by then, had much less strength to prepare her children for what was to come. Paisley would have hated that. If no one could cure her, what Paisley would have wanted most was exactly what Julianne gave her—the chance to say a proper goodbye.

Julianne doesn't know how Eudora Nestor, the other patient who died, spent her final months. Did she have a family? A business? Does it really matter? If she realized she'd been given a chance to settle her accounts, Julianne senses she, too, would have been grateful.

Even so, the idea that it will happen again, as she's sure it will, makes Julianne shudder. The tingling that magnifies itself into liquid fire, into darkness incarnate, the sense that death is running through her veins, is something she'll always dread. Anyone would. It is a brief enough blackness, but horrible all the same.

Yet if she's really able to help people finish what they came here for, perhaps the pain is worth the price. There are times when you allow it, even choose it, for what lies on the other side. Bill is right when he says it's not death she carries in her fingers, but knowledge. What she wants—maybe what she has always wanted—is this. *This.* The frightening, transcendent power in her hands that she wouldn't give back even if she could.

The next morning, Iona wakes up to the sight of two inches of snow on the ground, not unheard of so early in the season, but not common, either. It seems like a benediction. By the time she pulls on her boots and ventures outside, the younger children are already out in force, bored with their new indoor toys and anxious for sledding and snowmen and snowball fights.

Iona walks around Hazelwood Way and the full length of Brightwood Circle and is still too full of energy to go inside. She climbs the hill to Lindenwood Court, trespasses through the

Honeywells' yard, and stands in the field behind it. As always after a snowstorm, the landscape has been transformed. A long, white, pristine snowfield glistens where yesterday there had been an unbroken vista of drab, brown, dormant weeds and grass. After more than ten years, Iona's feet know the field by heart, its small crests and valleys left by a plow before Iona's time, the round sinkhole no wider than a yardstick and about a foot deep, treacherous if you don't know where it is in summer, when it gets so overgrown. Iona walks under the bare sycamores, around the perimeter of the field. She stops briefly at the place where all those years ago she spotted Paisley and Eddie Logan having sex under the sugar maple, which had just turned a gorgeous yellow-edged-with-orange, and was idly dropping leaves onto the scene below it, as if it were part of a movie set. There they were, Eddie stretched out on a blanket and a naked Paisley straddling him, Eddie's hands reaching up to cup her fine round breasts. The remains of a picnic lunch were strewn around the blanket, and Paisley's clothes were in a jumbled pile next to it. Eddie was busy doing what he was doing and never saw Iona. But Paisley did. She gazed at Iona not with the panicky expression of someone caught having illicit sex, but with the wild-eyed zeal of a missionary driven to complete a conversion. Iona would have bet money that the act was never repeated again.

Iona had never held it against her, though she'd always thought a little less of Eddie. She could not admire a man who would have sex with a pregnant woman who was not his wife. Or at least she thinks Paisley was pregnant with Melody by then. The timing was a little iffy. But Melody looks so much like Mason, it's hard to question her parentage. Even so, there's some mystery here. Iona is never going to know the half of it. She supposes it's none of her business.

At the end of her circle of the field, Iona passes the Lamms' backyard, where Melody is building a snowman while her little dog paws the snow. The back door opens and Brynne calls out, arms crossed over her thin sweater against the cold. "Want some help?"

"No. Me and Mom always do this," Melody says.

"Okay." Brynne closes the door.

Melody keeps packing snow onto what is surely the belly of the snowman, chattering either to the dog or to her mother, Iona can't tell which. She's too far away to make out the words. A kid, eight years old, talking to her dead mother in the backyard—it makes her sick.

What galls her is that she can't imagine any good coming of Paisley's death, for the children who've lost their mother or the husband who's lost his wife. How can this possibly make sense?

But when she tries to pursue this line of thinking, she is stopped by the memory of whatever it was that happened at that prayer meeting in Marie Coleman's kitchen. That unmistakable sense of a presence moving among them. The warmth in the cold room. The *something*. She still loves Richard and mourns for him, but if he hadn't died she would have had a different life she can no longer imagine. She never would have had Jeffrey and Lori and Rosalie the way she has them now, and they would never have had her. You never know how being a grandmother will soften you up.

Not that she's letting down her guard. Not a chance.

She crunches through the snow until she is too winded to think. Then comes a time when she is aware, for one of the few times in her life, that what she is experiencing is not happiness, exactly, but joy.

Odd, how in the afterglow of someone else's life, your own looks so much brighter.

Back on the street, the adults have emerged now and are pelting each other with snowballs. Paisley would be sorry to miss this.

Are they thinking about her?

Iona hopes so.

What is the measure of a person's life? How will they remember her? As the pretty mother of two who once drank too much? As the vivacious hostess who gave the best parties in the neighborhood? Who flirted and played tennis and listened to golden oldies?

Well, all of those things. But above all, Iona thinks they will remember her on one perfect fall afternoon, when she sat in a wheelchair, too weak to walk, perched atop the ruined foundation of her life, yet with her arms outstretched to the blue enormity of sky.

"Look at this!" they will remember her saying. "Just look!"

Dear Reader,

Let me start by thanking you for picking up *The Art of Saying Goodbye*. It's a book close to my heart because it began with something that really happened many years ago in the suburban neighborhood where I lived.

A woman in her midforties—the beautiful one with the beautiful children, the one who was always nice to everyone, the one whom all of us loved, admired, and even envied a little—was diagnosed with terminal cancer. We, her neighbors who knew her well or knew her only casually, went through an astonishing range of emotions. Her one close friend was devastated. The rest of us were saddened, sorry, sometimes even disbelieving, because she'd always been such an upbeat, vibrant woman who'd played such a cheerful role in our lives. The seriousness of the situation didn't truly dawn on us until a beautiful fall afternoon, when the trees were in full color, and her husband took her on a leaf tour, guiding her through the neighborhood in a wheelchair. Although she greeted everyone with her usual good-natured jokes, she was frighteningly thin and jaundiced, and clearly too weak to walk.

It was a dreadful moment. Like her, most of us were mothers raising children. It struck us then that she wasn't going to be able to watch hers grow up. And because each of us wanted above all to be around for *our* children, we were all secretly relieved that, if someone had to be sick, it was her and not us. This was an emotion we couldn't help but were deeply ashamed of.

All of us felt too guilty to confess our thoughts to our neighbors. The white ribbons we tied around the trees in our yards seemed a paltry gesture of support—so did the awkward visits we paid and the casseroles we brought, which she grew too sick to eat. We offered to take her children to their after-school activities, but our friend's mother had come to help and the family wanted to be self-sufficient. We felt helpless and terribly, terribly sad. As she grew sicker, we grieved for her. Already, we missed her. Our hearts ached for her daughters, who didn't fully understand what was going on, and for her husband, who did. What else could we do? Even the prayer meeting we had did nothing to stay her illness, though it offered the rest of us an hour of shared serenity none of us had expected.

Our friend handled her decline with a grace that amazed and humbled us, and forced us to appreciate the preciousness of our own healthy lives. In the stark glare of our shared mortality, we shed hurtful old habits and fears. We acknowledged what was really important to us. By the time she died, each of us had gone through a transformation that seemed like a gift she'd given us, the legacy she'd left behind.

I decided to write about this time in my life after I realized how many other people I knew who had gone through a similar experience. The four main characters I invented have very different reactions to their neighbor's illness, but in each case it throws her life into perspective. And the sick woman turns out to have strengths and depths that most of the others never suspected she had. I hope you'll enjoy the story and be moved by it, and perhaps recognize something of yourself in it that you'll find both familiar and comforting.

Ellyn Bache

QUESTIONS FOR DISCUSSION

1. In many ways, Paisley is the star of the suburban development where she lives—the pretty one who's nice to everyone, who gives the best parties, who seems to enjoy raising her daughters and living her conventional life. In what ways does her "stardom" inspire varying emotions in her neighbors? Overall, how do they regard her before she gets sick? How does this affect the way they feel after they learn she's ill?

2. Julianne is horrified by what she sees as her dark "gift" of diagnosis. Her ex-husband thinks it has a more rational explanation. Which one do you agree with? Why?

3. Although Paisley's illness causes her neighbors to experience a wide range of emotions—everything from disbelief to sadness—at times some of them feel less than sympathetic. Which ones struggle with this most? In what ways do their feelings rise directly from Paisley's situation, and in what ways do they rise from their own, personal issues?

4. Who is the most selfish, and who is the most unselfish, in terms of the way she feels about Paisley? How is this reflected in the way she acts?

5. Ginger has never been as close with Paisley as some of her neighbors, but when Paisley gets sick, she feels helpless. How does she finally resolve this? Discuss how the theme of helplessness is played out with some of the other characters.

6. Iona is older than the other women in the novel, and more cynical. Yet early on, Paisley brings her into their circle by inviting her to her hot tub party. Why do you think she does this?

7. What do you make of Iona's shifting relationship with her stepson and his wife? Why does she respond so powerfully to the prayer meeting she doesn't want to attend? At the end of the book, do you think she is a different person than she was at the beginning? If so, what caused her transformation?

8. Andrea is grateful to Paisley for her kindness when her daughter was sick. She wants to play the same role for Paisley, but she feels shut out. Is she, really?

9. Early in the novel, Julianne muses that Andrea's life is still dominated by the illness of a child who got well ten years ago. Why do you think Andrea is finally able to take action and free herself from that bondage?

10. Paisley helps people in some unconventional ways. What is your sense of the rightness or wrongness of her approach in various situations?

11. What do we learn about Paisley in the sections told from Paisley's point of view? How do those sections influence the way you think about her?

12. Which of Paisley's neighbors do you like best? Least? Why?

13. To the people in the neighborhood, Andrea's daughter, Courtney, seems such an angry, unappealing teenager that the little children call her "growly-face." Is she as unsympathetic as she seems? Overall, what is your assessment of her?

14. On the outside, Brynne is amazingly self-contained for a girl of fourteen. She tries to ease her mother's pain and to explain things to her younger sister. How do you account

for her calm exterior and apparent maturity? Julianne fears for her. Should she?

15. Discuss the roles of the other young people in the book. Ginger's twelve-year-old daughter, Rachel, has always idolized Brynne. How does Paisley's illness change that? Is Ginger's son, Max, as clueless as he seems? What function does eight-year-old Melody play?

16. Given that we see the men in the novel only through the eyes of the women, what do you think of Paisley's husband, Mason, and Ginger's husband, Eddie? Is there a hero in the book? A villain?

17. Julianne's relationship with her ex-husband, Bill, is complicated by his niceness, which Julianne resents. Does Bill provide a powerful, if unwanted, support system, or is he as meddlesome as Julianne sometimes believes?

18. If you had to take one of these women out to lunch, which one would it be, and why?

Center Point Publishing
600 Brooks Road ● PO Box 1
Thorndike ME 04986-0001 USA

(207) 568-3717

US & Canada:
1 800 929-9108
www.centerpointlargeprint.com